# AN ABUNDANCE OF KATHERINES

ALSO BY JOHN GREEN:

*Looking for Alaska*

*Paper Towns*

*Will Grayson, Will Grayson*
WITH DAVID LEVITHAN

*The Fault in Our Stars*

*Turtles All the Way Down*

JOHN GREEN

# AN ABUNDANCE OF KATHERINES

PENGUIN BOOKS

PENGUIN BOOKS
An imprint of Penguin Random House LLC, New York

First published in the United States of America by Dutton Books,
a member of Penguin Group (USA) Inc., 2006
Published by Speak, an imprint of Penguin Group (USA) Inc., 2008
Published by Speak, an imprint of Penguin Group (USA) Inc., 2012
Published by Penguin Books, an imprint of Penguin Random House LLC, 2019



Visit us online at penguinrandomhouse.com

THE LIBRARY OF CONGRESS HAS CATALOGED THE DUTTON BOOKS EDITION AS FOLLOWS:
Green, John, date.
An abundance of Katherines / John Green.
p. cm.
Summary: Having been recently dumped for the nineteenth time by a girl named Katherine, recent high school graduate and former child prodigy Colin sets off on a road trip with his best friend to try to find some new direction in life.
ISBN 0-525-47688-1 (hc)
[1. Interpersonal relations—Fiction. 2. Self-perception—Fiction. 3. Graphic methods—Fiction.]
I. Title. PZ7.G8233Abu 2006 [Fic]—dc22 2006004191

Penguin Books ISBN 9780142410707

Edited by Julie Strauss-Gabel
Designed by Irene Vandervoort

Printed in the United States of America



48 49 47

To my wife, Sarah Urist Green, anagrammatically:

Her great Russian
Grin has treasure—
A great risen rush.
She is a rut-ranger;
Anguish arrester;
Sister; haranguer;
Treasure-sharing,
Heart-reassuring
Signature Sharer
Easing rare hurts.

"But the pleasure isn't owning the person. The pleasure is this.
Having another contender in the room with you."
—Philip Roth, *The Human Stain*

# AN ABUNDANCE OF KATHERINES

# (one)

**The morning after** noted child prodigy Colin Singleton graduated from high school and got dumped for the nineteenth time by a girl named Katherine, he took a bath. Colin had always preferred baths; one of his general policies in life was never to do anything standing up that could just as easily be done lying down. He climbed into the tub as soon as the water got hot, and he sat and watched with a curiously blank look on his face as the water overtook him. The water inched up his legs, which were crossed and folded into the tub. He did recognize, albeit faintly, that he was too long, and too big, for this bathtub—he looked like a mostly grown person playing at being a kid.

As the water began to splash over his skinny but unmuscled stomach, he thought of Archimedes. When Colin was about four, he read a book about Archimedes, the Greek philosopher who'd discovered that volume could be measured by water displacement when he sat down in the bathtub. Upon making this discovery, Archimedes supposedly shouted "Eureka!"[1] and then ran naked through the streets. The book said that many important discoveries contained a "Eureka moment." And even then, Colin very much wanted to have some important discoveries, so he asked his mom about it when she got home that evening.

"Mommy, am I ever going to have a Eureka moment?"

"Oh, sweetie," she said, taking his hand. "What's wrong?"

---

[1] Greek: "I have found it."

"I wanna have a *Eureka moment*," he said, the way another kid might have expressed longing for a Teenage Mutant Ninja Turtle.

She pressed the back of her hand to his cheek and smiled, her face so close to his that he could smell coffee and makeup. "Of course, Colin baby. Of course you will."

But mothers lie. It's in the job description.

Colin took a deep breath and slid down, immersing his head. *I am crying*, he thought, opening his eyes to stare through the soapy, stinging water. *I feel like crying, so I must be crying, but it's impossible to tell because I'm underwater.* But he wasn't crying. Curiously, he felt too depressed to cry. Too hurt. It felt as if she'd taken the part of him that cried.

He opened the drain in the tub, stood up, toweled off, and got dressed. When he exited the bathroom, his parents were sitting together on his bed. It was never a good sign when both his parents were in his room at the same time. Over the years it had meant:

1. Your grandmother/grandfather/Aunt-Suzie-whom-you-never-met-but-trust-me-she-was-nice-and-it's-a-shame is dead.
2. You're letting a girl named Katherine distract you from your studies.
3. Babies are made through an act that you will eventually find intriguing but for right now will just sort of horrify you, and also sometimes people do stuff that involves baby-making parts that does not actually involve making babies, like for instance kiss each other in places that are not on the face.

It never meant:

4. A girl named Katherine called while you were in the bathtub. She's sorry. She still loves you and has made a terrible mistake and is waiting for you downstairs.

• • •

But even so, Colin couldn't help but hope that his parents were in the room to provide news of the Number 4 variety. He was a generally pessimistic person, but he seemed to make an exception for Katherines: he always felt they would come back to him. The feeling of loving her and being loved by her welled up in him, and he could taste the adrenaline in the back of his throat, and maybe it wasn't over, and maybe he could feel her hand in his again and hear her loud, brash voice contort itself into a whisper to say I-love-you in the very quick and quiet way that she had always said it. She said *I love you* as if it were a secret, and an immense one.

His dad stood up and stepped toward him. "Katherine called my cell," he said. "She's worried about you." Colin felt his dad's hand on his shoulder, and then they both moved forward, and then they were hugging.

"We're very concerned," his mom said. She was a small woman with curly brown hair that had one single shock of white toward the front. "And stunned," she added. "What happened?"

"I don't know," Colin said softly into his dad's shoulder. "She's just—she'd had enough of me. She got tired. That's what she said." And then his mom got up and there was a lot of hugging, arms everywhere, and his mom was crying. Colin extricated himself from the hugs and sat down on his bed. He felt a tremendous need to get them out of his room immediately, like if they didn't leave he would blow up. Literally. Guts on the walls; his prodigious brain emptied out onto his bedspread.

"Well, at some point we need to sit down and assess your options," his dad said. His dad was big on assessing. "Not to look for silver linings, but it seems like you'll now have some free time this summer. A summer class at Northwestern, maybe?"

"I really need to be alone, just for today," Colin answered, trying to convey a sense of calm so that they would leave and he wouldn't blow up. "So can we assess tomorrow?"

"Of course, sweetie," his mom said. "We'll be here all day. You just come down whenever you want and we love you and you're so so special, Colin, and you can't possibly let this girl make you think otherwise because you are the most magnificent, brilliant boy—" And right then, the most special, magnificent, brilliant boy bolted into his bathroom and puked his guts out. An explosion, sort of.

"Oh, Colin!" shouted his mom.

"I just need to be alone," Colin insisted from the bathroom. "Please."

When he came out, they were gone.

For the next fourteen hours without pausing to eat or drink or throw up again, Colin read and reread his yearbook, which he had received just four days before. Aside from the usual yearbook crap, it contained seventy-two signatures. Twelve were just signatures, fifty-six cited his intelligence, twenty-five said they wished they'd known him better, eleven said it was fun to have him in English class, seven included the words "pupillary sphincter,"[2] and a stunning *seventeen* ended, "Stay Cool!" Colin Singleton could no more *stay* cool than a blue whale could *stay* skinny or Bangladesh could *stay* rich. Presumably, those seventeen people were kidding. He mulled this over—and considered how twenty-five of his classmates, some of whom he'd been attending school with for twelve years, could possibly have wanted to "know him better." As if they hadn't had a chance.

But mostly for those fourteen hours, he read and reread Katherine XIX's inscription:

> Col,
>
> Here's to all the places we went. And all the places we'll go. And here's me, whispering again and again and again and again: iloveyou.
>
> yrs forever, K-a-t-h-e-r-i-n-e

---

[2] More on that later.

Eventually, he found the bed too comfortable for his state of mind, so he lay down on his back, his legs sprawled across the carpet. He anagrammed "yrs forever" until he found one he liked: *sorry fever*. And then he lay there in his fever of sorry and repeated the now memorized note in his head and wanted to cry, but instead he only felt this aching behind his solar plexus. Crying *adds* something: crying is you, plus tears. But the feeling Colin had was some horrible opposite of crying. It was you, minus something. He kept thinking about one word—*forever*—and felt the burning ache just beneath his rib cage.

It hurt like the worst ass-kicking he'd ever gotten. And he'd gotten plenty.

# (two)

**It hurt like this** until shortly before 10 P.M., when a rather fat, hirsute guy of Lebanese descent burst into Colin's room without knocking. Colin turned his head and squinted up at him.

"What the hell is this?" asked Hassan, almost shouting.

"She dumped me," answered Colin.

"So I heard. Listen, *sitzpinkler*,[3] I'd love to comfort you, but I could put out a house fire with the contents of my bladder right now." Hassan breezed past the bed and opened the door to the bathroom. "God, Singleton, what'd you eat? It smells like—AHHH! PUKE! PUKE! AIIIIEEE!" And as Hassan screamed, Colin thought, *Oh. Right. The toilet. Should have flushed.*

"Forgive me if I missed," Hassan said upon returning. He sat down on the edge of the bed and softly kicked Colin's prostrate body. "I had to hold my nose with both fugging hands, so Thunderstick was swinging freely. A mighty pendulum, that fugger." Colin didn't laugh. "God, you must be in some state, because (a) Thunderstick jokes are my best material, and (b) who forgets to flush their own hurl?"

"I just want to crawl into a hole and die." Colin spoke into the cream carpet with no audible emotion.

"Oh, boy," Hassan said, exhaling slowly.

---

[3] A German word, slang for "wimp," that literally means "a man who sits to pee." Those wacky Germans—they've got a word for everything.

"All I ever wanted was for her to love me and to do something meaningful with my life. And look. I mean, look," he said.

"I am looking. And I'll grant you, *kafir*,[4] that I don't like what I'm seeing. Or what I'm smelling, for that matter." Hassan lay back on the bed and let Colin's misery hang in the air for a moment.

"I'm just—I'm just a failure. What if this is it? What if ten years from now I'm sitting in a fugging cubicle crunching numbers and memorizing baseball statistics so I can kick ass in my fantasy league and I don't have her and I never do anything significant and I'm just a complete waste?"

Hassan sat up, his hands on his knees. "See, this is why you need to believe in God. Because I don't even expect to have a *cube*, and I'm happier than a pig in a pile of shit."

Colin sighed. Although Hassan himself was not *that* religious, he often jokingly tried to convert Colin. "Right. Faith in God. That's a good idea. I'd also like to believe that I could fly into outer space on the fluffy backs of giant penguins and screw Katherine XIX in zero gravity."

"Singleton, you need to believe in God worse than anyone I ever met."

"Well, *you* need to go to college," Colin muttered. Hassan groaned. A year ahead of Colin in school, Hassan had "taken a year off" even though he'd been admitted to Loyola University in Chicago. Since he hadn't enrolled in classes for the coming fall, it seemed his one year off would soon turn into two.

"Don't make this about me," Hassan said through a smile. "I'm not the one who's too fugged up to get off the carpet or flush my own puke, dude. And you know why? I got me some God."

"Stop trying to convert me," Colin moaned, unamused. Hassan jumped up and straddled Colin on the floor and pinned his arms down and started shouting, "There is no God but God and Muhammad is His

---

[4] "Kafir" is a not-nice Arabic word meaning "non-Muslim" that is usually translated as "infidel."

Prophet! Say it with me, *sitzpinkler*! *La ilaha illa-llah*!"[5] Colin started laughing breathlessly beneath Hassan's weight, and Hassan laughed, too. "I'm trying to save your sorry ass from hell!"

"Get off or I'm going there quite soon," Colin wheezed.

Hassan stood up and abruptly moved to serious mode. "So, what's the problem exactly?"

"The problem exactly is that she *dumped* me. That I'm alone. Oh my God, I'm alone again. And not only that, but I'm a total failure in case you haven't noticed. I'm washed up, I'm *former*. Formerly the boyfriend of Katherine XIX. Formerly a prodigy. Formerly full of potential. Currently full of shit." As Colin had explained to Hassan countless times, there's a stark difference between the words *prodigy* and *genius*.

Prodigies can very quickly learn what other people have already figured out; geniuses discover that which no one has ever previously discovered. Prodigies learn; geniuses do. The vast majority of child prodigies don't become adult geniuses. Colin was almost certain that he was among that unfortunate majority.

Hassan sat down on the bed and tugged at his stubbly second chin. "Is the real problem here the genius thing or the Katherine thing?"

"I just love her so much," was Colin's answer. But the truth was that, in Colin's mind, the problems were related. The problem was that this most special, magnificent, brilliant boy was—well, not. The Problem itself was that *He* didn't matter. Colin Singleton, noted child prodigy, noted veteran of Katherine Conflicts, noted nerd and *sitzpinkler*, didn't matter to Katherine XIX, and he didn't matter to the world. All of a sudden, he wasn't anyone's boyfriend or anyone's genius. And that—to use the kind of complex word you'd expect from a prodigy—blew.

"Because the genius thing," Hassan went on as if Colin hasn't just professed his love, "is nothing. That's just about wanting to be famous."

---

[5] The Islamic statement of faith, in transliterated Arabic: there is no God but God.

"No, it's not. I want to *matter*," he said.

"Right. Like I said, you want fame. Famous is the new popular. And you're not going to be America's fugging Next Top Model, that's for goddamned sure. So you want to be America's Next Top Genius and now you're—and don't take this personally—whining that it hasn't happened yet."

"You're not helping," Colin muttered into the carpet. Colin turned his face to look up at Hassan.

"Get up," Hassan said, reaching a hand down. Colin grabbed it, pulled himself up, and then tried to let go of Hassan's hand. But Hassan gripped tighter. "*Kafir*, you have a very complicated problem with a very simple solution."

# (three)

**"A road trip,"** Colin said. He had an overstuffed duffel bag at his feet and a backpack stretched taut, which contained only books. He and Hassan were sitting on a black leather couch. Colin's parents sat across from them on an identical couch.

Colin's mother shook her head rhythmically, like a disapproving metronome. "To *where?*" she asked. "And *why?*"

"No offense, Mrs. Singleton," Hassan said, putting his feet up on the coffee table (which you were not allowed to do), "but you're sort of missing the point. There is no where or why."

"Think of all you could *do* this summer, Colin. You could learn Sanskrit," said his dad. "I know how you've been wanting to learn Sanskrit.[6] Will you really be happy just driving around aimlessly? That doesn't seem like you. Frankly, it seems like *quitting.*"

"Quitting what, Dad?"

His dad paused. He always paused after a question, and then when he did speak, it was in complete sentences without ums or likes or uhs—as if he'd memorized his response. "It pains me to say this, Colin, but if you wish to continue to grow intellectually, you need to work harder right now than you ever have before. Otherwise, you risk wasting your potential."

"Technically," Colin answered, "I think I might have already wasted it."

---

[6] Which, pathetically enough, was true. Colin really *had* been wanting to learn Sanskrit. It's sort of the Mount Everest of dead languages.

• • •

Maybe it was because Colin had never once in his life disappointed his parents: he did not drink or do drugs or smoke cigarettes or wear black eyeliner or stay out late or get bad grades or pierce his tongue or have the words "KATHERINE LUVA 4 LIFE" tattooed across his back. Or maybe they felt guilty, like somehow they'd failed him and brought him to this place. Or maybe they just wanted a few weeks alone to rekindle the romance. But five minutes after acknowledging his wasted potential, Colin Singleton was behind the wheel of his lengthy gray Oldsmobile known as Satan's Hearse.

Inside the car, Hassan said, "Okay, now all we have to do is go to my house, pick up some clothes, and miraculously convince my parents to let me go on a road trip."

"You could say you have a summer job. At, like, a camp or something," Colin offered.

"Right, except I'm not going to lie to my mom, because what kind of bastard lies to his own mother?"

"Hmm."

"Well, although, *someone else* could lie to her. I could live with that."

"Fine," said Colin. Five minutes later, they double-parked on a street in Chicago's Ravenswood neighborhood, and jumped out of the car together. Hassan burst into the house with Colin trailing. In the well-appointed living room, Hassan's mom sat in an easy chair, sleeping.

"Hey, Mama," said Hassan. "Wake up." She jolted awake, smiled, and greeted both of the boys in Arabic. Colin answered in Arabic, saying, "My girlfriend dumped me and I'm really depressed, and so Hassan and I are going to go on a, a, uh, vacation where you drive. I don't know the word in Arabic."

Mrs. Harbish shook her head and pursed her lips. "Don't I tell you," she said in accented English, "not to mess with girls? Hassan is a good boy, doesn't do this 'dating.' And look how happy he is. You should learn from him."

"That's what he's going to teach me on this trip," Colin said, although nothing could have been further from the truth. Hassan barreled back into the room carrying a half-zipped duffel bag overflowing with clothes. "*Ohiboke,*[7] Mama," he said, leaning down to kiss her cheek.

Suddenly a pajama-clad Mr. Harbish entered the living room and in English said, "You're not going anywhere."

"Oh, Dad. We *have* to. Look at him. He's all screwed up." Colin stared up at Mr. Harbish and tried to look as screwed up as he possibly could. "He's going with or without me, but with me at least I can watch out for him."

"Colin is a good boy," Mrs. Harbish said to her husband.

"I'll call you every day," Hassan added. "We won't even be gone long. Just until he gets better."

Colin, now completely improvising, had an idea. "I'm going to get Hassan a job," he said to Mr. Harbish. "I think we both need to learn the value of hard work."

Mr. Harbish grunted in agreement, then turned to Hassan. "You need to learn the value of not watching that awful Judge Judy, for starters. If you call me in a week and have a job, you can stay wherever you want as long as you want, as far as I'm concerned."

Hassan seemed not to notice the insults, only meekly mumbling, "Thanks, Dad." He kissed his mother on both cheeks and hurried out the door.

"What a dick," Hassan said once they were safely inside the Hearse. "It's one thing to accuse me of laziness. But to malign the good name of America's greatest television judge—that's below the belt."

Hassan fell asleep around one in the morning and Colin, half-drunk on well-creamed gas station coffee and the exhilarating loneliness of a freeway at nighttime, drove south on I-65 through Indianapolis. It was a warm night

---

[7] Arabic: "I love you."

for early June, and since the AC in Satan's Hearse hadn't worked in this millennium, the windows were cracked open. And the beautiful thing about driving was that it stole just enough of his attention—*car parked on the side, maybe a cop, slow to speed limit, time to pass this sixteen-wheeler, turn signal, check rearview, crane neck to check blind spot and yes, okay, left lane*—to distract from the gnawing hole in his belly.

To keep his mind occupied, he thought of other holes in other stomachs. He thought of the Archduke Franz Ferdinand, assassinated in 1914. As he looked down at the bloody hole in his middle, the Archduke had said, "It is nothing." He was mistaken. There's no doubt that the Archduke Franz Ferdinand mattered, although he was neither a prodigy nor a genius: his assassination sparked World War I—so his death led to 8,528,831 others.

Colin missed her. Missing her kept him awake more than the coffee, and when Hassan had asked to drive an hour back, Colin had said no, because the driving kept him going—*stay under seventy; God, my heart racing; I hate the taste of coffee; so wired though; okay, and clear of the truck; okay yes; right lane; and now just my own headlights against the darkness*. It kept the loneliness of crushlessness from being entirely crushing. Driving was a kind of thinking, the only kind he could then tolerate. But still, the thought lurked out there, just beyond the reach of his headlights: he'd been dumped. By a girl named Katherine. For the nineteenth time.

When it comes to girls (and in Colin's case, it so often did), everyone has a type. Colin Singleton's type was not physical but linguistic: he liked Katherines. And not Katies or Kats or Kitties or Cathys or Rynns or Trinas or Kays or Kates or, God forbid, Catherines. K-A-T-H-E-R-I-N-E. He had dated nineteen girls. All of them had been named Katherine. And all of them—every single solitary one—had dumped him.

Colin believed that the world contained exactly two kinds of people: Dumpers and Dumpees. A lot of people will claim to be both, but those people miss the point entirely: You are predisposed to either one fate or the other. Dumpers may not *always* be the heartbreakers, and the Dumpees may not always be the heartbroken. But everyone has a tendency.[8]

Perhaps, then, Colin ought to have grown accustomed to it, to the rise and fall of relationships. Dating, after all, only ends one way: poorly. If you think about it, and Colin often did, all romantic relationships end in either (1) breakup, (2) divorce, or (3) death. But Katherine XIX had been different—or had seemed different, anyway. She had loved him, and he had loved her back, ferociously. And he still did—he found himself working the words through his mind as he drove: I love you, Katherine. The name sounded different in his mouth when spoken to her; it became not the name with which he had been so long obsessed, but a word that described only her, a word that smelled like lilacs, that captured the blue of her eyes and the length of her eyelashes.

As the wind rushed in through the cracked windows, Colin thought of Dumpers and Dumpees and of the Archduke. In the back Hassan grunted and sniffled as if he were dreaming he was a German shepherd, and Colin felt the ceaseless burning in his gut, thinking, *This is all so CHILDISH. PATHETIC. YOU'RE EMBARRASSING. GET OVER IT GET OVER IT GET OVER IT.* But he did not quite know what "it" was.

---

[8] It might be helpful to think about this graphically. Colin saw the Dumper/Dumpee dichotomy on a bell curve. The majority of people are lumped somewhere in the middle; i.e., they're either slight Dumpees or slight Dumpers. But then you have your Katherines and your Colins:

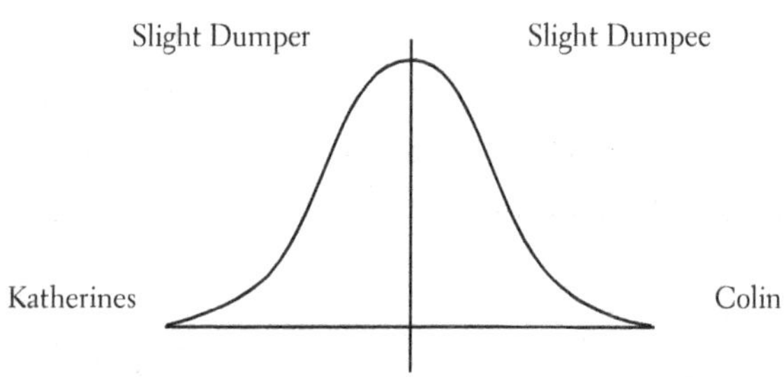

**Katherine I: The Beginning (of the Beginning)**

Colin's parents never considered him to be anything but normal until one June morning. Twenty-five-month-old Colin sat in a high chair, eating a breakfast of indeterminate vegetative origin while his father read the *Chicago Tribune* across their small kitchen table. Colin was skinny for his age, but tall, with tight brown curls that erupted from his head with an Einsteinian unpredictability.

"Three deed on West Side," Colin said after swallowing a bite. "No want more greenies," he added, referring to his food.

"What'd ya say, bud?"

"Three deed on West Side. I want french fries please thank you." [9]

Colin's dad flipped the paper around and stared at the large headline above the fold on the front page. This was Colin's first memory: his dad slowly lowering the paper and smiling at him. His dad's eyes were wide with surprise and pleasure, and his smile was uncontainable. "CINDY! THE BOY IS READING THE PAPER!" he shouted.

His parents were the sort of parents who really, really enjoyed reading. His mom taught French at the prestigious and expensive Kalman School downtown, and his dad was a sociology professor at Northwestern University, just north of the city. So after three died on the West Side, Colin's parents began to read with him, everywhere and always—primarily in English but also from French-language picture books.

Four months later, Colin's parents sent him to a preschool for gifted children. The preschool said that Colin was too advanced for their school and anyway, they didn't accept children who weren't yet fully potty-trained. They sent Colin to a psychologist at the University of Chicago.

---

[9] Like a smart monkey, Colin possessed an extensive vocabulary, but very little grammar. Also, he didn't know "dead" was pronounced *ded*. Forgive him. He was two.

And so the periodically incontinent prodigy ended up in a small, windowless office on the South Side, talking to a woman with horn-rimmed glasses, who asked Colin to find patterns in strings of letters and numbers. She asked him to flip polygons. She asked him which picture did not fit with the rest of the pictures. She asked him an endless string of wonderful questions, and Colin loved her for it. Up until that time, most of the questions Colin had been asked centered around whether or not he had pissed himself, or whether he could please eat one more bite of the miserable greenies.

After an hour of questions, the woman said, "I want to thank you for your extraordinary patience, Colin. You're a very special person."

*You're a very special person.* Colin would hear this a lot, and yet—somehow—he could never hear it enough.

The horn-rimmed-glasses woman brought his mom into the office. As the professor told Mrs. Singleton that Colin was brilliant, was a very special boy, Colin played with wooden alphabet blocks. He gave himself a splinter rearranging p-o-t-s into s-t-o-p—the first anagram he remembered making.

The professor told Mrs. Singleton that Colin's gifts must be encouraged but not pushed, and she warned, "You shouldn't have unreasonable expectations. Children like Colin process information very quickly. They show a remarkable ability to focus on tasks. But he's no more likely to win a Nobel Prize than any other reasonably intelligent child."

That night at home his father brought him a new book—*The Missing Piece* by Shel Silverstein. Colin sat down on the couch beside his dad and his small hands flipped through the big pages as he read it quickly, pausing only to ask whether "lookin'" was the same as "looking." Colin emphatically pushed the book cover shut when he finished reading.

"Did you like it?" his dad asked.

"Yup," Colin said. He liked all books, because he liked the mere act of reading, the magic of turning scratches on a page into words inside his head.

"What was it about?" his dad asked.

Colin placed the book in his dad's lap and said, "This circle is missing a piece. The missing piece is shaped like a pizza."

"Like a pizza or a pizza *slice*?" Smiling, his dad placed his big hands on top of Colin's head.

"Right, Daddy. A slice. So the circle goes looking for his piece. He finds a lot of wrong pieces. Then he finds the right piece. But then he leaves it behind. Then it ends."

"Do you sometimes feel like a circle missing a piece?" his dad wondered.

"Daddy, I am not a circle. I am a boy."

And his dad's smile faded just a bit—the prodigy could read, but he could not see. And if only Colin had known that he was missing a piece, that his inability to see himself in the story of a circle was an unfixable problem, he might have known that the rest of the world would catch up with him as time passed. To borrow from another story he memorized but didn't really get: if only he'd known that the story of the tortoise and the hare is about more than a tortoise and a hare, he might have saved himself considerable trouble.

Three years later, he enrolled in first grade—for free, because his mom taught there—at the Kalman School, merely one year younger than most of his classmates. His dad pushed him to study more and harder, but he wasn't the kind of prodigy who goes to college at eleven. Both Colin's parents believed in keeping him on a semi-normal educational track for the sake of what they referred to as his "sociological well-being."

But his sociological being was never all that well. Colin didn't excel at making friends. He and his classmates just didn't enjoy similar activities. His favorite thing to do during recess, for instance, was to pretend to be a robot. He'd walk up to Robert Caseman with a knees-locked gait, his arms swinging stiffly. In a monotone voice, Colin would say, "I AM A ROBOT. I CAN ANSWER ANY QUESTION. DO YOU WANT TO KNOW WHO THE FOURTEENTH PRESIDENT WAS?"

"Okay," said Robert. "My question is, Why are you such a tard, Colon Cancer?" Even though Colin's name was pronounced like *call in*, Robert Caseman's favorite game in first grade was calling Colin "Colon Cancer" until Colin cried, which usually didn't take very long, because Colin was what his mother called "sensitive." He just wanted to play robot, for God's sake. Was that so wrong?

In second grade, Robert Caseman and his ilk matured a bit. Finally recognizing that words can never hurt, but sticks and stones can sure break bones, they invented the Abdominal Snowman.[10] They would order him to lie on the ground (and for some reason he'd agree), and then four guys would take a limb apiece and pull. It was a kind of drawing-and-quartering, but with seven-year-olds tugging it wasn't fatal, just embarrassing and dumb. It made him feel like no one liked him, which, in fact, no one did. His single consolation was that one day, he would matter. He'd be famous. And none of them ever would. That's why, his mom said, they made fun of him in the first place. "They're just *jealous*," she said. But Colin knew better. They weren't jealous. He just wasn't likable. Sometimes it's that simple.

And so both Colin and his parents were utterly pleased and relieved when, just after the start of third grade, Colin Singleton proved his sociological well-being by (briefly) winning the heart of the prettiest eight-year-old girl in all Chicago.

---

[10] Which, for the record, *Colin* actually named. The others called it "The Stretch," but then one time when they were about to do it to him, Colin shouted, "Don't give me an abdominal snowman!" And the name was so clever that it stuck.

# (four)

**Colin pulled into a rest stop** near Paducah, Kentucky, around three in the morning, leaned his seat back until it pressed against Hassan's legs in the backseat, and slept. Some four hours later, he awoke—Hassan was kicking him through the seat.

"*Kafir*—I'm paralyzed back here. Lean that shit forward. I gotta pray."

He'd been dreaming his memories of Katherine. Colin reached down and pulled the lever, his seat snapping forward.

"Fug," Hassan said. "Did something die in my throat last night?"

"Um, I'm sleeping."

"Because my mouth tastes like an open grave. Did you pack any toothpaste?"

"There's a word for that, actually. *Fetor hepaticus*. It happens during late st—"

"Not interesting," said Hassan, which is what he said whenever Colin started going off on a random tangent. "Toothpaste?"

"Toiletry kit in the duffel in the trunk," Colin answered.[11]

Hassan slammed the door behind him, then slammed the trunk shut a few moments later, and as Colin wiped the sleep from his eyes, he figured he might as well wake up. While Hassan knelt on the concrete outside,

---

[11] But anyway, it's called *fetor hepaticus*, and it's a symptom of late-stage liver failure. Basically, what happens is that your breath literally smells like a rotting corpse.

facing Mecca, Colin went to the bathroom (there graffiti in the stall read: CALL DANA FOR BLOW. Colin wondered whether Dana provided fellatio or cocaine, and then, for the first time since he'd been lying motionless on the carpet of his bedroom, he indulged his greatest passion. He anagrammed: Call Dana for blow; Ballad for a clown).

He walked out into the warmth of Kentucky and sat down at a picnic table across from Hassan, who seemed to be attacking the table with the pocketknife attached to his key chain.

"What are you doing?" Colin folded his arms on the table and then put his head down.

"Well, while you were in the bathroom, I sat down at this picnic table here in Bumblefug, Kentucky, and noticed that someone had carved that GOD HATES FAG, which, aside from being a grammatical nightmare, is absolutely ridiculous. So I'm changing it to 'God Hates Baguettes.' It's tough to disagree with that. *Everybody* hates baguettes."

*"J'aime les baguettes,"* Colin muttered.

"You *aime* lots of stupid crap."

While Hassan worked to make God hates baguettes, Colin's mind raced like this: (1) baguettes (2) Katherine XIX (3) the ruby necklace he'd bought her five months and seventeen days before (4) most rubies come from India, which (5) used to be under control of the United Kingdom, of which (6) Winston Churchill was the prime minister, and (7) isn't it interesting how a lot of good politicians, like Churchill and also Gandhi, were bald while (8) a lot of evil dictators, like Hitler and Stalin and Saddam Hussein, were mustachioed? But (9) Mussolini only wore a mustache sometimes, and (10) lots of good scientists had mustaches, like the Italian Ruggero Oddi, who (11) discovered (and named for himself) the intestinal tract's sphincter of Oddi, which is just one of several lesser-known sphincters like (12) the pupillary sphincter.

And speaking of which: when Hassan Harbish showed up at the Kalman

School in tenth grade after a decade of home-schooling, he was plenty smart, albeit not prodigiously so. That fall, he was in Calculus I with Colin, who was a ninth-grader. But they never spoke, because Colin had given up on pursuing friendships with individuals not named Katherine. He hated almost all the students at Kalman, which was just as well, since by and large they hated him back.

About two weeks into class, Colin raised his hand and Ms. Sorenstein said, "Yes, Colin?" Colin was holding his hand underneath his glasses, against his left eye, in obvious discomfort.

"May I be excused for a moment?" he asked.

"Is it important?"

"I think I have an eyelash in my pupillary sphincter," replied Colin, and the class erupted into laughter. Ms. Sorenstein sent him on his way, and then Colin went into the bathroom and, staring in the mirror, plucked the eyelash from his eye, where the pupillary sphincter is located.

After class, Hassan found Colin eating a peanut butter and no jelly sandwich on the wide stone staircase at the school's back entrance.

"Look," Hassan said. "This is my ninth day at a school in my entire life, and yet somehow I have already grasped what you can and cannot say. And you cannot say anything about your own sphincter."

"It's part of your eye," Colin said defensively. "I was being clever."

"Listen, dude. You gotta know your audience. That bit would kill at an ophthalmologist convention, but in calculus class, everybody's just wondering how the hell you got an eyelash *there*."

And so they were friends.

"I've gotta say, I don't think much of Kentucky," Hassan said. Colin tilted his head up, resting his chin on his arms. He scanned the rest-stop parking lot for a moment. His missing piece was nowhere to be found.

"Everything here reminds me of her, too. We used to talk about going to Paris. I mean, I don't even want to go to Paris, but I just keep imagining how excited she'd be at the Louvre. We'd go to great restaurants and maybe drink red wine. We even looked for hotels on the Web. We could have done that on the *KranialKidz* money."[12]

"Dude, if Kentucky is going to remind you of Paris, we're in a hell of a pickle."

Colin sat up and looked across the poorly kept lawn of the rest stop. And then he looked down at Hassan's clever handiwork. "*Baguettes,*" Colin explained.

"Oh, my God. Give me the keys." Colin reached into his pocket and tossed the keys lazily across the picnic table. Hassan snatched them as he stood, then made his way to Satan's Hearse. Colin followed, forlorn.

Forty miles down the road, still in Kentucky, Colin had curled up against the passenger window and was starting to fall asleep when Hassan announced, "World's Largest Wooden Crucifix—Next Exit!"

"We're not stopping to see the World's Largest Wooden Crucifix."

"We shitsure are," Hassan said. "It must be huge!"

"Hass, why would we stop and see the World's Largest Wooden Crucifix?"

"It's a *road trip*! It's about *adventure*!" Hassan pounded on the steering wheel to emphasize his excitement. "It's not like we have somewhere to *go*. Do you really want to die having never seen the World's Largest Wooden Crucifix?"

Colin thought it over. "Yes. First off, neither of us is Christian. Second off, spending the summer chasing after idiotic roadside attractions is not going to fix anything. Third off, crucifixes remind me of her."

"Of who?"

"Of *her*."

---

[12] More on that later, but basically: about a year before, Colin had come into some cash.

"*Kafir*, she was an *atheist*!"

"Not always," Colin said softly. "She used to wear one a long time ago. Before we dated." He stared out the window, pine trees rushing past. His immaculate memory called forth the silver crucifix.

"Your sitzpinkling disgusts me," Hassan said, but he gave the Hearse some extra gas and shot past the exit.

# (five)

**Two hours after** passing the World's Largest Wooden Crucifix, Hassan brought it back up.

"Did you already know that the World's Largest Wooden Crucifix was in Kentucky?" he shouted, his window down and his left hand waving through the fast-passing air.

"Not before today," Colin answered. "But I did know that the world's largest wooden *church* is in Finland."

"Not interesting," Hassan said. Hassan's not-interestings had helped Colin figure out what other people did and did not enjoy hearing about. Colin had never gotten that before Hassan, because everyone else either humored or ignored him. Or, in the case of Katherines, humored then ignored. Thanks to Colin's collected list of things that weren't interesting,[13] he could hold a halfway normal conversation.

Two hundred miles and one pit stop later, safely removed from Kentucky, they were midway between Nashville and Memphis. The wind through the open windows dried their sweat without actually cooling them much, and Colin was wondering how they could get to a place with air-

---

[13] Among many, many others, the following things were definitely not interesting: the pupillary sphincter, mitosis, baroque architecture, jokes that have physics equations as punch lines, the British monarchy, Russian grammar, and the significant role that salt has played in human history.

conditioning when he noticed the hand-painted billboard towering above a field of cotton or corn or soybeans or something.[14] EXIT 212—SEE THE GRAVE OF ARCHDUKE FRANZ FERDINAND—THE CORPSE THAT STARTED WORLD WAR I.

"That just doesn't seem plausible," Colin noted quietly.

"I'm just saying that I think we should go *somewhere*," Hassan said, not hearing him. "I mean, I like this interstate as much as the next guy, but the farther south we go, the hotter it gets, and I'm already sweating like a whore in church."

Colin rubbed his sore neck, thinking he would never spend another night in the car when he had plenty of money to pay for hotels. "Did you see that sign?" he asked.

"What sign?"

"The one about the grave of Archduke Franz Ferdinand."

With little regard for the road, Hassan turned to Colin, smiled broadly, and punched him softly on the shoulder. "Excellent. *Excellent.* And anyway, it's lunchtime."

As Colin climbed out of the passenger's seat in the Hardee's parking lot at Exit 212 in Carver County, Tennessee, he called his mom.

"Hey, we're in Tennessee."

"How are you feeling, buddy?"

"Better, I guess. I don't know. It's hot. Did, um, did anyone call?"

His mom paused, and he could just *feel* her wretched pity. "Sorry, love. I'll tell, uh, anyone, to call your cell."

"Thanks, Mom. I gotta go eat lunch at Hardee's."

"Sounds delightful. Wear your seat belt! I love you!"

"You too."

---

[14] Crop identification not being among Colin's talents.

• • •

After a relentlessly greasy Monster Thickburger in the empty restaurant, Colin asked the woman behind the cash register, whose body seemed to have suffered from perhaps a few too many meals at her place of employment, how to get to Franz Ferdinand's grave.

"Who?" she asked.

"The Archduke Franz Ferdinand."

The woman stared at him blankly for a moment, and then her eyes lit up. "Oh y'all are looking for Gutshot. Boy, you're headed for the sticks, aren't you?"

"Gutshot?"

"Yes. Now what you want to do is you pull out of the parking lot and you turn right—away from the highway I mean, and then in about two miles, the road's gonna T. There's a closed-down Citgo there. You take a right onto that road and then you're gonna drive past a whole lot of nothing for ten or fifteen miles. You'll go up a bit of a hill and then that's Gutshot."

"Gutshot?"

"Gutshot, Tennessee. That's where they got the Archduke."

"So a right and then a right."

"Yup. Y'all have fun now, y'hear?"

"Gutshot," Colin repeated to himself. "Okay, thanks."

Since its last paving, the ten- or fifteen-mile-long road in question seemed to have been at the epicenter of an earthquake. Colin drove cautiously, but still, the worn shocks of the Hearse creaked and groaned at the endless potholes and waving undulations of pavement.

"Maybe we don't need to see the Archduke," said Hassan.

"We're on a *road trip*. It's about *adventure*," Colin mimicked.

"Do you think the people of Gutshot, Tennessee, have ever seen an actual, living Arab?"

"Oh, don't be so paranoid."

"Or for that matter do you think they've ever seen a Jew-fro?"

Colin thought that over for a moment, and then said, "Well, the woman at Hardee's was nice to us."

"Right, but the woman at Hardee's called Gutshot 'the sticks,'" Hassan said, imitating the woman's accent. "I mean, if Hardee's is urban, I'm not sure I want to see rural." Hassan rolled on with his diatribe, and Colin laughed and smiled at all the right places, but he just kept driving, calculating the odds that the Archduke, who died in Sarajevo more than ninety years before, and who'd randomly popped into Colin's brain the previous night, would end up between Colin and wherever he was heading. It was irrational, and Colin hated thinking irrationally, but he couldn't help but wonder whether perhaps being in the presence of the Archduke might reveal something to Colin about his missing piece. But of course the universe does not conspire to put you in one place rather than another, Colin knew. He thought of Democritus: "Everywhere man blames nature and fate, yet his fate is mostly but the echo of his character and passions, his mistakes and weaknesses."[15]

And so it was not fate, but Colin Singleton's character and passions, his mistakes and weaknesses, that finally brought him to Gutshot, Tennessee—POPULATION 864, as the roadside sign read. At first, Gutshot looked like everything that came before it, only with a better-paved road. On each side of the Hearse, fields of squat, luminously green plants stretched out into a gray forever, broken up only by the occasional horse pasture, barn, or stand of trees. Eventually, Colin saw before him on the side of the road a two-story cinder-block building painted a ghastly pink.

"I think that's Gutshot," he said, nodding toward the building.

On the side of the building, a hand-painted sign read THE KINGDOM OF

[15] The original Greek, for the curious: Όπου το άτομο κατηγορείτη φύση και τη μοίρα, όμως η μοίρα του είναι συνήθως αλλά η ηχώ του χαρακτήρα και των παθών του, των λαθών και των αδυναμιών του.

GUTSHOT—ETERNAL RESTING PLACE OF THE ARCHDUKE FRANZ FERDINAND / ICE-COLD BEER / SODA / BAIT.

Colin pulled into the store's gravel driveway. Unbuckling his seat belt, he said to Hassan, "I wonder if they keep the Archduke with the soda or the bait."

Hassan's deep laugh filled the car. "Shit, Colin made a funny. This place is like magic for you. Shame about how we're gonna die here, though. I mean, seriously. An Arab and a half-Jew enter a store in Tennessee. It's the beginning of a joke, and the punch line is 'sodomy.'" Nonetheless, Colin heard Hassan shuffling his feet on the gravel parking lot behind him.

They walked through a screen door into the Gutshot General Store. From behind the counter, a girl with a long, straight nose and brown eyes the size of some lesser planets looked up from an issue of *Celebrity Living* magazine and said, "How y'all doing?"

"We're okay. Yourself?" Hassan asked while Colin was trying to think whether a worthwhile soul in all of human history had ever read a single copy of *Celebrity Living*.[16]

"Just fine," said the girl.

For a while, they walked around the store, pacing the dusty, varnished two-by-fours that comprised a floor, pretending to consider various snacks, drinks, and minnows swimming in bait tanks. Half-crouched behind a chest-high rack of potato chips, Colin tugged on Hassan's T-shirt, cupped his hand over Hassan's ear, and whispered, "*Talk* to her." Except in point of fact Colin did not whisper, because he had never quite mastered the art of whispering—he just sort of talked in a slightly softer voice directly into Hassan's eardrum.

---

[16] To put it Venn Diagrammatically, Colin would have argued that the world looked like this:

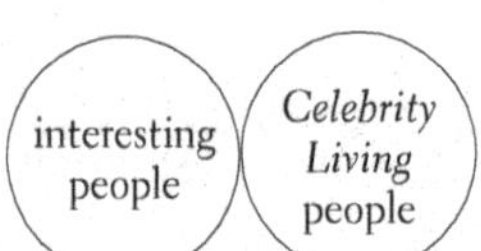

Hassan winced and shook his head. "What's the total area, in square miles, of the state of Kansas?" he whispered.

"Um, around 82,200; why?"

"I just find it amusing that you know that but can't figure out a way to speak without using your vocal cords." Colin started to explain that even whispering involves the *use* of the vocal cords, but Hassan just rolled his eyes. So Colin brought his hand to his face and nibbled on the inside of his thumb while staring at Hassan hopefully, but Hass had turned his attention to the potato chips and so finally it fell to Colin. He walked to the desk and said, "Hi, we're wondering about the Archduke."

The *Celebrity Living* reader smiled at him. Her puffy cheeks and too-long nose disappeared. She had the sort of broad and guileful smile in which you couldn't help but believe—you just wanted to make her happy so you could keep seeing it. But it passed in a flash. "Tours start every hour on the hour, cost eleven dollars, and frankly aren't worth it," she answered in a monotone.

"We'll pay," Hassan said, suddenly behind him. "The kid needs to see the Archduke." And then Hassan leaned forward and stage-whispered, "He's having a nervous breakdown." Hassan placed twenty-two dollars on the counter, which the girl promptly slid into a pocket of her shorts, flagrantly disregarding the cash register before her.

The girl blew a lock of mahogany hair from her face and sighed. "Sure is hot out," she noted.

"Is this, like, a guided tour?" Colin asked.

"Yeah. And much to my ever-loving chagrin, I am your tour guide." She stepped out from behind the counter. Short. Skinny. Her face not pretty so much as interesting-looking.

"I'm Colin Singleton," he said to the tour guide/grocery store clerk.

"Lindsey Lee Wells," she answered, reaching out a small hand, the fingernails a chipped metallic pink. He shook, and then Lindsey turned to Hassan.

"Hassan Harbish. Sunni Muslim. Not a terrorist."

"Lindsey Lee Wells. Methodist. Me neither." The girl smiled again. Colin wasn't thinking about anything but himself and K-19 and the piece of his gut he'd misplaced—but there was no denying her smile. That smile could end wars and cure cancer.

For a long time, they walked silently through knee-high grass behind the store, which irritated the sensitive skin of Colin's exposed calves, and he thought to mention it and ask whether maybe there was some kind of recently mowed patch through which they might walk, but he knew Hassan would think that "sitzpinklery," so he stayed quiet as the grass tickled at his skin. He thought of Chicago, where you can go days without ever once stepping on a single patch of actual earth. That well-paved world appealed to him, and he missed it as his feet fell on uneven clumps of hardened dirt that threatened to twist his ankles.

As Lindsey Lee Wells walked ahead of them (typical *Celebrity Living*–reader crap; avoiding talking to them), Hassan just padded along next to Colin, and even though he hadn't technically called Colin a *sitzpinkler* for being allergic to grass, Colin knew that he *would* have, which annoyed him. And so Colin again brought up Hassan's least favorite subject.

"Have I mentioned today that you should go to college?" Colin asked.

Hassan rolled his eyes. "Right, I know. I mean, just look where academic excellence got you."

Colin couldn't think of a comeback. "Well, but you should this year. You can't just not go forever. You don't even have to register until July fifteenth." (Colin had looked this up.)

"I actually *can* not go forever. I've said it before and I'll say it again: I like sitting around on my ass, watching TV, and getting fatter. It's my life's work, Singleton. That's why I love road trips, dude. It's like doing something without actually doing anything. Anyway, my dad didn't go to college, and he's rich as balls."

Colin wondered just how rich balls were, but only said, "Right, but your dad doesn't sit on his ass, either. He works, like, a hundred hours a week."

"True. True. And it's all thanks to him that I don't have to go to work *or* college."

Colin had no response to that. But he just didn't get Hassan's apathy. What is the point of being alive if you don't at least try to do something remarkable? How very odd, to believe God gave you life, and yet not think that life asks more of you than watching TV.

Although then again, when you have just gone on a road trip to escape the memory of your nineteenth Katherine and are traipsing through south-central Tennessee on your way to see the grave of a dead Austro-Hungarian Archduke, maybe you don't have a right to go and think anything odd.

And he was busy anagramming *anything odd—any odd night, handy dog tin, doing thy* DNA—when Colin did his DNA proud: he stumbled on a molehill and fell. He became so disoriented by the fast-approaching ground that he didn't even reach his hands out to break the fall. He just fell forward like he'd been shot in the back. The very first thing to hit the ground were his glasses. They were closely followed by his forehead, which hit a small jagged rock.

Colin rolled over onto his back. "I fell," he noted quite loudly.

"Shit!" Hassan shouted, and when Colin opened his eyes, he saw fuzzily that Hassan and Lindsey Lee Wells were kneeling, peering down at him. She smelled strongly of a fruity perfume, which Colin believed to be called Curve. He'd purchased it once, for Katherine XVII, but she hadn't liked it.[17]

"I'm bleeding, aren't I?" Colin asked.

"Like a stuck pig," she said. "Don't move." She turned to Hassan and said, "Give me your T-shirt," and Hassan promptly said no, which Colin

[17] "It smells like I rubbed chewed raspberry Bubblicious on my neck," she said, but it didn't, exactly. It smelled like raspberry Bubblicious-flavored *perfume*, which actually smelled very good.

figured had something to do with Hassan's man-boobs. "We need to apply pressure," Lindsey explained to Hassan, and then Hassan calmly said no again, and then Lindsey said, "Jesus Christ—fine," and took off her shirt.

Colin squinted through his glassesless fuzziness but couldn't see much. "We should probably save this for the second date," Colin said.

"Right, perv," she responded, but he could hear her smiling. As she wiped at his forehead and cheek softly with the T-shirt, then pressed hard on a tender spot above his right eyebrow, she kept talking. "Some friend you've got, by the way. Stop moving your neck. The two concerns we've got here are some kind of vertebral injury or a subdural hematoma. I mean, slight-slight-slight chances, but you've gotta be cautious, 'cause the nearest hospital's an hour away." He closed his eyes and tried not to wince as she pressed hard against the cut. Lindsey told Hassan, "Apply pressure with the shirt here. I'll be back in eight minutes."

"We should call a doctor or something," Hassan said.

"I'm a paramedic," Lindsey answered as she turned away.

"How the hell old are you?" he asked.

"Seventeen. Okay. Fine. A paramedic *in training*. Eight minutes. I swear." She ran off. It was not the way Curve smelled that Colin liked—not exactly. It was the way the air smelled just as Lindsey began to jog away from him. The smell the perfume left behind. There's not a word for that in English, but Colin knew the French word: *sillage*. What Colin liked about Curve was not its smell on the skin but its *sillage*, the fruity sweet smell of its leaving.

Hassan sat down beside him in the tall grass, pushing hard at the cut. "Sorry I wouldn't take off my shirt."

"Man-boobs?" asked Colin.

"Yeah, well. I just feel like I should know a girl a little before I trot out the man-tits. Where are your glasses?"

"I was just asking myself that very question when the girl took her shirt off," Colin said.

"So you couldn't see her?"

"I couldn't see her. Just that her bra was purple."

"Was it ever," Hassan replied.

And Colin thought of K-19 sitting over him on his bed wearing her purple bra as she dumped him. And he thought of Katherine XIV, who wore a black bra and also a black everything else. And he thought of Katherine XII, the first who wore a bra, and all the Katherines whose bras he'd seen (four, unless you count straps, in which case seven). People thought he was a glutton for punishment, that he liked getting dumped. But it wasn't like that. He could just never see anything coming, and as he lay on the solid, uneven ground with Hassan pressing too hard on his forehead, Colin Singleton's distance from his glasses made him realize the problem: myopia. He was nearsighted. The future lay before him, inevitable but invisible.

"I found 'em," Hassan said, and awkwardly tried to place the glasses on Colin's face. But it's hard to put glasses on someone else's head, and finally Colin reached up and nudged them up the bridge of his own nose, and he could see.

"*Eureka*," he said softly.

### Katherine XIX: The End (of the End)

She dumped him on the eighth day of the twelfth month, just twenty-two days shy of their one-year anniversary. They'd both graduated that morning, although from different schools, so Colin's and Katherine's parents, who were old friends, took them out to a celebratory lunch. But that evening was for them alone. Colin prepared by shaving and wearing that Wild Rain deodorant she liked so much that she'd nestle up against his chest to catch its scent.

He'd picked her up in Satan's Hearse and they drove south down

Lakeshore Drive, the windows down so they could hear, over the rumble of the engine, the waves of Lake Michigan beating against the rocky shore. Before them, the skyline towered. Colin had always loved Chicago's skyline. Although he was not a religious person, seeing the skyline made him feel what is called in Latin the *mysterium tremendum et fascinans*—that stomach-flipping mix of awestruck fear and entrancing fascination.

They drove downtown, winding through the soaring buildings of Chicago's Loop, and they were already late, because Katherine was always late to everything, and so after ten minutes spent searching for a parking meter, Colin paid eighteen dollars for a garage spot, which annoyed Katherine.

"I'm just saying we could have found a spot on the street," she said as she pressed the elevator button in the parking garage.

"Well, I've got the money. And we're late."

"You shouldn't spend money you don't need to spend."

"I'm about to spend fifty bucks on sushi," he answered. "For *you*." The doors opened. Exasperated, he leaned against the wood paneling of the elevator and sighed. They hardly spoke until they were inside the restaurant, seated at a tiny table near the bathroom.

"To graduating, and to a wonderful dinner," she said, raising her glass of Coke.

"To the end of life as we've known it," Colin replied, and they clinked glasses.

"Jesus, Colin, it's not the end of the world."

"It's the end of *a* world," he pointed out.

"Worried you won't be the smartest boy at Northwestern?" She smiled and then sighed. He felt a sudden twinge in his gut—in retrospect, it was the first hint that some piece of him might soon go missing.

"Why are you sighing?" he asked.

The waitress came then, interrupting with a rectangular plate of California *maki* and smoked salmon *negiri*. Katherine pulled apart her chopsticks, and Colin grabbed his fork. He knew a little conversational Japanese, but chopsticks eluded him.

"Why did you sigh?" he asked again.

"Jesus, no reason."

"No, just tell me why," he said.

"You're just—you spend all your time worrying about losing your edge or getting dumped or whatever and you're never for a second grateful. You're the valedictorian. You're going to a great school next year, for free. So maybe you're not a child prodigy. That's *good*. At least you're not a *child* anymore. Or, you're not supposed to be, anyway."

Colin chewed. He liked the seaweed wrapped around the sushi roll: how tough it was to chew, the subtleness of the ocean water. "You don't understand," he said.

Katherine placed her chopsticks against the saucer containing her soy sauce and stared at him with something beyond frustration. "Why do you always have to say that?"

"It's true," he said simply, and she *didn't* understand. She was still beautiful, still funny, still adept with chopsticks. Prodigy was what Colin had, the way language has words.

With all the nasty back-and-forth, Colin fought the urge to ask Katherine whether she still loved him, because the only thing she hated more than his saying she didn't understand was his asking whether she still loved him. He fought the urge and fought it and fought it. For seven seconds.

"Do you still love me?"

"Oh my God, Colin. Please. We graduated. We're happy. Celebrate!"

"What, are you afraid to say it?"

"I love you."

She would never—not ever—tell him those words in that order ever again.

"Can sushi be anagrammed?" she asked.

"Uh, sis," he answered immediately.

"Sis is three letters; sushi is five," she said.

"No. 'Uh, sis.' The uh and the sis. There are others, but they don't make grammatical sense."

She smiled. "Do you ever get tired of me asking?"

"No. No. I never get tired of anything you do," he said, and then he wanted to say he was sorry, but just that sometimes he felt un-understandable and sometimes he worried when they bickered and she went a while without saying she loved him, but he restrained himself. "Anyway, I like that sushi becomes 'uh, sis.' Imagine a situation."

"Imagine a situation" was a game she'd invented where Colin found the anagrams and then Katherine imagined an anagrammatic situation.

"Okay," she said. "Okay. So a guy goes out fishing on the pier, and he catches a carp, and of course it's all riddled with pesticides and sewage and all the nasty Lake Michigan shit, but he takes it home anyway because he figures if you fry a carp long enough, it won't matter. He cleans it, fillets it, and then the phone rings, so he leaves it on the kitchen counter. He talks on the phone for a bit, and then he comes back into the kitchen and sees that his little sister has a big hunk of raw Lake Michigan carp in her hand, and she's chewing, and she looks up at her brother and says, 'Sushi!' And he says, 'Uh, sis . . .'"

They laughed. He had never loved her so much as he did then.

Later, after they tiptoed into the apartment and Colin walked upstairs to tell his mom he was home, leaving out the possibly relevant information that he wasn't alone, and after they'd climbed into bed downstairs, and after she pulled off his shirt and he hers, and after they kissed until his lips were numb except for tingling, she said, "Do you really feel sad about graduating?"

"I don't know. If I'd done it differently—if I'd gone to college at ten or whatever—there's no way of knowing if my life would be better. We probably wouldn't be together. I wouldn't have known Hassan. And a lot of prodigies who push and push and push end up even more fugged up than me. But a few of them end up like John Locke[18] or Mozart or whatever. And my chances at Mozartdom are done."

"Col, you're *seventeen.*" She sighed again. She sighed a lot, but nothing could be wrong, because it felt so good to have her nestled up against him, her head on his shoulder, his hand brushing the soft blond hair from her face. He looked down and could see the strap of her purple bra.

"It's the tortoise and the hare, though, K.[19] I learn faster than other people, but they keep learning. I've slowed down, and now they're coming. I know I'm seventeen. But I'm past my prime." She laughed. "Seriously. There are studies about this shit. Prodigies tend to hit their peak at, like twelve or thirteen. What have I done? I won a fugging game show a year ago? That's my indelible mark on human history?"

She sat up, looking down at him. He thought of her other sighs, the better and different ones of his body moving against hers. For a long time she stared at him, and then she bit her lower lip and said, "Colin, maybe the problem is us."

"Oh. Shit," he said. And so it began.

The end occurred mostly in her whispers and his silence—because he couldn't whisper and they didn't want to wake Colin's parents. They succeeded in staying quiet, in part because it felt like the air had been shocked out of him. Paradoxically, he felt as if his getting dumped was the only thing happening on the entire dark and silent planet, and also as if it weren't happening at all. He felt himself drifting away from the one-sided whispered conversation, wondering if maybe everything big and heartbreaking and incomprehensible is a paradox.

He was a dying man staring down on the surgeons trying to save him.

---

[18] A British philosopher and political scientist who could read and write in Latin and Greek before the rest of us can tie our shoes.

[19] Although you'll no doubt notice that Colin still doesn't *quite* get what the tortoise and the hare story is about, he had figured out by now that it was about more than a turtle and a rabbit.

With an almost comfortable distance from the thing itself as it really was, Colin thought about the dork mantra: sticks and stones may break my bones, but words will never hurt me. What a dirty lie. This, right here, was the true abdominal snowman: it felt like something freezing in his stomach.

"I love you so much and I just want you to love me like I love you," he said as softly as he could.

"You don't need a girlfriend, Colin. You need a robot who says nothing but 'I love you.'" And it felt like being stoned and sticked from the inside, a fluttering and then a sharp pain in his lower rib cage, and then he felt for the first time that a piece of his gut had been wrenched out of him.

She tried to get out as quickly and painlessly as possible, but after she begged curfew, he began to cry. She held his head against her collarbone. And even though he felt pitiful and ridiculous, he didn't want it to end, because he knew the absence of her would hurt more than any breakup ever could.

But she left anyway, and he was alone in his room, searching out anagrams for *mymissingpiece* in a vain attempt to fall asleep.

# (six)

**It always happened like this:** he would look and look for the keys to Satan's Hearse and then finally he'd just give up and say, "*Fine. I'll take the fugging bus,*" and on his way out the door, he'd see the keys. Keys show up when you reconcile yourself to the bus; Katherines appear when you start to disbelieve the world contains another Katherine; and, sure enough, the Eureka moment arrived just as he began to accept it would never come.

He felt the thrill of it surge through him, his eyes blinking fast as he fought to remember the idea in its completeness. Lying there on his back in the sticky, thick air, the Eureka moment felt like a thousand orgasms all at once, except not as messy.

"Eureka?" Hassan asked, the excitement evident in his voice. He'd been waiting for it, too.

"I need to write this down," Colin said. He sat up. His head hurt like hell, but he reached into his pocket and pulled out the little notebook he kept at all times, and a #2 pencil, which was broken in the middle from his fall, but still wrote okay. He sketched:

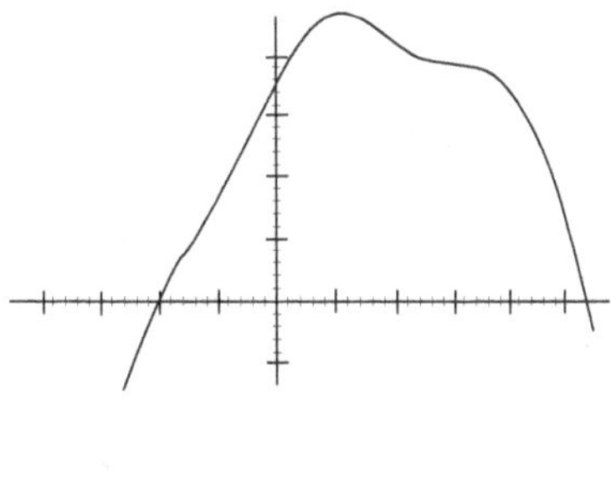

*Where $x$ = time, and $y$ = happiness, $y = 0$ beginning of relationship and breakup, $y$ negative = breakup by m, and $y$ positive = breakup by f: my relationship with K-19.*

• • •

He was still sketching when he heard Lindsey Lee Wells coming and opened his eyes to see her wearing a fresh T-shirt (it read GUTSHOT!) and toting a first-aid box with an honest-to-God red cross on it.

She knelt beside him and pulled the T-shirt off his head slowly, and then she said, "This is going to sting," and dug into the cut with a long Q-tip soaked in what seemed to be cayenne pepper sauce.

"FUG!" shouted Colin, wincing, and he looked up and saw her round, brown eyes blinking away sweat as she worked.

"I know. I'm sorry. Okay, done. You don't need stitches, but you're going to have a little scar, I bet. Is that okay?"

"What's another scar?" he said absentmindedly as she pulled a wide gauze bandage taut against his forehead. "I feel like someone punched me in the brain."

"Possible concussion," Lindsey noted. "What day is it? Where are you?"

"It's Tuesday, and I'm in Tennessee."

"Who was the junior senator from New Hampshire in 1873?" asked Hassan.

"Bainbridge Wadleigh," answered Colin. "I don't think I have a concussion."

"Is that for real?" asked Lindsey. "I mean, did you really know that?"

Colin nodded slowly. "Yeah," he said. "I know all the senators. Also, that's an easy one to remember—because I always think about how much your parents have to fugging hate you to name you Bainbridge Wadleigh."

"Seriously," said Hassan. "I mean, you've already got the last name Wadleigh. That's a bad sitch, just to be a Wadleigh. But then you take that Wadleigh and you raise it to the power of Bainbridge—no wonder the poor bastard never became president."

Lindsey added, "Well but then again, a guy named Millard Fillmore became president. No loving mother would ever make a Fillmore a Millard, either." She fell into conversation with them so quickly and so naturally that Colin was already revising his *Celebrity Living* theorem. He'd always thought people in Nowhere, Tennessee, would be, well, *dumber* than Lindsey Lee Wells.

Hassan sat down next to Colin and grabbed the notebook from him. He held it above his head to block the sun, which had darted out from behind a cloud to further bake the cracked orange dirt.

Hassan only glanced at the paper before saying, "You just got me all riled up and your big revelation is that you like getting dumped? Shit, Colin, I could have told you that. In fact, I have."

"Love is graphable!" Colin said defensively.

"Wait." Hassan looked down at the paper again, and then back to Colin. "Universally? You're claiming this will work for anyone?"

"Right. Because relationships are so predictable, right? Well, I'm finding a way to predict them. Take any two people, and even if they've never met each other, the formula will show who's going to break up with whom if they ever date, and approximately how long the relationship will last."

"Impossible," Hassan said.

"No, it's not, because you can see into the future if you have a basic understanding of how people are likely to act."

Hassan's long and slow exhalation broke into a whisper. "Yeah. Okay. That's interesting." Hassan could give Colin no higher compliment.

Lindsey Lee Wells reached down and grabbed the notebook from Hassan. She read it slowly. Finally, she said, "What the hell is K-19?"

Colin put a hand down in the caked-dry earth and pushed himself up. "The what's a who," he answered. "Katherine XIX. I've dated nineteen girls named Katherine."

Lindsey Lee Wells and Colin stared at each other dead in the eye for a very long time, until finally her smile collapsed into a gentle laugh. "What?" Colin asked.

She shook her head but couldn't stop laughing. "Nothin'," she said. "Let's go see the Archduke."

"No, tell me," he said insistently. He didn't like secrets kept from him. Being on the outside of something annoyed him—more than it should have, really.

"It's nothing. Just—I've only dated one boy."

"Why's that funny?" Colin asked.

"It's funny," she explained, "because his name is Colin."

### The Middle (of the Beginning)

By third grade, his failure to achieve "sociological well-being" had become so obvious to everyone that Colin attended regular school at Kalman only three hours a day. The rest of his day was spent with his lifelong tutor, Keith Carter, who drove a Volvo with the license plate KRAZZZY. Keith was one of those guys who never grew out of his ponytail. He also maintained (or, as the case was, failed to maintain) a thick, broad mustache that extended to his lower lip when his mouth was closed, which was very rarely the case. Keith enjoyed talking, and his favorite audience was Colin Singleton.

Keith was a friend of Colin's dad and a psychology professor. His interest in Colin wasn't exactly unselfish—over the years, Keith would publish a number of articles about Colin's prodigy. Colin liked being so special that scholars would take note of him. And also, Krazy Keith was the closest thing Colin had to a best friend. Every day, Keith drove down into the city and he and Colin went to a broom-closet-of-an-office on the third floor of the Kalman School. Colin pretty much got to read whatever he wanted in silence for the next four hours, with Keith occasionally breaking in to discuss something, and then on Fridays they'd spend the day talking about what Colin had learned. Colin liked it a great deal better than regular school. For one thing, Keith never gave him an Abdominal Snowman.

Krazy Keith had a daughter, Katherine, who was Colin's year in school but eight months older in actual life. She went to a school north of the city, but every so often Colin's parents would have Krazy Keith and his wife and Katherine over to dinner to discuss Colin's "progress" and the like. And then after those dinners, the parents would sit in the living room laughing louder as time passed, Keith shouting that he couldn't *possibly* drive home, that he needed a cup of coffee after all that wine—*your home is an Alamo for oenophiles*, he'd cry.

One night in November of his third-grade year, after it got cold but before his mom put up the holiday decorations, Katherine came over. After a dinner of lemon chicken and brown rice, Colin and Katherine went into the living room, where Colin lay across the couch and studied Latin. He had just recently learned that President Garfield, who was not even particularly noted for his intelligence, had been able to write simultaneously in Latin and Greek—Latin with his left hand and Greek with his right. Colin intended to match this feat.[20] Katherine, a tiny blond with both her father's ponytail and his fascination with prodigies, sat watching him quietly. Colin was aware of her, but it did not distract him, because people often watched him when he studied, like there was some secret in his approach to academia. The secret, in truth, was that he just spent more time studying, and paid more attention, than everyone else.

"How come you learned Latin already?"

"I study hard," he answered.

"Why?" she asked, coming over to sit by his feet on the couch.

"I like it."

"Why?" she asked.

---

[20] But never did, because try as he might, he just wasn't ambidextrous.

He paused for a moment. Unfamiliar with the "why game," he took her questions seriously. "I like it because it makes me different and better. And because I'm quite good at it."

"Why?" she asked, her voice singing the monosyllable, almost smiling.

"Your dad says it's because I remember things better than other people on account of how I pay very close attention and care very much."

"Why?"

"Because it is important to know things. For an example, I just recently learned that Roman Emperor Vitellius once ate one thousand oysters in one day, which is a very impressive act of *abligurition*,"[21] he said, using a word he felt sure Katherine wouldn't know. "And also it is important to know things because it makes you special and you can read books that normal people cannot read, such as Ovid's *Metamorphoses*, which is in Latin."

"Why?"

"Because he lived in Rome when they spoke and wrote Latin."

"Why?"

And that one tripped him up. Why *had* Ovid lived in Ancient Rome in 20 BCE[22] and not Chicago in 2006 CE? Would Ovid still have been Ovid if he had lived in America? No, he wouldn't have been, because he would have been a Native American or possibly an American Indian or a First Person or an Indigenous Person, and they did not have Latin or any other kind of written language then. So did Ovid matter because he was Ovid or because he lived in Ancient Rome? "That," Colin said, "is a very good question and I will try to find out the answer for you," he said, which is what Krazy Keith said when Krazy Keith did not know an answer.

"Do you want to be my *boyfriend*?" Katherine asked.

---

[21] An actual, if very obscure, English word, which means "the spending of too much money on food."

[22] One no longer says AD or BC. It's just not hip anymore. These days, one says either CE (for Common Era) or BCE (for Before Common Era).

Colin sat up quickly and looked at her, her bright blue eyes staring down into her lap. He would come, eventually, to call her The Great One. Katherine I. Katherine the Magnificent. Even seated, she was noticeably shorter than he, and she looked quite serious and nervous, her lips pulled in tight as she looked down. Something surged through him. The nerve endings exploded into shivers on his skin. His diaphragm fluttered. And of course it couldn't have been lust or love and it didn't feel like *like*, so it must have been what the kids at school called *like-like*. And he said, "Yes, yes, I do." She turned to him, her face round and her cheeks full and freckled and she leaned toward him, her lips pursed, and she kissed him on the cheek. It was his first kiss, and her lips felt like the coming winter—cold and dry and chapped—and it occurred to Colin that the kiss didn't feel nearly as good as the sound of her asking if she could be his girlfriend.

# (seven)

**Quite out of nowhere,** just over the crest of a tiny slope, the grassy field broke out into a graveyard. It contained perhaps forty gravestones and was surrounded by a knee-high stone wall covered in slippery moss. "This would be the last and final resting place of the Archduke Franz Ferdinand," Lindsey Lee Wells said, her voice suddenly affected with a new cadence, that of the bored tour guide who long ago memorized her speech. Colin and Hassan followed her to a six-foot-tall obelisk—a kind of miniature Washington Monument—before which lay a plethora of not-new pink silk roses. Though obviously fake, the flowers still seemed wilted.

Lindsey sat down on the mossy wall. "Ah, screw the speech. You probably already know this anyway," she said, nodding toward Colin. "But I'll tell the story: the Archduke was born in December 1863 in Austria. His uncle was the emperor Francis Joseph, but being the Austro-Hungarian emperor's nephew don't matter much. *Unless*, say, the emperor's only son, Rudolph, happens to shoot himself in the head—which is what, in fact, happened in 1889. All of a sudden, Franz Ferdinand was next in line for the throne."

"They called Franz 'the loneliest man in Vienna,'" Colin said to Hassan.

"Yeah, well no one liked him because he was a total nerd," Lindsey said, "except he was one of those nerds who isn't even very smart. Your average inbred ninety-six-pound weakling type. His family thought he was a liberal wuss; Viennese society thought he was an idiot—like an actual tongue-hanging-out-of-your-mouth idiot. And then he went and made matters worse by marrying for love. He married this girl named Sophie in 1900, and everyone thought she was just totally low-rent. But, you know, in the guy's defense, he really loved her. That's what I never tell in the tour, but from everything I've read about Franzy, he and Sophie had about the happiest marriage in the whole history of royalty. It's sort of a cute story, except for how on their fourteenth wedding anniversary—June twenty-eighth, 1914—they were both shot dead in Sarajevo. The emperor had them buried outside of Vienna. He didn't even bother to attend the funeral. But he cared enough about his nephew to go ahead and start World War I, which he did by declaring war on Serbia a month later." She stood up. "Thus ends the tour." She smiled. "Tips are appreciated."

Colin and Hassan clapped politely, and then Colin walked over to the obelisk, which read only: ARCHDUKE FRANZ FERDINAND. 1863–1914. LIE LIGHTLY UPON HIM EARTH, THO' HE / LAID MANY A HEAVY BURDEN UPON THEE. Heavy burdens, indeed—millions of them. Colin reached out and felt the granite, cool despite the hot sun. And what had the Archduke Franz Ferdinand done that he might have done differently? If he hadn't obsessed over love, hadn't been so tactless, so whiny, so nerdy—maybe if he hadn't been, Colin thought, so much like *me* . . .

In the end, the Archduke had two problems: no one gave a shit about him (at least not till his corpse started a war), and one day he got a piece taken out of his middle.

But now Colin would fill his own hole *and* make people stand up and take notice of him. He would stay special, use his talent to do something more interesting and important than anagramming and translating Latin. And yes, again the Eureka washed over him, the yes-yes-yes of it. He would use his past—and the Archduke's past, and the whole endless past—to inform the future. He would impress Katherine XIX—she had always loved the idea of him being a genius—and he would make the world safer for Dumpees everywhere. He would matter.

From which reverie he was awoken by Hassan asking, "So how the fug did a perfectly good Austrian Archduke end up in Shitsberg, Tennessee?"

"We bought him," Lindsey Lee Wells said. "Around 1921. The owner of the castle where he was buried needed money and put him up for sale. And we bought him."

"How much did a dead Archduke cost in those days?" Hassan wondered.

"'Bout thirty-five hundred bucks, they say."

"That's a lot of money," Colin said, his hand still on the granite obelisk. "The dollar rose by a factor of more than ten between 1920 and now, so that's more than thirty-five thousand dollars in today's dollars. A lot of tours at eleven bucks apiece."

Lindsey Lee Wells rolled her eyes. "Okay, okay—I am sufficiently impressed. Enough already. You know, we got these things down here—I don't know if you have 'em where you're from, but they're called calculators, and they can do all that work for you."

"I wasn't trying to impress anyone," Colin insisted defensively.

And then Lindsey's eyes lit up and she cupped her hands over her mouth and shouted, "Hey!" Three guys and one girl were trudging up the slope, just their heads visible. "Kids from school," Lindsey explained. "And my boyfriend." Lindsey Lee Wells took off running toward them. Hassan and Colin stood still, and began chatting quickly back and forth.

Hassan said, "I'm a Kuwaiti exchange student; my dad's an oil baron."

Colin shook his head. "Too obvious. I'm a Spaniard. A refugee. My parents were murdered by Basque separatists."

"I don't know if Basque is a thing or a person and neither will they, so no. Okay, I just got to America from Honduras. My name is Miguel. My parents made a fortune in bananas, and you are my bodyguard, because the banana-workers' union wants me dead."

Colin shot back, "That's good, but you don't speak Spanish. Okay, I was abducted by Eskimos in the Yukon Terr—no, that's crap. We're cousins from France visiting the United States for the first time. It's our high-school graduation trip."

"That's boring, but we're out of time. I'm the English speaker?" asked Hassan.

"Yeah, fine." By now, Colin could hear the group chatting, and see Lindsey Lee Wells's eyes staring up at a tall, muscular boy wearing a Tennessee Titans jersey. The boy was a hulking mass of muscle with spiked hair and a smile that was all top teeth and gums. The success of the game depended on Lindsey having not talked about Colin and Hassan, but Colin figured it was a safe bet, as she seemed pretty enthralled with the boy.

"Okay, they're coming," said Hassan. "What's your name?"

"Pierre."

"Okay. I'm Salinger, pronounced SalinZHAY."

"Y'all here for the tour, are ya," Lindsey's boyfriend said.

"Yes. I am Salinzhay," Hassan said, his accent passable if not magnificent. "This is my cousin Pierre. We visit your country for the first time, and we wish to see the Archduke, who started our—how you say—first Earth war." Colin glanced at Lindsey Lee Wells, who suppressed a smile as she smacked orange gum.

"I'm Colin," the boyfriend said, his hand extended. Hassan leaned over to Pierre/Colin and whispered, "His name is 'The Other Colin.'" Hassan then said, "My cousin, he speak very little English. I am his man of translate." The Other Colin laughed, as did the two other boys, who quickly introduced themselves as Chase and Fulton. ("We will call Chase, Jeans Are Too Tight, and Fulton shall be Short One Chewing Tobacco," Hassan whispered to Colin.)

"*Je m'appelle Pierre,*" Colin blurted out after the boys had introduced themselves. "*Quand je vais dans le métro, je fais aussi de la musique de prouts.*"[23]

"We get a lot of foreign tourists here," said the only girl besides Lindsey,

---

[23] "My name is Pierre. When I go to the metro, I also make fart music."

who was tall and thoroughly Abercrombified in her tight tank top. The girl also had—how to put this politely—gigantic gazoombas. She was incredibly hot—in that popular-girl-with-bleached-teeth-and-anorexia kind of way, which was Colin's least favorite way of being hot. "I'm Katrina, by the way." *Close*, Colin thought, *but no cigar*.

"*Amour aime aimer amour!*"[24] Colin announced quite loudly.

"Pierre," said Hassan. "He has the disease with the talking. The, uh, with the bad words. In France, we say it the *Toorettes*. I do not know how you say in English."

"He has Tourette's?" asked Katrina.

"*MERDE!*"[25] shouted Colin.

"Yes," said Hassan excitedly. "Same word both language, like hemorrhoid. That one we learned yesterday because Pierre had the fire in his bottom. He has the *Toorettes*. And the hemorrhoid. But, is good boy."

"*Ne dis pas que j'ai des hémorroïdes! Je n'ai pas d'hémorroïde,*"[26] Colin shouted, at once trying to continue the game and get Hassan on to a different topic.

Hassan looked at Colin, nodded knowingly, and then told Katrina, "He just said that your face, it is beautiful like the hemorrhoid." At which point Lindsey Lee Wells burst out laughing and said, "Okay. Okay. Enough."

Colin turned to Hassan and said, "Why'd it have to be hemorrhoids? How the hell did that idea pop into your mind?" And then The Other Colin (TOC) and Jeans Are Too Tight (JATT) and Short One Chewing Tobacco (SOCT) and Katrina were all abuzz, talking and laughing and asking Lindsey questions.

"My dad went to France last year, dude," explained Hassan, "and he told this story about getting a hemorrhoid and having to point at his butt and say the French word for fire over and over again until it came out that

---

[24] "Love loves to love love." A quote, translated into French, from James Joyce's *Ulysses*.
[25] "Shit!"
[26] "Don't say I have hemorrhoids! I don't have hemorrhoids."

the word was hemorrhoid in both languages. And I didn't know any other fugging French words. Plus that's some funny shit, you having Tourette's *and* hemorrhoids."

"Whatever," Colin said, his face flushed. And then he overheard TOC saying, "That's awful funny. Hollis would love them, huh?" And Lindsey laughed and reached up on her tiptoes to kiss him and then said, "I got you good, baby," and he said, "Well, *they* got me," and Lindsey faked like she was pouting, and TOC leaned down to kiss her forehead, and she brightened. The same scene had played out in Colin's own life frequently—although he'd usually been the fake pouter.

They trudged back through the field as a group, Colin's sweat-soaked T-shirt sticky and tight against his back, his eye still throbbing. *The Theorem of Underlying Katherine Predictability*, he thought. Even the name rang true. He had waited so long for his breakthrough, despaired so many times, and he just wanted to be alone for a little while with a pencil and some paper and a calculator and no talking. In the car would work. Colin tugged softly on Hassan's shirt and gave him a meaningful look.

"I just need some Gatorade," Hassan responded. "Then we'll go."

"I'll need to open up the store for ya, then," Lindsey said. She turned to TOC. "Come with me, baby." The gooey softness of her voice reminded Colin of K-19.

"I would," TOC said, "'cept Hollis is sitting out on the steps. Me and Chase is supposed to be at work, but we skipped out." TOC picked her off her feet and squeezed her tight, his biceps flexing. She squirmed a little but kissed him hard, her mouth open. Then he dropped her down, winked, and trudged off with his entourage toward a red pickup truck.

When Lindsey, Hassan, and Colin arrived back at the Gutshot General Store, a large woman wearing a pink floral dress was sitting on the steps talking to a man with a bushy brown beard. As they approached, Colin could hear the woman telling a story.

"So Starnes is out there to mow the lawn," she was saying. "And he turns off the mower and looks up and appraises the situation for a bit and then calls out to me, 'Hollis! What the hell is wrong with that dog?' and I says to him that the dog's got inflamed anal sacs that I just drained, and Starnes chews that one over for a while and then finally he says, 'I reckon you could go ahead and shoot that dog and git you another one with regular anal sacs and wouldn't nobody be the wiser.' And I tell him, 'Starnes, this town ain't got any men worth loving, so I might as well love my dog.'" The bearded guy bent over in laughter, and then the storyteller looked over at Lindsey.

"You were on a tour?" Hollis asked. When Lindsey nodded, Hollis went on. "Well, you sure-God took your time."

"Sorry," mumbled Lindsey. Nodding to the guys, she said, "Hollis, this is Hassan and Colin. Boys, this is Hollis."

"Also known as Lindsey's mother," Hollis explained.

"Christ, Hollis. Don't go bragging about it," Lindsey said. She walked past her mom, unlocked the store, and everyone walked into the sweet air-conditioning. As Colin passed, Hollis put a hand on his shoulder, spun him around, and stared at his face.

"I know you," she said.

"I don't know you," Colin responded, and then added, by way of explanation, "I don't forget many faces." Hollis Wells continued to stare at him, but he was sure they had never met.

"He means that literally," Hassan added, peering up from behind a rack of comic books. "Do you guys get newspapers here?" From behind the counter, Lindsey Lee Wells produced a *USA Today*. Hassan paged through the front section and finally folded the paper carefully to reveal only a small black-and-white picture of a thick-haired bespectacled white male. "Do you know this guy?" Hassan asked.

Colin squinted at the paper and thought for a moment. "I don't personally know him, but his name is Gil Stabel and he is the CEO of a company called Fortiscom."

"Good work. Except he's not the CEO of Fortiscom."

"Yes, he is," Colin said, quite confident.

"No, he's not. He's not the CEO of anything. He's dead." Hassan unfolded the paper, and Colin leaned in to read the caption: FORTISCOM CEO DIES IN PLANE CRASH.

"*KranialKidz*!" Hollis shouted triumphantly.

Colin looked up at her, wide-eyed. He sighed. *No one* watched that show. Its Nielsen share was 0.0. The show had been on for one season and not a single soul among Chicago's three million residents had ever recognized him. And yet, here in Gutshot, Tennessee . . .

"Oh my God!" Hollis shouted. "What are you doing *here*?"

Colin, flushed for a moment with a feeling of famousness, thought about it. "I cracked up; then we went on a road trip; then we saw the sign for the Archduke; then I cut my head; then I had a Eureka moment; then we met her friends; now we're going back to the car, but we haven't left yet."

Hollis stepped forward and examined his bandage. She smiled, and with one hand reached up for his Jew-fro and mussed his hair like she was his aunt and he was a seven-year-old who'd just done something exceedingly cute. "You're not leaving yet, either," she said, "because I'm going to cook you dinner."

Hassan clapped his hands together. "I *am* hungry."

"Close her down, Linds." Lindsey rolled her eyes and walked slowly out from behind the register. "You drive with Colin in case he gets lost," Hollis told Lindsey. "I'll take—what did you say your name was?"

"I'm not a terrorist," Hassan said by way of answering.

"Well. That's a relief." Hollis smiled.

Hollis drove a new and impressively pink pickup truck, and Colin followed in the Hearse with Lindsey riding shotgun. "Nice car," she said sarcastically.

Colin didn't respond. He liked Lindsey Lee Wells, but sometimes it felt like she was trying to get his goat.[27] He had the same problem with Hassan. "Thanks for not saying anything when I was Pierre and Hassan was Salinger."

"Yeah, well. It was pretty funny. And plus Colin was being sort of a dick and needed to be taken down a peg."

"I see," said Colin, which is what he had learned to say when he had nothing to say.

"So," she said. "You're a genius?"

"I'm a washed-up child prodigy," Colin said.

"What are you good at, other than just already knowing everything?"

"Um, languages. Word games. Trivia. Nothing useful."

He felt her glance at him. "Languages are useful. What do you speak?"

"I'm pretty good in eleven. German, French, Latin, Greek, Dutch, Arabic, Spanish, Russian—"

"I get the picture," she said, cutting him off. "I think that *meine Mutter denkt, daß sie gut für mich sind,*"[28] she said. "That's why we're in this car together."

"*Warum denkt sie das?*"[29]

"Okay, we've both proven we speak German. She's been on my ass like crazy to go to college and become, I don't know, a doctor or something. Only I'm not going. I'm staying here. I already made up my mind about that. So I'm thinking maybe she wants you to inspire me or something."

"Doctors make more money than paramedics-in-training," Colin pointed out.

"Right, but I don't need money." She paused, and the car rumbled beneath them. Finally, he glanced over at her. "I need my life," she explained,

---

[27] Which is what Colin's mom always called teasing, even though it never made a lick of sense to Colin.
[28] "My mother thinks that you are good for me."
[29] "Why would she think that?"

"which is good and which is here. Anyway, I might go to the community college in Bradford to shut Hollis up, but that's it." The road took a sharp, banked turn to the right and, past a stand of trees, a town emerged. Small but well-kept houses lined the road. They all had porches, it seemed, and a lot of people were sitting out on them, even though it was hotter than hell in summertime. On the main road, Colin noted a newish combination gas station and Taco Bell, a hair salon, and the Gutshot, TN, Post Office, which appeared from the road to be the size of a spacious walk-in closet. Lindsey pointed out Colin's window. "Out there's the factory," she said, and in the middle distance Colin saw a complex of low-lying buildings. It didn't look much like a factory—no towering steel silos or smokestacks billowing carbon monoxide, just a few buildings that vaguely reminded him of airplane hangars.

"What does it make?" Colin asked.

"It makes jobs. It makes all the good jobs this town has. My great-grandfather started the plant in 1917." Colin slowed down, pulling to the shoulder so that a speeding SUV could pass him while he looked out at the factory with Lindsey.

"Right, but what gets *made* there?" he asked.

"You'll laugh."

"I won't laugh."

"Swear not to laugh," she said.

"I swear."

"It's a textile mill. These days we mostly make, uh, tampon strings."

Colin did not laugh. Instead, he thought, *Tampons have strings? Why?* Of all the major human mysteries—God, the nature of the universe, etc.—he knew the least about tampons. To Colin, tampons were a little bit like grizzly bears: he was aware of their existence, but he'd never seen one in the wild, and didn't really care to.

In lieu of Colin's laugh came a period of unbreachable silence. He followed Hollis's pink truck down a newly paved side street that sloped up precipitously, causing the Hearse's worn-out engine to rev for its very life. As they climbed the hill, it became clear that the street was actually a long driveway, which dead-ended into the largest single-family residence that Colin had ever personally laid eyes upon. Also, it was glaringly, bubble-gummingly, Pepto-Bismolly pink. He pulled into the driveway. Colin was staring at it somewhat slack-jawed when Lindsey poked him softly on the arm. Lindsey shrugged, as if embarrassed. "It ain't much," she said. "But it's home."

A broad staircase led up to a heavily columned front porch. Hollis opened the door and Colin and Hassan walked into a cavernous living room outfitted with a couch long enough for both of them to lie down without touching. "Y'all make yourselves at home. Lindsey and I are going to get dinner ready."

"You can probably handle that on your own," Lindsey said, leaning against the front door.

"I probably could, but I ain't gonna."

Hassan sat down on the couch. "That Hollis is a riot, man. On the way over here she was telling me that she owns a factory that makes tampon strings." Colin still did not find this fact particularly hilarious.

"You know," Colin said, "the movie star Jayne Mansfield lived in a pink mansion." He walked around the living room, reading the spines of Hollis's books and looking at framed photographs. A picture on the mantel above their fireplace caught Colin's eye, and he walked over to it. A slightly younger, slightly thinner Hollis was standing in front of Niagara Falls. Beside her stood a girl who looked a little like Lindsey Lee Wells, except the girl wore a black trench coat over a ratty old Blink-182 T-shirt. Her eyeliner was thick and stretched back toward her temples, her black jeans tight and tapered, her Doc Martens well-polished. "Does she have a sister?" asked Colin.

"What?"

"Lindsey," Colin elaborated. "Come here and look at this."

Hassan came over and briefly appraised the picture before saying, "That's the most pathetic attempt I've ever seen to be goth. Goth kids don't like Blink-182. God, even I know that."

"Um, do you like green beans?" Lindsey asked, and Colin suddenly realized she was behind them.

"Is this your sister?" asked Colin.

"Uh, no," she said to Colin. "I'm an only child. Can't you tell by how adorably self-involved I am?"

"He was too busy being adorably self-involved to notice," Hassan interjected.

"So who is this?" Colin asked Lindsey.

"It's me in eighth grade."

"Oh," said Colin and Hassan simultaneously, both embarrassed. "Yeah, I like green beans," Hassan said, trying to change the subject as quickly as possible. Lindsey pulled shut the kitchen door behind her, and Hassan shrugged toward Colin and smirked, then returned to the couch.

"I need to work," Colin said. He found his way down a pink-wallpapered hallway and into a room with a huge wooden desk that looked like the kind of place where a president might sign a bill into law. Colin sat down, pulled from his pocket his broken #2 pencil and omnipresent notebook, and began to scribble.

*The Theorem rests upon the validity of my long-standing argument that the world contains precisely two kinds of people: Dumpers and Dumpees. Everyone is predisposed to being either one or the other, but of course not all people are* COMPLETE *Dumpers or Dumpees. Hence the bell curve:*

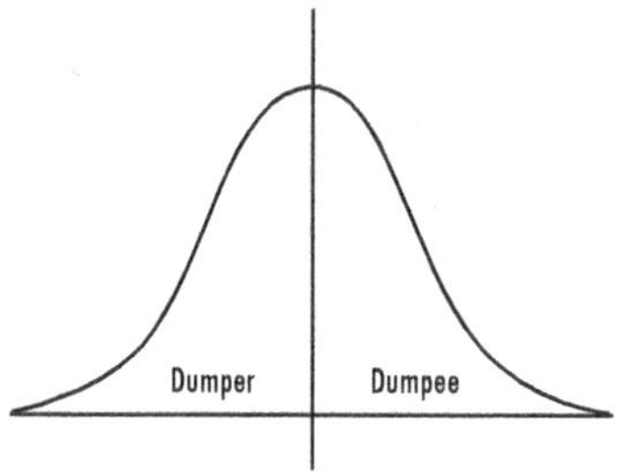


*The majority of people fall somewhere close to the vertical dividing line with the occasional statistical outlier (e.g., me) representing a tiny percentage of overall individuals. The numerical expression of the graph can be something like 5 being extreme Dumper, and 0 being me. Ergo, if the Great One was a 4 and I am a 0, total size of the Dumper/Dumpee differential = -4. (Assuming negative numbers if the guy is more of a Dumpee; positive if the girl is.)*

And then he sought a graphable equation that would express his relationship with the Great One (the simplest of all his romances) as it actually was: nasty, brutish, and short.

For some reason, as he discarded equations left and right, the room seemed to grow warmer. Sweat pooled in the gauze bandage over his eyes, so he tore it off. He removed his shirt, wiping still-trickling blood from his face. Naked from the waist up, his vertebrae extruded from his skinny back as he hunched over the desk, working. He felt as he had never felt before—that he was close to an original concept. Plenty of people, Colin included, had noted the Dumper/Dumpee dichotomy before. But no one had ever used it to show the arc of romantic relationships. He doubted anyone had ever even imagined that a single formula could predict the rise and fall of romances universally. He knew it wouldn't be easy. For one thing, turning concepts into numbers was a sort of anagramming to which he was unaccustomed. But he had confidence. He'd never been all that good at math,[30] but he was a goddamned world-famous expert in getting dumped.

---

[30] Although of course he was certainly better than most people.

He kept at the formula, haunted by the feeling that his head was just about to wrap around something big and important. And when he proved he mattered, she would miss him, he knew. She would see him as she had in the beginning: as a genius.

Within an hour, he had an equation:

$$f(x) = D^3x^2 - D$$

which made Katherine I look like this:

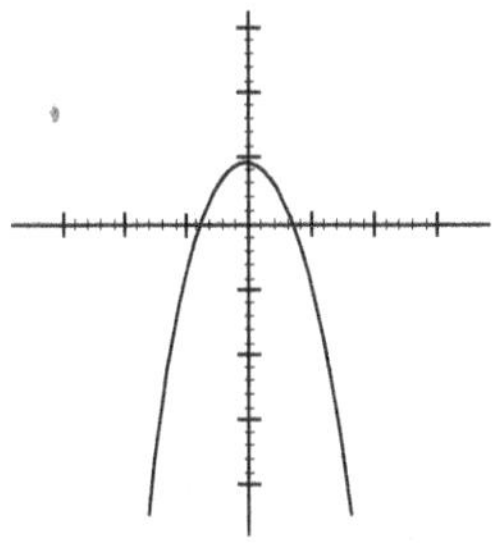

That was nearly perfect—an uncomplicated graphical representation of an uncomplicated relationship. It even captured the relationship's brevity. The graphs didn't need to represent time accurately; they merely needed to give an idea of length *by comparison*, i.e., she'll date me longer than K-14 but not as long as K-19.[31]

But Katherine II came out all wrong—only touching the x-axis once. Clearly, it wasn't refined enough yet to send out a notice to *The Annals of Mathematics* or anything, but Colin felt good enough to slink back into his shirt. Happier than he'd been in, well, at least two days, Colin hurried down

[31] A fuller explanation of the math involved here would be really boring and also really long. There is a part of books specifically designed for the very long and the very boring, and that part is called "The Appendix," which is precisely where one can find a semi-exhaustive explanation of the math invoked herein. As for the actual story itself: there will be no more math. None. Promise.

the hallway and burst into the coolness of the living room, where he saw through a doorway that Lindsey and Hassan and Hollis were seated in the dining room. He walked in and sat down before a plate of rice, green beans, and what appeared to be very small chickens.

Hassan was laughing about something, and so were both the Wellses. Already, they seemed to love him. People just liked Hassan, the way people like fast food and celebrities. It was a gift Colin found amazing.

The moment Colin sat down, Hollis asked Hassan, "Would you like to say grace?"

"Sure thing." Hassan cleared his throat. "*Bismillah.*" Then he picked up his fork.

"That's it?" Hollis wondered.

"That's it. We are a terse people. Terse, and also hungry."

The Arabic seemed to render everyone uncomfortable or something, because no one talked for a few minutes except Hassan, who kept saying that the quail (it was quail, not tiny chicken) was *excellent*. And it *was* good, Colin supposed, if you happened to enjoy searching through an endless labyrinth of bones and cartilage for the occasional sliver of meat. He hunted around with his fork and knife for the edible parts and finally located one entire bite of meat. He chewed slowly so as to relish it, chewing and chewing and *ouch. Christ. What the hell was that?* Chew. Chew. Chew. And *again. Fug. Is that a bone?* "Ow," he said softly.

"Birdshot," Lindsey told him.

"Birdshot?"

"Birdshot," Hollis agreed.

"The bird was shot?" Colin asked, spitting out a tiny metal pellet.

"Yup."

"And I'm eating the *bullets*?"

Lindsey smiled. "Nope. You're spitting them out."

And so it was that Colin dined that evening primarily on rice and green beans. After everyone had finished, Hollis asked, "So how did it feel to win *KranialKidz?* I remember on the show you didn't seem that, uh, excited."

"I felt really bad about the other kid losing. She was really nice. The kid I played against—she took it kind of hard."

"I was happy enough for the both of us," said Hassan. "I was the only member of the studio audience dancing a jig. Singleton beat that little fugger like she'd stole something."[32]

*KranialKidz* reminded Colin of Katherine XIX, and he stared straight ahead and tried hard to think of as little as possible. When Hollis spoke, it seemed to break a long quiet, the way alarm clocks do. "I think y'all should work for me this summer in Gutshot. I'm starting a project, and you'd be perfect for it."

Over the years, people had occasionally sought to employ Colin in a manner befitting his talents. But (a) summers were for smart-kid camp so that he could further his learning and (b) a real job would distract him from his real work, which was becoming an ever-larger repository of knowledge, and (c) Colin didn't really have any marketable skills. One rarely comes across, for instance, the following want ad:

> *Prodigy*
>
> *Huge, megalithic corporation seeks a talented, ambitious prodigy to join our exciting, dynamic Prodigy Division for summer job. Requirements include at least fourteen years' experience as a certified child prodigy, ability to anagram adeptly (and alliterate agilely), fluency in eleven languages. Job duties include reading, remembering encyclopedias, novels, and poetry; and memorizing the first ninety-nine digits of pi.*[33]

[32] Stole*n* something, Colin wanted to say. But grammar isn't interesting.

[33] Which Colin did when he was ten, by making up a 99-word sentence in which the first letter of each word corresponded to the digit of pi (a=1, b=2, etc.; j=0). The sentence, if

And so every summer Colin went to smart-kid camp and with each passing year it became increasingly clear to him that he wasn't qualified to do *anything*, which is what he told Hollis Wells.

"I just need you to be reasonably smart and not from Gutshot, and you both fit the bill. Five hundred dollars a week for both y'all, plus free room and board. You're hired! Welcome to the Gutshot Textiles family!"

Colin shot a glance at his friend, who held a quail daintily in his hands, his teeth gnawing at the bone in a vain search for a half-decent meal. Hassan placed the quail carefully back on the plate and looked back at Colin.

Hassan nodded subtly; Colin's lips pursed; Hassan rubbed at his five-o'clock shadow; Colin bit at the inside of his thumb; Hassan smiled; Colin nodded.

"Okay," said Colin finally. They had decided to stay. *Like it or not*, Colin thought, *road trips have destinations*. Or at least his kind of road trip always would. And this seemed a fair end point—sweet, if ceaselessly pink, accommodations; reasonably nice people, one of whom made him feel slightly famous; and the home of his first-ever Eureka. Colin didn't need the money, but he knew how much Hassan hated begging spending money off his parents. And also, they could both use a job. Neither of them, it occurred to Colin, had ever, technically, worked for money before. Colin's only worry was the Theorem.

Hassan said, *"La ureed an uz'ij rihlatik—wa lakin min ajl khamsu ma'at doolar amreeki fil usbu', sawfa afa'al."*[34]

---

you're curious: Catfish always drink alcoholic ether if begged, for every catfish enjoys heightened intoxication; gross indulgence can be calamitous, however; duly, garfish babysit for dirty catfish children, helping catfish babies get instructional education just because garfish get delight assisting infants' growth and famously inspire confidence in immature catfish, giving experience (and joy even); however, blowfish jeer insightful garfish, disparaging inappropriately, doing damage, even insulting benevolent, charming, jovial garfish, hurting and frustrating deeply; joy fades but hurt feelings bring just grief; inevitable irritation hastens feeling blue; however, jovial children declare happiness, blowfishes' evil causes dejection, blues; accordingly, always glorify jolly, friendly garfish!

[34] "I don't want to ruin your road trip—but for five hundred American dollars a week, I will."

*"La ureed an akhsar kulla wakti min ajl watheefa. Yajib an ashtaghil ala mas'alat al-riyadiat."*[35]

"Can we just make sure Singleton has time to doodle?" asked Hassan in English.

"Is that some kind of gibberish?" Lindsey interrupted, incredulous.

Colin ignored her, responding in English to Hassan. "It's not doodling, which you'd know if you—"

"Went to college, right. God, so predictable," Hassan said. Then he turned to Lindsey and said, "We are not speaking *gibberish*. We're speaking the sacred language of the *Qur'an*, the language of great *calipha* and Saladin, the most beautiful and intricate of all human tongues."

"Well, it sounds like a raccoon clearing its throat," Lindsey noted. Colin stopped for a moment to ponder that.

"I need time to do my work," Colin said, and Hollis just nodded.

"Splendid," Lindsey said, seemingly genuine. "Splendid. But you can't have my room."

His mouth half-full of rice, Hassan said, "I think we'll be able to find a place to hunker down somewhere in this house."

After awhile Hollis announced, "We should play Scrabble." Lindsey groaned.

"I've never played," Colin said.

"A genius who's never played Scrabble?" Lindsey asked.

"I'm not a genius."

"Okay. A *smartypants*?"

Colin laughed. It suited him. No longer a prodigy, not yet a genius—but still a smartypants. "I don't play games," Colin said. "I don't really *play* much."

"Well, you should. Playing is fun. Although Scrabble isn't really the A#1 way of doing it," Lindsey said.

---

[35] "The road trip has kind of sucked anyway, but I don't want the job to take my time. I need to do the Theorem."

*Final Score:*
*Hollis: 158*
*Colin: 521*
*Lindsey: 293*
*Hassan: 0*[36]

After he called his parents and told them he was in a town called Gutshot but failed to mention he was boarding with strangers, Colin stayed up late working on the Theorem in his new bedroom on the second floor, which featured a nice oak desk with empty drawers. Colin, for whatever reason, had always loved desks with empty drawers. But the Theorem didn't go well; he was beginning to worry that he might lack the math expertise for the job when he glanced up to see the bedroom door opening. Lindsey Lee Wells was wearing paisley pajamas.

"How's the head?" she asked, sitting down on his bed.

He closed his right eye, then opened it, and then pressed a finger against his cut. "It hurts," he responded. "Thanks for your treatment, though."

She folded her legs beneath her, smiled, and sang, "That's what friends are for." But then she turned serious, almost shy. "Listen, I wonder if I can just tell you something." She bit at the inside of her thumb.

"HeyIDoThat," Colin said, pointing.

"Oh, weird. It's like the poor man's thumb sucking, isn't it? Anyway, I only do it in private," Lindsey said, and it occurred to Colin that being around him was not really "private," but he didn't pursue it. "Right so anyway. This will sound retarded, but can I just tell you about that picture so you don't think I'm an absolute asshole? Because I've been lying in bed thinking about what an asshole you probably think I am, and how you and Hassan are probably talking about what an asshole I am and everything."

[36] "I'm not playing *Scrabble* against *Singleton*. God, if I want to be reminded of how dumb I am, I'll just consult my verbal SAT scores, thanks."

"Um, okay," he said, although frankly he and Hassan had plenty of other things to talk about.

"So I was ugly. I was never fat, really, and I never wore headgear or had zits or anything. But I was ugly. I don't even know how ugly and pretty get decided—maybe there's like a secret cabal of boys who meet in the locker room and decide who's ugly and who's hot, because as far as I can remember, there was no such thing as a hot fourth-grader."

"Clearly, you never met Katherine I," interrupted Colin.

"Rule 1 of stories: no interrupting. But, ha ha. Perv. Anyway, I was ugly. I got picked on a lot. I'm not going to bore you with stories about how bad it was, but it was pretty bad. I was miserable. And so in eighth grade I went all alternative. Hollis and I drove to Memphis and bought me a whole new wardrobe, and I got me a Zelda haircut and dyed it black and stopped going outside in the sun, and I was like half-emo and half-goth and half-punk and half-nerd chic. Basically, I didn't know what the hell I was doing, but it didn't matter because the middle school in Milan, Tennessee, had never seen emo or goth or punk or nerd chic. I was *different*, that was all. And I hated all of them, and they hated all of me for an entire year. And then high school started, and I decided to make them like me. I just decided. It was so easy, dude. It was so, so easy. I just became it. If it walks like a cool kid and talks like a cool kid and dresses like a cool kid and has the right mix of naughtyandnastyandnice like a cool kid, it becomes a cool kid. But I'm not an asshole to people. There's not even really *popularity* at my school."

"That," Colin said emphatically, "is a sentence that has only ever been spoken by popular people."

"Well, okay. But I'm not just some former ugly girl who sold her soul to date hotties and go to the finest keg parties the Greater Gutshot Area has to offer." She repeated it, almost defensively. "I didn't sell my soul."

"Um, okay. I wouldn't care if you did," Colin acknowledged. "Nerds always say they don't give a shit about popularity; but—not having friends sucks. I never liked quote unquote cool kids, personally—I thought they were all dumb little shits. But I'm probably like them in some ways. Like, the other day, I told Hassan I wanted to *matter*—like, be remembered. And he said, 'famous is the new popular.' Maybe he's right, and maybe I just want to be famous. I was thinking about this tonight, actually, that maybe I want strangers to think I'm cool since people who actually know me don't. I was at the zoo once when I was ten on a class trip and I really needed to pee, right? I actually had repeated urges to urinate that day, probably due to overhydration. Incidentally, did you know that the whole eight glasses a day thing is complete bullshit and has no scientific basis? So many things are like that. Everyone just assumes they're true, because people are basically lazy and incurious, which incidentally is one of those words that sounds like it wouldn't be a word but is."[37]

"It's very weird to watch your brain work," Lindsey said, and Colin sighed. He knew he couldn't tell stories, that he always included extraneous details and tangents that interested only him. "Anyway, the end of that story is that I came relatively close to having a lion bite off my penis. And my point was that shit like that never happens to popular people. Ever."

Lindsey laughed. "That sounds like a hell of a good story if only you knew how to tell it." She bit at her thumb again. Her private habit. From behind her hand she said, "Well, I think you're cool, and I want you to think I'm cool, and that's all popular is."

### The End (of the Beginning)

After their first kiss, Colin and Katherine I sat in silence for perhaps two minutes. Katherine watched Colin carefully, and he tried to continue translating Ovid. But he found himself with an unprecedented problem. Colin

---

[37] That's absolutely true, about the eight glasses a day. There's no reason whatsoever to drink eight glasses of water a day unless you, for whatever reason, particularly like the taste of water. Most experts agree that unless there's something horribly wrong with you, you should just drink water whenever you're—get this—thirsty.

couldn't focus. He kept glancing up at her. Her big blue eyes, too big for her young face really, stared unceasingly at him. He figured he was in love. Finally, she spoke.

"Colin," she said.

"Yes, Katherine?"

"I'm breaking up with you."

At the time, of course, Colin did not fully understand the significance of the moment. He immersed himself in Ovid, grieving his loss in silence, and she continued to watch him for the next half hour until her parents came into the living room to take her home. But it only took a few more Katherines for him to look back nostalgically upon The Great One as the perfect spokesperson for the Katherine Phenomenon. Their three-minute relationship was the thing itself in its most unadulterated form. It was the immutable tango between the Dumper and the Dumpee: the coming and the seeing and the conquering and the returning home.

# (eight)

**When you spend** your entire life in and around the city of Chicago, as it turns out, you fail to fully apprehend certain facets of rural life. Take, for example, the troubling case of the rooster. To Colin's mind, the rooster crowing at dawn was nothing more than a literary and cinematic trope. When an author wanted a character to be awoken at dawn, Colin figured the author just used the literary tradition of the crowing rooster to make it happen. It was, he thought, just like how authors always wrote things in ways other than how they actually happened. Authors never included the whole story; they just got to the point. Colin thought the truth should matter as much as the point, and he figured that was why he couldn't tell good stories.

That morning, he learned that roosters really *don't* start crowing at dawn. They start well *before* dawn—around 5 A.M. Colin rolled over in the foreign bed, and for a few slow seconds, as he squinted into the darkness, he felt good. Tired, and annoyed with the rooster. But good. And then he remembered that she'd dumped him, and he thought of her in her big fluffy bed asleep, not dreaming of him. He rolled over and looked at his cell phone. No missed calls.

The rooster crowed again. "Cock-a-doodle-don't, motherfugger," Colin mumbled. But the rooster cock-a-doodle-did, and by dawn, the crowing created a kind of weird dissonant symphony when mingled with the muffled sounds of a Muslim's morning prayers. Those hours of unsleepthroughable loudness allowed him ample time to wonder about everything from when

Katherine last thought of him to the number of grammatically correct anagrams of *rooster.*[38]

Around 7 A.M., as the rooster (or perhaps there was more than one—perhaps they crowed in shifts) entered its third hour of shrieking cries, Colin stumbled into the bathroom, which also connected to Hassan's bedroom. Hassan was already in the shower. For all its luxury, their bathroom contained no bathtub.

"Morning, Hass."

"Hey." Hassan shouted over the water. "Dude, Hollis is asleep in the living room watching the Home Shopping Network. She's got a billion-dollar house and she sleeps on the couch."

"Bees feefle are weird," Colin said, pulling out his toothbrush mid-sentence.

"Whatever—Hollis loves me. She thinks I hung the moon. And that you're a genius. And at five hundred dollars a week, I'll never have to work again. Five hundred dollars can last me five months at home, dude. I can survive on this summer till I'm, like, thirty."

"Your lack of ambition is truly remarkable."

Hassan's hand reached out from behind the shower and grabbed a towel monogrammed HLW. He emerged moments later, and walked into Colin's room, towel around his sizable waist.

"Listen, *kafir*. Seriously. Lay off about me going to school. Let me be happy; I'll let you be happy. Giving each other shit is fine, but there comes a point."

"Sorry. I didn't know the point had come." Colin sat down on the bed, pulling on a *KranialKidz* T-shirt he'd been given.

"Well, you've brought it up like 284 consecutive days."

"Maybe we should have a word," Colin said. "For when it's gone too far. Like, just a random word and then we'll know to back off."

---

[38] He found forty, of which he only really liked two: "rose rot" and "to err so."

Standing there in his towel, Hassan looked up at the ceiling and finally said, "Dingleberries."

"Dingleberries." Colin agreed, anagramming in his head. Dingleberries was an anagrammatic jackpot.[39]

"You're anagramming, aren't you, motherfugger?" asked Hassan.

"Yeah," Colin said.

"Maybe that's why she dumped you. Always anagramming, never listening."

"Dingleberries," said Colin.

"Just wanted to give you a chance to use it. Okay, let's go eat. I'm hungrier than a kid on his third day of fat camp." As they made their way down a hall to a spiral staircase that led to the living room, Colin asked—as close to a whisper as he could muster—"So why do you think Hollis wants to give us jobs, really?"

Hassan stopped on the staircase, and Colin with him. "She wants to make me happy. We fatties have a bond, dude. It's like a Secret Society. We've got all kinds of shit you don't know about. Handshakes, special fat people dances—we got these secret fugging lairs in the center of the earth and we go down there in the middle of the night when all the skinny kids are sleeping and eat cake and fried chicken and shit. Why d'you think Hollis is still sleeping, *kafir*? Because we were up all night in the secret lair injecting butter frosting into our veins. She's giving us jobs because a fatty always trusts another fatty."

"You're not fat. You're pudgy."

"Dude, you *just* saw my man-tits when I got out of the shower."

"They're not that bad," said Colin.

"Oh, that's it! You asked for it!" Hassan pulled his T-shirt up to his collarbone and Colin glanced over at Hass's hairy chest, which featured—

---

[39] See inbred girl; lie breeds grin; leering debris; greed be nil, sir; be idle re. rings; ringside rebel; residing rebel; etc.

okay, there's no denying it—minor breasts. An A cup, but still. Hassan smiled with great satisfaction, pulled down his shirt, and headed down the stairs.

It took an hour for Hollis to get ready, during which time Hassan and Lindsey chatted and watched *The Today Show* while Colin sat at the far edge of the couch and read one of the books he'd stuffed in his backpack—a Lord Byron anthology including the poems *Lara* and *Don Juan*. He liked it pretty well. When Lindsey interrupted him, he'd just come to a line in *Lara* he liked quite a lot: "Eternity bids thee to forget."

"Whatcha reading there, smartypants?" asked Lindsey. Colin held up the cover. "Don Juan," she said, pronouncing the *Juan* like *Wan*. "Trying to learn how to avoid getting dumped?"

"*Jew-un*," Colin corrected. "It's pronounced *Don Jew-un*," he said.[40]

"Not interesting," Hassan pointed out. But Lindsey seemed to find it more aggravating than not-interesting. She rolled her eyes and picked up the breakfast plates from the coffee table. Hollis Wells came downstairs, wrapped in what looked, for all the world, like a flowery toga.

"What we're doing," she spoke quickly, "is we're putting together an oral history of Gutshot, for future generations. I've been pulling people off the line to do interviews for a couple of weeks, but I ain't gotta now that you're here. Anyway, the downfall of this whole operation so far has been gossip—everybody chattering 'bout what everyone else says or doesn't say. But y'all don't have a reason in the world to talk about whether or not Ellie Mae liked her husband when she married him in 1937. So—it's you two. And Linds, who everybody trusts—"

"I'm very honest," Lindsey explained, cutting off her mom.

"To a fault, dear. But yes. So, you get these people talking and they won't shut up, I assure you. I want six hours of new tape turned in to me

---

[40] That's true. Much of the meter in *Don Juan* only works if you read *Juan* as bi-syllabic.

every day. But steer them toward real *history*, if you can. I'm doing this for my grandkids, not for a gossip fest."

Lindsey coughed, mumbled, "Bullshit," and then coughed again.

Hollis's eyes grew wide. "Lindsey Lee Wells, you put a quarter in the swear jar right this minute!"

"Shit," Lindsey said. "Dick. Craptastic." She glided over to the fireplace mantel, and placed a dollar bill in a glass Mason jar. "Don't have any change, Hollis," she said. Colin couldn't help but laugh; Hollis glowered.

"Well," she said, "y'all should head out. Six hours of tape, and be back by supper."

"Wait, who's gonna open up the store?" asked Lindsey.

"I'll just send Colin out there for a while."

"I'm supposed to be tape recording strangers," Colin pointed out.

"The other Colin," Hollis said. "Lindsey's," and then she sighed, "boyfriend. He hasn't been showing up at work half the time, anyway. Now, y'all git."

In the Hearse, with Hassan driving down the exceedingly long driveway away from the Pink Mansion, Lindsey said, "Lindsey's, sigh, boyfriend. It's always Lindsey's, sigh, boyfriend. Jesus Christ. Anyway, listen, just drop me off at the store."

Hassan looked up and spoke to Lindsey through the rearview mirror. "No fugging way. That's how horror movies start. We drop you off, walk into some stranger's house, and five minutes later some psycho's lobbing off my nuts with a machete while his schizophrenic wife makes Colin do push-ups on a bed of hot coals. You're coming with us."

"No offense to y'all, but I haven't seen Colin since yesterday."

"No offense to that fugger," Hassan responded, "but *Colin* is sitting in the passenger seat reading Don JEW-UN. You're dating *The Other Colin*, aka TOC."

Colin wasn't reading anymore; he was listening to Hassan defend him.

Or at least he thought Hassan was defending him. You could never quite tell with Hassan. "I mean, my boy over here is clearly the Primary Colin. There's no one like him. Colin, say 'unique' in as many languages as you can."

Colin brought them forth quickly. This was a word he knew. "Um, único,[41] unico,[42] einzigartig,[43] unique,[44] уникáљнњій,[45] μουαδκός,[46] singularis,[47] farid."[48]

Hassan was good at his job, no doubt—Colin felt a rush of affection toward him, and the recitation of the words caused something to wash over the omnipresent hole in his gut. It felt, just for a moment, like medicine.

Lindsey smiled at Colin through the rearview mirror. "Lord, my cup of Colins runneth over." She smiled. "One to teach me French, one to French me." She laughed at her own joke, then said, "Well, okay. I'll go. I wouldn't want to see Colin get his nuts chopped off, after all. Either Colin, really. But you gotta take me to the store after." Hassan agreed, and then Lindsey led them down past what she called the "Taco Hell" to a little side street lined with small, single-story houses. They pulled into a driveway. "Most people're at work," she explained. "But Starnes should be home."

He greeted them at the door. Starnes's lower jaw was missing; he appeared to have a kind of duck bill covered in skin instead of a chin or jaw or teeth. And yet he still tried to smile for Lindsey. "Sugar," he said, "how are you?"

"I'm always good when I get to see you, Starnes," she said, hugging him. His eyes lit up, and then Lindsey introduced him to Colin and Hassan. When the old man noticed Colin staring, Starnes explained, "Cancer. Now, y'all come in and sit."

---

41 Spanish.
42 Italian.
43 German.
44 French and English.
45 Russian.
46 Greek.
47 Latin.
48 Arabic.

The house smelled like musty old couches and unfinished wood. It smelled, Colin thought, like cobwebs or hazy memories. It smelled like K-19's basement. And the smell brought him back so viscerally, to a time when she loved him—or he at least felt like she did—that his gut ached anew. He closed his eyes tight for a second and waited for the feeling to pass, but it wouldn't. For Colin, nothing ever passed.

**The Beginning (of the End)**

Katherine XIX wasn't quite yet the XIX when they hung out alone together for the third time. Although the signs seemed positive, he couldn't bring himself to ask her if she wanted to date him, and he certainly couldn't just lean in and kiss her. Colin frequently faltered when it came to the step of actual kissing. He had a theory on this subject, actually, entitled the Rejection Minimization Theorem (RMT):

The act of leaning in to kiss someone, or asking to kiss them, is fraught with the possibility of rejection, so the person least likely to get rejected should do the leaning in or the asking. And that person, at least in high-school heterosexual relationships, *is definitely the girl*. Think about it: boys, basically, want to kiss girls. Guys want to make out. Always. Hassan aside, there's rarely a time when a boy is thinking, "Eh, I think I'd rather not kiss a girl today." Maybe if a guy is actually, literally, on fire he won't be thinking about hooking up. But that's about it. Whereas girls are very fickle about the business of kissing. Sometimes they want to make out; sometimes they don't. They're an impenetrable fortress of unknowability, really.

Ergo: girls should always make the first move, because (a) they are, on the whole, less likely to be rejected than guys, and (b) that way, girls will never get kissed unless they want to be kissed.

Unfortunately for Colin, there is nothing logical about kissing, and so his theory never worked. But because he always waited so incredibly long to kiss a girl, he rarely faced rejection.

He called the future Katherine XIX that Friday after school and asked her out for coffee the next day, and she said yes. It was the same coffee shop where they'd had their first two meetings—perfectly pleasant events filled with so much sexual tension that he couldn't help but get a little bit turned on just from her casually touching his hand. He would put his hands up on the table, in fact, because he wanted them within her reach.

The coffee shop was a few miles from Katherine's house and four buildings down from Colin's. Called *Café Sel Marie,* it served some of the best coffee in Chicago, which didn't matter at all to Colin, because Colin didn't like coffee. He liked the *idea* of coffee quite a lot—a warm drink that gave you energy and had been for centuries associated with sophisticates and intellectuals. But coffee itself tasted to him like caffeinated stomach bile. So he did an end-around on the unfortunate taste by drowning his java in cream, for which Katherine gently teased him that afternoon. It rather goes without saying that Katherine drank her coffee black. Katherines do, generally. They like their coffee like they like their ex-boyfriends: bitter.

Hours later, after four cups of coffee between them, she wanted to show him a movie. "It's called *The Royal Tenenbaums,*" she said. "It's about a family of prodigies."

Colin and Katherine took the Brown Line southeast toward Wrigleyville, and then walked five blocks to her house, a narrow, two-story building. Katherine led him down to her basement. Floored with wavy linoleum tiles, the damp, dank place featured an old couch, no windows, and very low ceilings (they were 6'3" to Colin's 6'1"). It made for a poor living area, but it was an awesome theater. It was so dark that you could sink into the couch and disappear into the movie.

Colin liked the movie pretty well; he laughed a lot, anyway, and he found comfort in a world where all the characters who had been smart children grew up to be really fascinating, unique adults (even if they were all screwed up). When it was over, Katherine and Colin sat in the dark together. The basement was the only genuinely dark place Colin had ever seen in Chicago—day and night, orange-gray light seeped through any place with windows.

"I just love the sound track," Katherine said. "It has such a cool feel."

"Yeah," Colin said. "And I liked the characters. I even liked the horrible dad a little."

"Right, me too," Katherine said. He could see her blond hair and the outline of her face but little else. His hand, which had been holding hers since about thirty minutes into the movie, was cramped and sweaty, but he didn't want to be the one to pull away. She went on, "I mean, he's selfish, but everyone is selfish."

"Right," Colin said.

"So is that what it's like? To be a, uh, prodigy or whatever?"

"Um, not really. All the prodigies in that movie were really hot, for instance," he joked, and she laughed and said, "So are all the ones I know," and then he exhaled sharply and looked up at her and almost—but no. He wasn't sure and couldn't handle the thought of rejection. "Anyway, plus in that movie it's like they are all just born talented. I'm not like that, you know. I mean, I've worked at least ten hours a day, every day, since I was three," he said, with no small measure of pride. He *did* think of it as work—the reading and the practicing of languages and pronunciation, the recitation of facts, the careful examination of every text laid before him.

"So what are you good at, exactly, anyway? I mean, I know you're good at everything, but what are you *so* good at besides languages?"

"I'm good with codes and stuff. And I'm good at, like, linguistic tricks like anagramming. That's my favorite thing, really. I can anagram anything." He'd never before told a Katherine about his anagramming. He'd always figured it would bore them.

"Anything?"

"Night, nay," he answered quickly, and she laughed and then said, "Katherine Carter."

He wanted so much to put his hand around the nape of her neck and pull her into him and taste her mouth, full and soft in the darkness. But not yet. He wasn't sure. His heart pounded. "Um, okay. Her karate cretin—um, oh. I like this one: their arcane trek."

She laughed and pulled her hand away and placed it flat against his knee. Her fingers were soft. He could suddenly smell her over the dank basement. She smelled like lilacs, and then he knew that it was almost time. But he didn't dare look at her, not yet. He just watched the blank TV screen. He wanted to draw out the moment before the moment—because as good as kissing feels, nothing feels as good as the anticipation of it.

"How do you *do* that?" she asked.

"Practice, mostly. I've been doing it a long time. I see the letters and pull out a good word first—like, karate, or arcane—and then I try to use the remaining letters to make—oh God, this is boring," he said, hoping it wasn't.

"No it's not."

"I just try to make grammatical sense with the remaining letters. Anyway, it's just a trick."

"Okay, so anagrams. That's one. Got any other charming talents?" she asked, and now he felt confident.

Finally, Colin turned to her, gathering in his gut the slim measure of courage available to him, and said, "Well, I'm a fair kisser."

# (nine)

**"Y'all make yourselves** at home. Hollis said you might'n come over here to interview me and find out about my fascinating life," Starnes said, and Colin sat down on a musty couch not unlike the one on which he and K-19 had shared their first kiss. Lindsey introduced Colin and Hassan, and then Colin started asking questions. The room was not air-conditioned, and as Colin pressed the record button of the digital mini-recorder and placed it on Starnes's coffee table, he felt the first bead of sweat form on his neck. It would be a long day.

"When did you come to Gutshot?" Lindsey asked.

"I was born in the country[49] nineteen hundred and twenty. Born here, raised up here, always lived here, and gonna die here, I'm sure," he said, and then winked at Lindsey.

"Aww, Starnes, don't say that," Lindsey said. "What the hell would I do 'round here without you?"

"Prob'ly run around with that Lyford boy," Starnes answered. Starnes turned to the boys and then said, "I don't think too highly of that boy's daddy."

"You just want me all to yourself," Lindsey said, laughing. "Tell us about the factory, Starnes. These boys ain't ever been." Around Starnes, for some reason, Lindsey spoke with a thick accent.

---

[49] It eventually became clear to Colin that Starnes did not mean "the United States of America" but rather "this general area of south-central Tennessee."

"The factory opened up three years 'fore I was born, and I worked there from when I was fourteen. I suppose if I hadn't, I would have farmed—that's what my father did until the factory came along. We made everything back then; T-shirts and handkerchiefs and bandannas, and it was hard work. But your family was always fair—first Dr. Dinzanfar and then his son-in-law Corville Wells. Then there was that sumbitch Alex, who I know was your daddy, Lindsey, so you'll have to forgive me. And then Hollis, who took good care of us every one. I worked in that factory sixty years to the day. I have the world record. They named the break room after me, because that's where I spent most of my time." His upper lip smiled, but Starnes's jawless chin couldn't follow suit.

Already, the house felt like a hot tub without the water and bubbles. *This is a hard way to make a hundred dollars,* Colin thought.

"Y'all want some tea?" Starnes asked. Without waiting for an answer, he stood up and walked into the kitchen.

At once sweet and bitter, it tasted a little like lemonade, except somehow more grown-up. Colin loved it—it was everything he'd hoped coffee would be—and helped himself to several glasses while Starnes talked, pausing only to take his medication (once) and go to the bathroom (four times; old people do that—they seem to love bathrooms).

"Well, the first thing that you have to understand is that in the country we weren't ever poor. Even in the Depression, I wasn't ever hungry, because when Dr. Dinzanfar had to lay people off, he never fired more than one person from a family."

Something about Dr. Dinzanfar led Starnes elsewhere. "You know they've been calling the country Gutshot for a long-ass time, and Lindsey, I bet you don't even know why." Lindsey shook her head politely, and Starnes leaned forward out of his La-Z-Boy and said, "Aw, see. Now y'all haven't heard a damn thing about the place then! Back in the old days, so old that even this old man weren't born yet, prizefighting was illegal. And if you wanted to break the law, Gutshot was a fine place to do it.

"Always has been, really. I saw the inside of the Carver County Jail a few times myself, you know. I was drunk in public in 1948; I was a public nuisance in 1956; and then I was in jail for two days on illegal discharging of a firearm when I killed Caroline Clayton's rat snake in 1974. Mary wouldn't bail me out after I kilt that God-forsaken snake, you know. But how on earth am I supposed to tell it's a pet? I go into Caroline Clayton's house looking for the hammer she borrowed from me six months before, and there's a by-God rat snake slitherin' across the kitchen. What would you do, son?" he asked Colin.

Colin mulled the situation over. "You went into someone else's house without knocking?" he asked.

"No, I knocked, but she wa'n't home."

"That's a crime also," Colin pointed out. "Trespassing."

"Well thank the Lord *you* didn't arrest me, boy," Starnes said. "Anyway, you see a snake, you kill it. That's just how I was raised up. So I shot it. Split it right in two. And that evening Caroline Clayton come over to my house—she's passed on now, bless her heart—and she's screaming and crying that I killed Jake, and I told her that someone else musta killed Jake, whoever the hell he was, 'cause all I did was shoot up a goddamned rat snake. But then turns out that Jake *was* the snake, and that she loved it like the child she never had. She never married, of course. Uglier than sin, bless her heart."

"The snake probably didn't care that she was ugly," Colin pointed out. "They have very poor eyesight."

Starnes look over at Lindsey Lee Wells. "Your friend here is a regular fountain of knowledge."

"He sure God is," she said, drawling.

"What was I talking about?" asked Starnes.

"Gutshot. Boxing. The old days," Colin answered quickly.

"Right, yes, well. It was a town for trouble back then before the factory brought in families. Just a rough sharecropper town. My mama told me the town didn't have no name. But then they started bringing in boxers. Boys from all over the country would come here and they'd fight for five or ten dollars, winner take all, and make extra money betting on themselves. But to get around the prizefighting laws, they had this rule: you couldn't hit below the belt or above the shoulders. Gutshot boxing. The town became famous for it, and that's what we got called."

Colin wiped the back of his sweaty palm against his sweaty forehead, spreading the moisture around rather than truly dealing with it, and took several gulps of tea.

"Mary and I got married in 1944," Starnes went on, "when I was supposed to go off to the war." And Colin thought that Starnes might benefit from a lesson from his eleventh-grade English teacher Mr. Holtsclaw, who taught them about *transitions*. Colin couldn't tell a story to save his life, admittedly, but at least he'd *heard of* transitions. Still, it was fun to listen to Starnes. "Anyway, I didn't go off to the war because I shot off two of my toes because I'm a coward. I'm an old man so I can tell you that frankly. I wasn't afraid of war, you know. War never scared me. I just didn't want to go all the way-hell over there to fight one. I had a reputation after that—I pretended I shot myself by accident, but everyone knew. I never did lose that reputation, but now most everyone is dead, and y'all ain't got any stories from them, so you have to believe mine by default: They were cowards, too. Everyone is.

"But we got married and oh Lord we sure loved each other. Always did till the very end. She never liked me much, but she sure loved me, if you know what I'm saying." Colin glanced at Hassan, who glanced back, his eyes wide in horror. They both feared they knew *exactly* what Starnes was saying. "She died in 1997. Heart attack. She was nothing but good and I was nothing but bad, but then she died, and I didn't."

He showed them pictures then; they crowded around his La-Z-Boy as his wrinkled hands flipped slowly through a photo album thick with memories. The oldest pictures were faded and yellowing, and Colin thought about how even in pictures of their youth, old people look old. He watched as the pictures moved to a crisp black-and-white and then to the bland color of Polaroids, watched as children were born and then grew up, as hair fell out and was replaced by wrinkles. And all the while Starnes and Mary stayed in the pictures together, from their wedding to their fiftieth anniversary. *I will have that*, Colin thought. *I will have it. I will. With Katherine. But I won't be only that*, he resolved. *I will leave behind something more than one photo album where I always look old.*

Later, Colin knew their six hours were up when Lindsey Lee Wells stood up and said, "Well we gotta get going, Starnes."

"All right," he said. "Good to have you. And Lindsey, you just look perfect."

"You need an air conditioner, bud? It's awful hot in here, and Hollis could get you one no problem," Lindsey said.

"I get by all right. She's done good by me." Starnes stood up and walked them to the door. Colin shook the old man's shaky hand.

In the Hearse Colin drove as fast as the roads would permit, with the windows down to try to cool off.

Hassan said, "I think I just lost sixty pounds in sweat."

"Then you could stand to stay out in the heat a while longer," Lindsey said. "That was the easiest hundred dollars anyone ever made in Gutshot. Hey, no, don't turn. I need you to take me to the store."

"So we can all hang out with The Other Colin in the sweet, sweet air-conditioning?"

Lindsey shook her head. "Uh-uh. You get to drop me off and then you make yourselves scarce till you pick me up in two hours and then we tell Hollis that we spent the afternoon running around the country."

"Well," said Hassan, sounding somewhat annoyed, "we will certainly miss your abundant charm and bubbly personality."

"Oh, I'm sorry," she said. "I'm just kidding around. Anyway, I like you,

Hassan; it's the Smartypants I find unbearable." Colin glanced through the rearview into the backseat. She was smiling at him with her lips closed. He knew she was kidding, or thought she was, but he still felt anger rise up in his throat, and he knew the hurt was betrayed in his eyes. "Jesus, Singleton, I'm just kidding."

"You've got to remember that usually when he hears a girl call him unbearable, it's the last words of a Katherine," explained Hassan, talking like Colin wasn't behind the wheel. "He's pretty touchy on the whole subject of his being unbearable."

"Dingleberries," said Colin.

"Gotcha."

After dropping off Lindsey, they ended up back at Hardee's, eating a midafternoon snack of double cheeseburgers and fries limp with the weight of their own grease. Colin read from Byron for the first thirty minutes while Hassan repeatedly sighed and said, "God, you're boring," until finally Colin put the book down.

They still had an hour to kill when the meal was over. Standing in the parking lot with the heat radiating in waves off the pavement, Hassan wiped his forehead and said, "I think we should stop by the Gutshot General Store."

They pulled into the store's dirt parking lot fifty minutes early and strode up the staircase and into a blast of air-conditioning. Behind the counter, Lindsey Lee Wells was sitting on what appeared to be a boy, who had an arm draped across her lap.

"Hello," said Colin. TOC peeked out from behind Lindsey. He nodded at Colin without smiling or blinking or in any way moving any of the muscles in his strong, round face.

"What's up," said TOC.

"Not much," said Colin.

"You're a lucky couple a guys, to get to live with Lindsey." Lindsey let loose a chirpy laugh and contorted herself to kiss her boyfriend sweetly on the neck. "Oh, we'll live together one day," she said.

"If you touch her," TOC said out of the blue, "I'll kill you."

"That's a little clichéd," Hassan called out from the candy aisle. "And if we *touch* her? I mean, what if I brush up against her as we walk through a hallway?"

TOC glowered. "Well," he said, "this has been fun. But Lindsey and I were in the middle of a very important talk, so if you wouldn't mind . . ."

To defuse the tension, Colin said, "Oh, sorry. Yeah, we'll just, uh, take a walk or something."

"Here," Lindsey said, and tossed them a set of keys. "Colin's truck has AC."

"Don't take that truck out of park," TOC said gruffly.

As they walked out the door, Colin heard TOC ask Lindsey, "Who's the genius—the fat one or the skinny one?" But he didn't hang around to hear Lindsey's response. As they walked across the dirt parking lot toward TOC's SUV, Hassan said, "God, he's built like a brick shithouse, isn't he? Listen, The Fat One's gonna take a piss in the field."

"The Skinny One will wait for The Fat One in the truck," Colin said. Colin climbed in, turned the key, and put the AC on full-blast, although at first it only pumped out hot air.

Hassan opened the passenger door and immediately started talking. "She's so bubbly around him, but then around us she's just one of the guys, just slinging shit, and then around Starnes she was all y'allin' it up and talking Southern."

"Do you have a crush on her or something?" asked Colin suddenly.

"No. I was just thinking aloud. For the last time, I'm not interested in dating a girl I'm not gonna marry. Dating Lindsey would be *haram*.[50] Also, she's got a big nose. I don't go in for noses."

---

[50] *Haram* is an Arabic word that means "forbidden by Islam."

"Well, not to start an argument, but you do all kinds of shit that is *haram*."

Hassan nodded. "Yeah, but the *haram* shit I do is, like, having a dog. It's not like smoking crack or talking behind people's backs or stealing or lying to my mom or fugging girls."

"Moral relativism," Colin said.

"No it's not. I don't think God gives a shit if we have a dog or if a woman wears shorts. I think He gives a shit about whether you're a good person."

The words "good person" made Colin immediately think about Katherine XIX. She would be leaving Chicago soon for a camp in Wisconsin where she worked every summer as a counselor. The camp was for kids with physical disabilities. They taught them how to ride horses. She was such a good person, and he missed her all over his body. He missed her like crazycakes.[51] But he felt, in the throbbing missing piece inside him, that she didn't long for him like that. She was probably relieved. If she were thinking of him, she'd call. *Unless* . . .

"I think I'm going to call her."

"That's the worst idea you've ever had," Hassan replied immediately. "The. Worst. Idea. Ever."

"No, it's not, because what if she's just waiting for me to call like I'm waiting for her to call?"

"Right, but you're the Dumpee. Dumpees don't call. You know that, *kafir*. Dumpees must never, never call. There's no exception to that rule. None. Never call. Never. You can't call." Colin reached into his pocket. "Don't do it, dude. You're pulling the pin on a grenade. You're covered in gasoline and the phone is a lit match."

Colin flipped open the phone. "Dingleberries," he said.

[51] It's cheesy, but that's what they always said to each other. "I love you like crazycakes; I miss you like crazycakes;" etc.

Hassan threw up his hands. "You can't dingleberry that! That's a flagrant misuse of the dingleberry! I dingleberry you calling her!"

Colin closed the phone and mulled it over. Pensive, he bit at the inside of his thumb. "Okay," he said, sliding the phone back into his pocket. "I won't."

Hassan sighed heavily. "That was a close one. Thank goodness for the Double Reverse Dingleberry."

They sat in silence for a moment and then Colin said, "I want to go home."

"To Chicago?"

"No, to Lindsey's. But we still have forty minutes to kill."

Hassan stared out through the windshield and nodded his head slowly. After a few quiet moments, he said, "Okay. Okay. Fat kid asthma attack. It's an oldie, but it's a goodie."

"What?"

Hassan rolled his eyes. "What, are you deaf? Fat kid asthma attack. It's the oldest trick in the whole fat kid book. Just follow my lead."

They got out of the car and Hassan started wheezing very loudly. His every inhalation sounded like the cry of a dying duck. *HEEEEEENH*; exhale; *HEEEENH*; exhale. He placed his hand against his chest, and ran into the Gutshot General Store.

"What's wrong with him?" Lindsey asked Colin. Before he could answer, Hassan started talking amid his wheezes.

"*HEEEEENH*. Asthma. *HEEEENH*. Attack. *HEEEENH*. Bad one. *HEEEENH*."

"Oh shit," said Lindsey. She hopped off TOC's lap, turned around, grabbed her first-aid box, and started looking through it in vain for asthma meds. The Other Colin sat silently on the stool, no doubt displeased by the interruption.

"He'll be fine," Colin said. "It happens. I just need to get him home to his inhaler."

"Hollis doesn't like it when people show up when she's working," Lindsey said.

"Well, she'll make an exception," said Colin.

Hassan kept up his wheezing for the drive home, and as he raced up the Pink Mansion's stairs toward his room. Colin sat with Lindsey in the living room. They could both hear Hollis in the kitchen saying, "This is an American product. It's made with American labor. That's a selling point. That's a marketable, promotable facet of our product. People buy American. I've got a study here . . ." Colin had wondered whether maybe Hollis just watched the Home Shopping Network all day and left other people to run the business, but obviously she *did* work.

Hollis came out then and the first thing she said was, "Please don't interrupt me during working hours," and then Lindsey said Hassan had an asthma attack and forgot his inhaler, and then Hollis took off running up the stairs. Colin followed quickly, shouting, "I hope you're okay, Hassan!" so that Hassan would know she was coming, and when they all got to his room, he was lying peacefully on the bed.

"Sorry I forgot my inhaler," he said. "It won't happen again."

They ate a dinner of hamburgers and steamed asparagus in the Wells family backyard. Colin's backyard in Chicago measured twelve feet by ten feet; this backyard went on for football fields. To their left, a hill rose to its peak, the forest broken up only by a few rocky outcroppings. To their right, a well-kept lawn stretched on down the hill toward a soybean field (he'd found out from Starnes that they were soybeans). As the sun set behind them, a citronella candle burned in a bucket in the center of the table to ward off mosquitoes. Colin liked how Gutshot felt wide open and endless.

When he finished eating, Colin's mind returned to Katherine XIX. He glanced at his phone to see if she'd called and noticed it was time to call his parents.

For whatever reason, Colin could never get reception in his house in the third-largest city in America but had all five bars in Gutshot, Tennessee. His father picked up.

"I'm still in the same town as yesterday. Gutshot, Tennessee," Colin began. "I'm staying with a woman named Hollis Wells."

"Thank you for calling on time. Should that name be familiar to me?" asked his dad.

"No, but she's listed in the phone book. I checked. She owns a factory here. I think we're going to stay here a few days," Colin said, fibbing. "Inexplicably, Hassan loves it here, and also we seem to have gotten jobs."

"You can't just *stay with strangers*, Colin."

Colin considered lying. Staying in a hotel. Working in a restaurant here. Getting my bearings. But he told the truth. "She's nice. I trust her."

"You trust everyone."

"Dad, I survived seventeen years in Chicago without ever getting mugged or stabbed or kidnapped or falling onto the third rail or get—"

"Talk to your mother," he said, which is what his dad always said. After a few moments (Colin could just see them talking while his dad held his hand over the receiver), his mom picked up. "Well, are you happy?"

"I wouldn't go that far."

"Happier?" his mom tried.

"Marginally," he allowed. "I'm not lying facedown on the carpet."

"Let me talk to this woman," his mom said. So Colin walked inside, found Hollis on the couch, and handed the phone to her.

And after talking to Hollis, it was decided: he could stay. He knew that his mom wanted him to have an adventure. She'd always wished he could be a normal kid. Colin suspected she'd be secretly pleased if he came home one night at three in the morning reeking of booze, because that would be *normal*. Normal kids come home late; normal kids drink warm forties of malt liquor in alleys with their friends (normal kids have more than one friend). His father wanted Colin to transcend all that stuff, but maybe even he was starting to see the unlikelihood of Colin ever becoming extraordinary.

Colin walked up to Hassan's room to tell him his parents were cool with him staying, but Hassan wasn't home. He hunted around the cavernous house, eventually making his way downstairs, where he found a closed door with Lindsey's voice emanating from behind it. He stood in front of the thin door and listened.

"Right, but how does he *do* it? Does he just *memorize* everything?" Lindsey was saying.

"No it's not like that. It's like, if you or me sat down and read a book about, say, the presidents, and we read that William Howard Taft was the fattest president and one time he got stuck in a bathtub,[52] that might click in our brains as interesting, and we'd remember it, right?" Lindsey laughed. "You and me will read a book and find like three interesting things that we remember. But Colin finds *everything* intriguing. He reads a book about presidents and he remembers more of it because everything he reads clicks in his head as fugging interesting. Honestly, I've seen him do it with the phone book. He'll be like, 'Oh, there are twenty-four listings for Tischler. How *fascinating*.'"

Colin felt an odd mix of feelings, like his talent was at once being inflated and ridiculed. It was true, he guessed. But it wasn't just that he found things fascinating in and of themselves and could memorize the whole phone book because it made for such excellent literature. He found stuff fascinating for a *reason*. Like, take for example the Tischler thing, which happened to be true (and Hassan remembered it correctly). "Tischler" was the German word for carpenter, and when he was looking in the phone book that day with Hassan, Colin thought, *How strange that there would be*

---

[52] True.

*exactly twenty-four German carpenters in Chicago when the all-night manicure place on the corner of Oakley and Lawrence is called "24/7 Nails."* And then he got to wondering whether there were exactly seven carpenters of some other language in the Chicago phone book, and it turned out that there were precisely seven Carpinteros. So it wasn't just that things interested him because he didn't know from boring—it was the connection his brain made, connections he couldn't help but seek out.

"But that doesn't explain why he's good at, like, Scrabble," Lindsey pointed out.

"Right, well, he's good at that because he's ridiculously good at anagramming. But anything he takes up, he just works insanely hard. Like, typing. He didn't learn to type until ninth grade, when we were friends. Our English teacher required typewritten papers, so over like two weeks, Singleton taught himself to type. And he didn't do it by typing his English papers, because then he wouldn't have been *good* enough at typing. What he did is he sat down at his computer every day after school and retyped Shakespeare's plays. All of them. Literally. And then he retyped *The Catcher in the Rye*. And he kept retyping and retyping until he could fugging type like a genius."

Colin backed away from the door then. It occurred to him that he'd never done anything else in his whole life. Anagramming; spitting back facts he'd learned in books; memorizing ninety-nine digits of an already known number; falling in love with the same nine letters over and over again: retyping and retyping and retyping and retyping. His only hope for originality was the Theorem.

Colin opened the door and found Hassan and Lindsey sitting on opposite sides of a green leather couch in a room dominated by a pool table with pink felt. They were watching poker on a huge, flat-screen TV hanging on the wall. Hassan turned around to face Colin. "Dude," he said, "you can see all their zits."

Colin sat down between them. Lindsey and Hassan talked about poker and zits and HD and DVR while Colin graphed his past. By the end of the night, a slightly tweaked formula had worked for two more K's: IX and XIV. He barely registered the change when they turned off the TV and started playing pool. He just kept scribbling. He loved the scratching of pencil against paper when he was this focused: it meant something was happening.

When the clock read midnight, Colin put his pencil down. He looked up at Lindsey, who was standing on one foot, bent over the pool table at an absurdly awkward angle. Hassan seemed to have left the room. "Hey," said Colin.

"Oh, you're out of the Twilight Zone," she said. "How's the Theorem?"

"Okay. I don't really know if it will work yet. Where's Hassan?"

"He went to bed. I asked you if you wanted to play, but I don't think you heard me, so I figured I'd just play against myself for a while. I'm beating me pretty handily."

Colin stood up and sniffed. "I think I'm allergic to this house."

"It could be Princess," Lindsey said. "This is actually Princess's room. *Shh*. She's sleeping." Colin followed Lindsey to the pool table and knelt down beside her. Beneath the table, a large sphere that initially seemed to be a ball of shaggy carpet grew and then shrunk rhythmically, breathing. "She's always sleeping."

"I'm allergic to pet dander," Colin announced.

She smirked. "Yeah, well, Princess lived here first." She sat back down with him, her legs tucked beneath her so that she seemed taller than Colin. "Hassan told me you're good at anagramming," she said.

"Yeah," Colin answered. "Good at anagramming—dragon maggot mania."

Lindsey's hand (she'd painted her fingernails an electric blue since yesterday) was suddenly against his forearm, and Colin tensed up from surprise. When he turned his head to look at her, she placed her hand back in her lap. "So," she went on, "you're a genius at making words out of other words, but you can't make new words out of thin air."

And yes, again, that was it exactly. A retyper and not a writer. A prodigy and not a genius. It was so quiet then that he could hear Princess breathing, and he felt the missing piece inside him. "I just want to do something that matters. Or *be* something that matters. I just want to matter."

Lindsey didn't answer right away, but she leaned in toward Colin and he could smell her fruity perfume, and then she lay down next to him on her back, the crown of her head just brushing against his shorts. "I think we're opposites, you and me," she said finally. "Because personally I think mattering is a piss-poor idea. I just want to fly under the radar, because when you start to make yourself into a big deal, that's when you get shot down. The bigger a deal you are, the worse your life is. Look at, like, the miserable lives of famous people."

"Is that why you read *Celebrity Living*?"

Lindsey nodded. "Yeah. Totally—there's a word in German for it. God, it's on the tip of—a . . ."

"Schadenfreude," Colin said. Finding pleasure in others' pain.

"Right! So, anyway," Lindsey went on, "take staying here. Hollis always tells me that nothing really good will ever happen to me if I stay in Gutshot; and maybe that's true. But nothing really bad will ever happen, either, and I'll take that bargain any day."

Colin didn't answer, but he was thinking that Lindsey Lee Wells, for all her coolness and whatever, was a bit of a wimp. But before he could figure a way to say so, Lindsey sat up, animated by a new topic.

"Okay," she said. "Here's the thing about storytelling: you need a beginning, and a middle, and an end. Your stories have no plots. They're like, here's something I was thinking and then the next thing I was thinking and then et cetera. You can't get away with rambling. You're Colin Singleton, Beginning Storyteller, so you've got to stick to a straight plot.

"And you need a good, strong moral. Or a theme or whatever. And the other thing is romance and adventure. You've got to put some of those in. If it's a story about peeing into a lion cage, give yourself a girlfriend who notices how gigantic your winky is and then saves you from the lion at the last second by tackling you, because she's desperate to save that gorgeous, ginormous winky." Colin blushed, but Lindsey kept going. "In the beginning, you need to pee; in the middle, you do; in the end, through romance and adventure, your winky is saved from the jaws of a hungry lion by the pluck of a young girl motivated by her abiding love for giant winkies. And the moral of the story is that a heroic girlfriend, combined with a giant winky, will save you from even the most desperate situations."

When Colin finished laughing, he placed his hand on top of Lindsey's. It stayed there for a moment, and he could feel the worn place on her thumb where she nibbled at it. He pulled his hand away after a moment and said, "My Theorem will tell the story. Each graph with a beginning and a middle and an end."

"There's no romance in geometry," Lindsey answered.

"Just you wait."

### The Beginning (of the Middle)

He never thought much about Katherine I. He only felt upset about the breakup because that's what you're *supposed* to feel. Little kids play house; they play war; they play relationships. I want to go with you; you dumped me; I'm sad. But none of it was really real.

Because Katherine's dad was Colin's tutor, Colin and Katherine continued to see each other periodically over the next several years. They got along well—but it's not like he burned with longing for her. He didn't miss her enough to become obsessed with her name, to date her namesakes over and over and over and over[53] again.

And yet, that's what happened. It didn't seem willful at first—it was

[53] And over and over and over and over and over and over and over and over and over and over and over and over and over and over and over.

just a series of odd coincidences. It just kept happening: he'd meet a Katherine, and like her. She'd like him back. And then it would end. And then, after it ceased being mere coincidence, it just became two streaks—one (dating Katherines) he wished to keep, and one (getting dumped by them) he wished to break. But it proved impossible to divorce one cycle from the other. It just kept happening to him, and after a while it felt almost routine. Each time, he'd cycle through feelings of anger, regret, longing, hope, despair, longing, anger, regret. The thing about getting dumped generally, and getting dumped by Katherines in particular, was how utterly *monotonous* it was.

That's why people grow weary of listening to Dumpees obsess over their troubles: getting dumped is predictable, repetitive, and boring. They want to stay friends; they feel smothered; it's always them and it's never you; and afterward, you're devastated and they're relieved; it's over for them and just starting for you. And to Colin's mind, at least, there was a deeper repetition: each time, Katherines dumped him because they just didn't *like* him. They each came to precisely the same conclusion about him. He wasn't cool enough or good-looking enough or as smart as they'd hoped—in short, he didn't matter enough. And so it happened to him again and again, until it was boring. But monotony doesn't make for painlessness. In the first century CE, Roman authorities punished St. Apollonia by crushing her teeth one by one with pliers. Colin often thought about this in relationship to the monotony of dumping: we have thirty-two teeth. After a while, having each tooth individually destroyed probably gets repetitive, even dull. But it never stops hurting.

# (ten)

**The next morning,** Colin felt tired enough to sleep through the rooster's squawking until eight. When he made his way downstairs, he found Hollis wearing a hot pink muumuu, passed out on the couch with papers strewn across her chest and the floor. Colin walked softly past her, and thought to add "muumuu" to his mental list of unanagrammable words.

Hassan sat in the kitchen, eating oatmeal and scrambled eggs. Without speaking, he handed Colin a note written on stationery embossed with the words HOLLIS P. WELLS / CEO & PRESIDENT, GUTSHOT TEXTILES:

> Boys,
>
> I'm probably sleeping, but hopefully y'all got up on time. You need to be down at the factory by 9. Ask for Zeke. I listened to your interview with Starnes—it's good work, but I've changed my mind about some things. At six hours per person, we'll never get through the whole town. I'd like you only to ask the following four questions: Where would you live if you could live anywhere? What would you do for a living if you didn't work for the factory? When did your people come to the country? and What do you think makes Gutshot special? I think that'll move things along nicely. They're expecting you at the factory. Lindsey will accompany you.
>
> See you tonight. Hollis.
>
> P.S. I'm writing this note at 5:30 A.M., so don't wake me up.

• • •

"Nice bedhead, by the way, *kafir*. You look like you stuck a fork in a light socket."

"Did you know that in 1887, Nikola Tesla's hair stood on end for an entire week after he passed fifty thousand volts through his body to prove that elec—"

"*Kafir*," Hassan said, putting his fork down on his plate. "Absolutely, completely not interesting. Now if Nikola Tesla, whoever the hell that is, had a long-term love affair with a one-legged chicken, and his chicken-lust made his hair stand on end—then, yes, by all means, share with me this bounty of hilarious history. But not electricity, *kafir*. You know better."[54]

Colin searched through a labyrinth of cabinets for a plate, a cup, and some silverware. He scooped eggs from the frying pan onto a plate and poured himself water through the fancy push-this-lever-and-water-comes-out refrigerator.

"How are the eggs?" asked Hassan.

"Good, dude. Good. You're a good cook."

"No shit. That's how Daddy got so fat. By the way, I've decided to start referring to myself exclusively as 'Daddy.' Every time Daddy would otherwise say 'I' or 'Me,' Daddy is now going to say 'Daddy.' You like?"

"Oh, yes. I love."

"Love what?" asked Lindsey Lee Wells as she came into the living room wearing her paisley pajamas, her brown hair pulled back in a ponytail. Colin noticed she looked different, but not quite how, and then he saw it. No makeup. She looked prettier than she ever had before—Colin always preferred girls without makeup.

---

[54] The odd thing about that is that Nikola Tesla actually *did* love birds, but not one-legged chickens. Tesla, who did at least as much for electricity as Thomas Edison, had a quasi-romantic fascination with pigeons. He really fell for one particular white pigeon. Of her, he wrote, "I loved that pigeon. I loved her as a man loves a woman."

Colin sneezed, and then noticed that Princess was following in Lindsey's wake. XIX had a dog, too—a miniature dachshund named Fireball Roberts.

No one looked more beautiful without makeup than Katherine. She never wore it, and never needed to. God, her blond hair in her face when the wind blew as they walked by the lake after school; the corners of her eyes crinkling when he first said "I love you"; the speed and assured softness with which she had replied, "And I love you." All roads led to her. She was the nexus of all the connections his brain made—the wheel's hub.

When Colin looked up, Lindsey was reading the note from Hollis. "Christ, I guess I better get some pants on, then," she said.

They piled into the Hearse after Lindsey successfully called shotgun. At the front door of Gutshot Textiles, they were met by a large man with a beard like Santa Claus's but browner.

He hugged Lindsey with one arm, saying, "How's my girl?" and she said, "I'm a'ight. How's my Zeke?" He laughed. He shook Hassan's hand, then Colin's. Zeke walked them past a very loud room where machines seemed to smack against each other and into a room with a small brown plastic sign that read, THE STARNES WILSON BREAK ROOM.

Colin put the tape recorder down on a coffee table. The room seemed to have been furnished with stuff that employees could no longer bear to keep in their homes: a stomach-bile-yellow corduroy couch, a couple of black leather chairs with foam peeking out from innumerable cracks, and a Formica dining room table with six chairs. Above two vending machines hung a portrait of Elvis Presley that had been painted on velvet. Colin, Lindsey, and Hassan took the couch and Zeke sat in one of the leather chairs. Before they could even start asking their questions from Hollis, Zeke started talking.

"Hezekiah Wilson Jones, aged forty-two, divorced, two sons aged eleven and nine, Cody and Cobi, both on the honor roll. I was raised up in

Bradford and moved here when I was thirteen on account of how my dad lost his gas station in a poker game—which is the kinda shit that happened to my old man regularly. He took a job at the factory. Started working here myself in the summers during high school and went full-time the day after I graduated. Worked here ever since. I've worked the line; I've worked quality control; and now I'm the day shift plant manager. What we do here, boys, is we take cotton—usually from Alabama or Tennessee." He stopped then and reached into his jeans pocket and pulled out an aluminum square. He unwrapped it, popped a square piece of chewing gum in his mouth and started talking again. "I quit smoking eleven years ago and still chew this Nicorette, which tastes like shit and ain't cheap either. Don't smoke. Now, the plant." For the next twenty minutes, Zeke walked them through the process of how cotton becomes string, and how those strings are then cut by a machine to a length of exactly two and one-eighth inches, and then how those strings are shipped off. A quarter of them, he said, get shipped directly to their biggest client, STASURE Tampons, and the rest go to a warehouse in Memphis and from there head out into the world of tamponery.

"Now, I got to get back to work, but what I'm going to do is I'm going to send in some people for twenty minutes, for their break, and you can ask them questions. You got any questions for me, by the way?"

"Yes, actually," said Hassan. "Where would you live if you could live anywhere; what would you do for a living if you didn't work for the factory; when did your people come to the country—wait you already answered that; and what do you think makes Gutshot special?"

Zeke pulled his bottom lip tight against his teeth, sucking on the Nicorette. "I'd live here," he said. "If I didn't work for the factory, I'd work for another one, probably. But maybe I'd start a tree-trimming business. My ex-brother-in-law's got one, and he does right well. And what makes it special? Well, shit. For starters, our Coke machine is free. Just push the button, and Coke comes out. They ain't got that at most jobs. Plus we got ourselves the lovely Miss Lindsey Lee, which most every town does not. All right, y'all. I've gotta get to work."

The moment Zeke left, Lindsey stood up. "This has been a blast, boys, but I'm going to walk to the store and go stare dreamily into the eyes of my boyfriend. Pick me up at five-thirty, okay?" And then she was gone. For a girl who'd be in deep shit if Colin or Hassan ratted her out to Hollis, Lindsey seemed quite confident. *And that*, Colin found himself thinking, *must mean that we are friends*. Almost by accident, and in just two days, Colin had made his second-ever friend.

Over the course of the next seven hours, Colin and Hassan interviewed twenty-six people, asking them all the same four questions. Colin listened to people who wanted to make a living with chain-saw sculpture or teaching elementary school. He found it mildly interesting that almost all of the interviewees said that of all the places in the world, they—just like Lindsey Lee Wells—would want to stay in Gutshot. But since Hassan asked most of the questions, Colin was free to focus in on his Theorem.

He remained convinced that romantic behavior was basically monotonous and predictable, and that therefore one could write a fairly straightforward formula that would predict the collision course of any two people. But he was worried that he might not be enough of a genius to make the connections. He just couldn't imagine a way to correctly predict the other Katherines without screwing up the ones he'd already gotten down pat. And for some reason, his feared lack of genius made him miss K-19 more than he had since his face was pressed flat against his bedroom carpet. The missing piece in his stomach hurt so much—and eventually he stopped thinking about the Theorem and wondered only how something that isn't there can hurt you.

At four-thirty, a woman walked in and announced she was the last uninterviewed employee of Gutshot Textiles currently at work. She removed a pair of thick gloves, blew her bangs up into the air with a puff of breath, and said, "They say one of you is a genius."

"I'm not a genius," Colin said dispassionately.

"Well, you're the closest thing I've got and I've got a question. How come the shower curtain always blows in when the water should be blowing it out?"

"That," Hassan acknowledged, "is one of the great unsolved mysteries of the human condition."

"Actually," Colin said, "I know." Colin smiled. It felt good to be useful again.

"No!" Hassan said. "Seriously?"

"Yeah. What happens is the water spray creates a vortex, kind of like a hurricane. And the center of the vortex—the eye of the hurricane—is a low-pressure area, which sucks the shower curtain in and up. This guy did a study on it. Honestly."

"Now, *that*," Hassan said, "is *really* interesting. It's like there's a little hurricane in every shower?"

"Exactly."

"Wow," said the woman. "I've been wondering that my whole life. Well, okay. So my name's Katherine Layne. I'm twenty-two, been working here ten months."

"Wait, how do you spell that?" Hassan asked.

"K-a-t-h-e-r-i-n-e L-a-y-n-e."

"Uh-oh," mumbled Hassan. She was quite attractive now that Colin took a look at her. But no. Colin didn't like Katherine Layne. And it wasn't the age gap. It was K-19. Colin knew the situation was dire, indeed, when he could sit across from a perfectly nice and attractive (and sexily older!) Katherine without feeling even the smallest hint of enchantment.

They left after interviewing Katherine Layne. They drove around in Satan's Hearse for a while, getting good and lost with the windows rolled down, driving down a two-lane highway toward absolutely nothing. They listened to a country radio station turned up so loud that the twangs of steel guitars were distorted in the Hearse's old speakers. When they could catch on to the chorus, they sang loud and off-key and didn't give a shit. And it felt so good to sing with those trumped-up, hound-dog country accents. Colin felt sad, but it was an exhilarating and infinite sadness, like it connected him to Hassan and to the ridiculous songs and mostly to her, and Colin was shouting, "Like Strawwwwwberry Wine," when all of a sudden he turned to Hassan and said, "Wait, stop here." Hassan pulled over on the gravel shoulder of the road and Colin hopped out and pulled out his telephone.

"What are you doing?" asked Hassan from the driver's seat.

"I'm going to walk out into that field until I get cell reception and I'm going to call her."

Hassan began pounding his head rhythmically against the steering wheel. Colin turned away. As he walked out into the field, he heard Hassan shout, "Dingleberries!" But Colin kept walking. "Daddy is leaving you here if you take one more step!" Colin took one more step, and behind him, he heard the car start. He didn't turn around. He heard the tires spinning in the gravel, and then they caught onto the asphalt, and Colin heard the rumble of the eternally struggling engine grow distant. After five minutes of walking, he found a spot where he had okay reception. It was awfully quiet. *Chicago only gets this quiet when it snows*, he thought. And then he flipped open the phone, pressed the voice button, and said "Katherine." He said it softly, reverently.

Five rings and then her voice mail. *Hey, it's Katherine*, he heard, and in the background cars rushed by. They'd been walking home together from the RadioShack[55] when she recorded the message. *I'm not, uh.* And she uhed, he remembered, because he'd goosed her butt as she tried to talk. *Uh, at my cell phone, I guess. Leave me a message and I'll call you back.* And

---

[55] A roach disk.

he remembered everything about it, and also everything about everything else, and why couldn't he forget and *beep*.

"Hey, it's Col. I'm standing in a soybean field outside of Gutshot, Tennessee, which is a long story, and it's hot, K. I'm standing here sweating like I had hyperhidrosis, that disease where you sweat a lot. Crap. That's not interesting. But anyway, it's hot, and so I'm thinking about cold to stay cool. And I was remembering walking through the snow coming back from that ridiculous movie. Do you remember that, K? We were on Giddings, and the snow made it so quiet, I couldn't hear a thing in the world but you. And it was so cold then, and so silent, and I loved you so much. Now it's hot, and dead quiet again, and I love you still."

Five minutes later, he was trudging back when his phone began vibrating. He raced back to the spot with good reception and, breathless, answered.

"Did you listen to the message?" he asked immediately.

"I don't think I need to," she answered. "I'm sorry, Col. But I think we made a really good decision." And he didn't even care to point out that *they* hadn't made a decision, because the sound of her voice felt so good—well, not good exactly. It felt like the *mysterium tremendum et fascinans*, the fear and the fascination. The great and terrible awe.

"Did you tell your mom?" he asked, because her mom had loved him. All moms loved him.

"Yeah. She was sad. But she said you always wanted to be attached to my hip, which wasn't healthy."

"A better fate than this," he said mostly to himself.

He could hear her eyes rolling as she said, "You are probably the only person I've ever known who *wants* to be a Siamese twin."

"Conjoined twin," Colin corrected. "Did you know that there is a word for a person who is not a conjoined twin?" he asked her.

"No. What is it? Normal person?"

"Singleton," he said. "The word is Singleton." And she said, "That's funny, Col. Listen, I really have to go. I've got to pack for camp. Maybe we shouldn't talk till I get back. Just some time away from it would be good for you, I think." And even though he wanted to say, *We're supposed to be FRIENDS, remember?* And *What is it? New boyfriend?* And *I love you entirely*, he just mumbled, "Just please listen to the message," and then she said, "Okay. Bye," and he didn't say anything because he wasn't going to be the person who ended the conversation or hung up, and then he heard the deadness in his ear and it was over. Colin lay down on the dry, orange dirt and let the tall grass swallow him up, making him invisible. The sweat pouring down his face was indistinguishable from his tears. He was finally—finally—crying. He remembered their arms entangled, their stupid little inside jokes, the way he felt when he would come over to her house after school and see her reading through the window. He missed it all. He thought of being with her in college, having the freedom to sleep over whenever they wanted, both of them at Northwestern together. He missed that, too, and it hadn't even happened. He missed his imagined future.

*You can love someone so much*, he thought. *But you can never love people as much as you can miss them.*

He waited on the side of the road for twenty minutes before Hassan came by, with Lindsey riding shotgun.

"You were right," Colin said. "Not a good idea."

"Daddy's sorry," Hassan said. "It's a shitty situation. Maybe you had to call her."

Lindsey turned around in her seat. "You really love this girl, huh?"

And then Colin started crying again, and Lindsey crawled into the backseat and put her arm around him, and Colin's head was up against the side of her head. He tried not to sob much, because the plain fact of the matter is that boy-sobbing is exceedingly unattractive. Lindsey said, "Let it out, let it out," and then Colin said, "But I can't, because if I let it out it'll sound like a bullfrog's mating call," and everyone, including Colin, laughed.

He worked on the Theorem from the time they got home until 11 P.M. Lindsey brought him some kind of chicken taco salad from Taco Hell, but Colin only ate a few bites. Generally, he didn't think all that highly of eating, particularly when he was working. But his work that night came to naught. He couldn't make the Theorem work, and he realized that his Eureka moment had been a false alarm. Imagining the Theorem only required a prodigy, but actually *completing* it would take a genius. Proving the Theorem, in short, required more mattering than Colin brought to the table.

"I'm going to burn you," he said out loud to the notebook. "I'm going to throw you in the fire." Which was a fine idea—only there was no fire. There don't tend to be a lot of crackling fireplaces during the Tennessee summer, and Colin didn't smoke, so no matches were on hand. He rousted about the empty drawers of his adopted desk for matches or a lighter, but he could find nothing. He was hell-bent on burning that goddamned notebook with all his Theoremizing, though. So he walked through the bathroom and cracked open the door to Hassan's darkened room.

"Dude, do you have a match?" Colin asked, failing at whispering.

"Your daddy is sleeping."

"I know, but do you have a lighter or a match or something?"

"Daddy is trying really fugging hard to think of a not-terrifying reason why you'd wake Daddy up in the middle of the night to ask that fugging question. But no. No. Daddy does not have a match or a lighter. And, okay, enough of the Daddy shit. Anyway, you'll just have to wait till morning to douse yourself in gasoline and self-annimilate."

"Self-immolate," Colin corrected, and then pulled the door shut.

He walked downstairs and shuffled past Hollis Wells, who was too distracted by all the papers around her and the blaring Home Shopping Network to notice him. Down a hallway, he came to what he believed to be Lindsey's room. He'd never technically seen it, but he'd seen her enter the living room from this approximate side of the house. Also, a light was on. He knocked softly.

"Yeah," she said. Lindsey was seated in a plush armchair beneath a giant wall-length bulletin board, on which she'd thumbtacked pictures of herself and Katrina, herself and TOC, herself in camouflage. It was like every single picture of Lindsey Lee Wells ever taken—except Colin noticed immediately that they were all from the last couple of years. No baby pictures, no kid pictures, and no emo-alternative-gothy-screamo-punk synthesis pictures. A four-poster queen-size bed jutted up against the wall opposite the bulletin board. Notably, the room lacked pink.

"It's not so pink in here," Colin commented.

"It's the only refuge in the entire house," she said.

"Do you have a match?"

"Sure, I got a shitload of 'em," Lindsey answered without looking up. "Why?"

"I want to burn this," he said, holding it up. "I can't finish my Theorem, and so I want to burn it."

Lindsey stood up, darted toward Colin, and snatched the notebook from his hand. She paged through it for a while. "Can't you just throw it away?"

Colin sighed. Clearly, she didn't get it. "Well, yeah, I *could*. But look, if I can't *be* a genius—and clearly I can't be—I can at least burn my work like one. Look at all the geniuses who either successfully or unsuccessfully tried to burn their papers."

"Yes," Lindsey said absentmindedly, still reading from the notebook. "Just look at all of them."

"Carlyle, Kafka, Virgil. It's hard to imagine better company, really."

"Yes. Hey, explain this to me," she said, sitting down on the bed and motioning for him to sit next to her. She was reading from a page with an early version of the formula and several inaccurate graphs.

"The idea is that you take two people and figure out if they're Dumpers or Dumpees. You use a scale that goes from -5 for a strong Dumpee to +5 for a strong Dumper. The difference between those numbers gives you the variable, D, and then by putting D into the formula, you get a graph that predicts the relationship. Only—" he paused, trying to think of a way to put his failure poetically. "Uh, it doesn't really work."

She didn't look up at him; just closed the notebook. "You can burn it," she said, "but not tonight. I want it for a couple days."

"Uh, okay," Colin said, and then he waited for Lindsey to say something more. Finally, she added, "It's just a cool-ass way to tell stories. I mean, I hate math. But this is cool."

"Okay. But soon, we burn it!" Colin said, his finger in the air, mock emphatic.

"For sure, yo. Now go to bed before your day gets any worse."

# (eleven)

**On their fifth night** in Gutshot, Hassan and Colin split up. Hassan went out with Lindsey to go "cruising," an activity that apparently involved driving in Hollis's pink truck from the Gutshot General Store to the gas station/Taco Hell and then back to the General Store, and then back to the gas station/Taco Hell, ad infinitum.

"You should come out," Hassan told him. He was standing beside Lindsey in the living room. She wore dangly blue earrings and quite a bit of rouge, which made her look flushed.

"I'm behind on my reading," Colin explained.

"Behind on your reading? All you *do* is read," Lindsey said.

"I've been way behind because I've worked so hard on the Theorem and because of oral historianing. I try to read four hundred pages a day—ever since I was seven."

"Even on weekends?"

"*Particularly* on weekends, because then I can really focus on pleasure reading."

Hassan shook his head. "Dude, you're such a geek. And that's coming from an overweight *Star Trek* fan who scored a 5 on the AP Calculus test. So you know your condition is grave." He rubbed Colin's Jew-fro as if for luck, and then turned away.

"You should go; keep them out of trouble," Hollis yelled from the couch.

Without a word, Colin grabbed his book (a biography of Thomas Edison)[56] and headed upstairs to his room, where he lay on his bed and read in peace. Over the next five hours, he finished that book and started one he found on the bookshelf in his room called *Foxfire*. *Foxfire* discussed how people did things in the old days of Appalachia.

The reading quieted his brain a little. Without Katherine and without the Theorem and without his hopes of mattering, he had very little. But he always had books. Books are the ultimate Dumpees: put them down and they'll wait for you forever; pay attention to them and they always love you back.

*Foxfire* had just taught Colin how to skin a raccoon and cure it into a hide when Hassan burst into his room, laughing loudly, with the slow-moving gray furball known as Princess sauntering after him.

"I'm not going to lie, *kafir*. I drank half a beer."

Colin scrunched his nose and sniffled. "See, drinking is *haram*. I told you, you do *haram* shit all the time."

"Yeah, well, when in Gutshot, do as the Gutshotians do."

"Your religious commitment is an inspiration to us all," Colin deadpanned.

"Come on. Don't make me feel guilty. I split a beer with Lindsey. I didn't feel anything. It's really *getting drunk* that's *haram*, not *drinking half a beer*. Anyway, cruising is fun. It's amazingly fun. I got to sit in a pickup truck with TOC and JATT and SOCT for about an hour and a half, and they're really not bad. I think I made them all like me. Plus Katrina, as it turns out, is very nice. And when I say nice, I mean gorgeous. Although it is ridiculous the way everyone hangs on TOC like he's God's gift to Gutshot.

---

[56] Who was not a child prodigy but did end up being something of a genius. Although a lot of Edison's discoveries were not actually made by Edison. Like the lightbulb, for instance, was technically invented by Sir Humphrey Davy in 1811, but his lightbulb sort of sucked and burned out all the time. Edison improved upon the idea. Edison also stole ideas from Nikola Tesla, the aforementioned pigeon lover.

I guess he's the quarterback or cornerback or something on the football team, except he just graduated, so I don't think he's anything anymore, but apparently being quarterback or cornerback is like being a Marine: it's a once/always thing. Also when Lindsey is not around, TOC talks about her ass constantly. He has no other topic of conversation. Apparently he spends a lot of his free time grabbing her ass, so that's a nice image. I never even noticed her ass."

"Me neither," Colin said. He never really thought to notice butts, unless they were unusually massive.

"Anyway," Hassan went on, "so there's this hunt camp in the woods, and we're going hunting with them and Lindsey and some guy from the factory. *Hunting*. With guns! *For pigs*!"

Colin had no desire to shoot pigs—or anything else, for that matter. "Um," Colin said. "I don't even know how to shoot a gun."

"Yeah, me neither, but how hard can it be? Complete fugging idiots shoot guns all the time. That's why there are so many dead people."

"Maybe, instead, you and I could just, like, go out in the woods that weekend and hang out. Like build a fire or something and go camping."

"Are you shitting me?"

"No, it could be fun. Reading by firelight and cooking our own food on the fire and stuff. I know how to build a fire even without a match. I read about it in this book," Colin said, gesturing to *Foxfire*.

"Do I *look* like an eighth-grade Boy Scout, *sitzpinkler*? We'll go out. We'll have fun. We'll get up early and drink coffee and hunt pigs and everyone will be drunk and hilarious except for us."

"You can't *make* me go with you," Colin shot back.

Hassan took a step toward the doorway. "That's true, *sitzpinkler*. You don't have to come. I won't begrudge you sitting on your ass. God knows I have always loved it. I just feel like a little adventure lately."

Colin felt vaguely like he'd been dumped. He'd tried to come up with a compromise. He *did* want to hang out with Hassan, but not with those oh-so-cool guys. "I don't get it," Colin said. "Do you want to make out with Lindsey or something?"

Hassan stood up, petting the fluff ball, releasing her pet dander into the air for Colin to sneeze at. "Again with that? No. God. I don't want to date *anyone*. I see what it's done to you. As you well know, I believe in saving Thunderstick for one very special lady."

"Also, you believe in not drinking."

"*Touché, mon ami*. Too fugging shay."

### The Middle (of the Middle)

The biggest study of highly gifted children ever undertaken was the brainchild (as it were) of one Lewis Terman, a psychologist in California. With the help of teachers around the state, Terman chose some seven thousand gifted children, who have now been followed for almost sixty years. Not all the kids were *prodigies*, of course—their IQs ranged from 145 to 190, and Colin, by comparison, had an IQ that sometimes measured above 200—but they represented many of the best and brightest children of that generation of Americans. The results were somewhat startling: the highly gifted kids in the study weren't much more likely to become prominent intellectuals than normal kids. Most of the children in the study became successful enough—bankers and doctors and lawyers and college professors—but almost none of them turned out to be real *geniuses*, and there was little correlation between a really high IQ and making a significant contribution to the world. Terman's gifted children, in short, rarely ended up being as special as they initially promised to be.

Take, for instance, the curious case of George Hodel. With one of the highest IQs in the study, one might have expected Hodel to discover the structure of DNA or something. Instead, he was a fairly successful doctor in California who later lived in Asia. He never became a genius, but Hodel did manage to become infamous: he was quite probably a serial killer.[57] So much for the benefits of prodigy.

As a sociologist, Colin's dad studied people, and he had a theory on how to transform a prodigy into a grown-up genius. He believed Colin's development ought to involve a delicate interplay between what he called "active, results-oriented parenting" and Colin's natural predisposition to studying. This basically meant letting Colin study and setting "markers," which were exactly like goals except they were called markers. Colin's father believed that this kind of prodigy—born and then made smarter by the right environment and education—could become a considerable genius, remembered forever. He told Colin this sometimes, when Colin would come home from school sullen, tired of the Abdominal Snowman, tired of pretending that his abject friendlessness didn't bother him.

"But you'll win," his dad would say. "You have to imagine that, Colin, that one day they will all look back on their lives and wish they'd been you. You'll have what everyone else wants in the end."

But it did not take until the end. It took until *KranialKidz*.

At the tail end of Christmas break his junior year, Colin received a call from a cable station he'd never heard of called CreaTVity. He didn't watch much TV, but it wouldn't have mattered, because *no one* had heard of CreaTVity. They'd gotten his number from Krazy Keith, who they'd contacted because of his scholarly articles about prodigy. They wanted Colin on their game show. His parents disapproved, but their "active, results-oriented" parenting meant that they gave Colin a measure of freedom to

---

[57] Hodel was likely guilty of the 1947 "Black Dahlia" murder, one of the most famous and long-unsolved murder cases in California history. (He was apparently pretty *good* at serial killing, as one might expect of a prodigy, since he never got caught and indeed probably no one would have ever known about Hodel except his son—true story—became a homicide detective in California, and through a series of amazing coincidences and some pretty solid police work, became convinced that his dad was a murderer.)

make his own decisions. And he wanted to go on the show, because (a) the ten-thousand-dollar first prize was a lot of money, and (b) he would be on television, and (c) 10K is a *lot* of money.

They gave Colin a makeover when he arrived for the first taping, turning him into the cool, snide, troublemaking prodigy. They bought him glasses with rectangular wire rims and caked his hair with endless product so that he had a kind of curly, mussy 'do like the coolest kids at school. They gave him five outfits—including a pair of designer jeans, which hugged his ass like they were a needy boyfriend, and a T-shirt that read, in a hand-printed scrawl: SLACKER. And then they taped all six preliminary rounds of the show in one day, pausing to change the prodigies into new outfits. Colin won all six rounds, leaving him ready for the finals. His opponent there was Karen Aronson, a towheaded twelve-year-old kid studying for her PhD in math. Karen had been cast as the adorable one. In the week between the first tapings and the final, Colin wore his new trendy kid button-downs and his designer jeans to school, and people asked him, *Are you really going to be on TV?* And then a cool kid named Herbie[58] told Hassan that this girl Marie Caravolli liked Colin. And since Colin had, not too long before, been dumped by Katherine XVIII, Colin asked Marie out on a date, because Marie, a perennially tan Italian beauty who would have won Homecoming Queen if the Kalman School did that kind of thing, was the hottest girl he had ever, or would ever, come across. Let alone talk to. Let alone date. He'd wanted to keep his Katherine streak alive, of course. But Marie Caravolli was the kind of girl you break streaks for.

And that's when the funny thing happened. He got off the train after school on the day of his date; everything was perfectly planned. He had just enough time to walk home, clean all the fast-food wrappers and soda cans out of the Hearse, take a shower, buy some flowers from the White Hen, and pick

[58] How does a kid named Herbie manage to be cool? This is one of life's enduring mysteries, how guys named Herbie or Dilworth or Vagina or whatever so easily overcome the burden of their names to achieve a kind of legendary status, but Colin is forever linked with Colon.

up Marie. But when he turned onto his street, he saw Katherine I sitting on the steps outside his house. As he squinted at her, watching her pull her knees up almost to her chin, he realized he'd never seen Katherine without Krazy Keith.

"Is everything okay?" Colin asked as he approached.

"Oh yeah," she said. "I'm sorry to drop by unannounced. It's just I've got this French test?" she said as if it were a question. "Tomorrow? And I don't want my dad to know what a dumbass I am in French and so I thought maybe—I tried to call, but I don't have your cell number. So anyway, I figured that since I know a world-famous TV quiz show star, I could maybe get tutoring from him." She smiled.

"Um," Colin said. And in the next few seconds, he tried to work out what it would really be like to date Marie. Colin had always been jealous of people, like Hassan, who just know how to make friends. But the risk of being able to win over anyone, he found himself thinking, was that you might pick the wrong people.

He imagined the best possible scenario: Marie actually, improbably, ends up *liking* him, whereupon Colin and Hassan vault up the social ladder and get to eat lunch at a different table, and get invited to some parties. Now, Colin had seen enough movies to know what happens when dorks go to cool-kid parties: generally, the dorks either get thrown into the pool[59] or they become drunk, vacuous cool kids themselves. Neither seemed like a good option. Also there was the fact that Colin did not, technically, *like* Marie. He didn't even know her.

"Hold on," he told Katherine I. And then he called Marie. She'd given him the number earlier that very day, during their second-ever conversation,[60] a remarkable fact considering they'd attended the same school together for nearly a decade. "I'm really sorry," he said. "But I've got a family

---

[59] Although there are admittedly not a lot of pools in Chicago.
[60] The first being the date-asking itself.

emergency. . . . Yeah, no, my uncle is in the hospital, and we have to go see him. . . . Well, yeah, I'm sure he'll be fine. . . . Okay. Cool. Sorry, again."

And so it came to pass that the only time Colin came anywhere close to ever dumping anyone, it was Marie Caravolli, who everyone agreed was the most attractive individual in American history. Instead, he tutored Katherine I. And one session turned into one each week, and then into two each week, and by the next month, she came over to his house with Krazy Keith to watch, with Colin's parents and Hassan, as Colin annihilated a poor sap named Sanjiv Reddy in the first episode of *KranialKidz*. Later that night, after Hassan had gone home, while Krazy Keith and Colin's parents were drinking red wine, Colin and Katherine Carter snuck out of the house to have a cup of coffee at *Café Sel Marie*.

# (twelve)

**The following Thursday,** Colin woke up to the sounds of the rooster mixing with Hassan's prayers. Colin rolled out of bed, pulled on a T-shirt, peed, and then entered Hassan's room through the bathroom. Hassan was back in bed, his eyes closed.

"Is there a way you could pray *less loudly*? I mean, shouldn't God be able to hear you even if you whisper?" he asked.

"I'm calling in sick," Hassan said without opening his eyes. "I think I have a sinus infection, and also I need a day off. Jesus. This working business is all right, but I need to sit in my boxers and watch *Judge Judy*. Do you realize that I haven't seen *Judge Judy* in, like, twelve days? Imagine if *you* were separated from the love of *your* life for twelve days." With his lips pursed, Colin stared at Hassan silently. Hassan blinked open his eyes. "Oh. Right. Sorry."

"You can't call in sick. Your boss works here. In the house. She'll know you're not sick."

"She spends Thursdays at the factory, dumbass. You need to pay better attention. It's the *perfect* day to call in sick. I just need to charge the emotional batteries."

"You've been charging the batteries all year! You haven't done anything in twelve months!"

Hassan smirked. "Don't you have to go to work or something?"

"At least call your mom and tell her to send a deposit to Loyola. The deposit deadline is in four weeks. I looked online for you."

Hassan didn't open his eyes. "I'm trying to think of a word. God, it's right on the tip of my tongue. Duh—doo—dii. Oh. Right. Dingleberries, motherfugger. Dingle. Berries."

When Colin got downstairs, he saw that Hollis was up already—or maybe she'd just stayed up all night—and dressed in a pink pantsuit.

"Beautiful day in the country," she said. "High's only 83 today. But Lord, I sure am glad Thursday only comes around once a week."

When Colin sat down beside her at the dining room table, he asked, "What do you do on Thursdays?"

"Oh, I just like to go in to the factory and check on things in the morning. And then around noon I drive to Memphis and visit our warehouse."

"Why is the warehouse in Memphis instead of Gutshot?" asked Colin.

"Lord, you ask a lot of questions," Hollis answered. "So listen. Y'all have interviewed most everyone who works at the factory now. So I'm gonna start sending you out to the other folks in Gutshot, factory retirees, and that sort of thing. I still just need you to ask the four questions, but you might want to stay a bit longer, just to look polite and all."

Colin nodded. After a bit of silence, he said, "Hassan is sick. He has a sinus infection."

"Poor thing. Okay, you'll go out with Lindsey. It's a bit of a drive today. You're going to see the oldsters."

"The oldsters?"

"That's what Lindsey calls them. The folks at the nursing home in Bradford—a lot of them live off pensions from Gutshot Textiles. Lindsey used to visit those folks all the time before she started," Hollis sighed, "dating that," Hollis sighed again, "boy." Hollis craned her neck around and shouted down the hall, "LINDSSSSEEEEY! GET YOUR LAZY ASS OUT OF BED!"

And even though the sound of Hollis's thick voice had to carry down the hallway and through two closed doors to reach Lindsey, Lindsey shouted back moments later, "PUT A QUARTER IN THE GODDAMNED SWEAR JAR, HOLLIS. I'M ABOUT TO TAKE A SHOWER."

Hollis got up, put a quarter in the swear jar on the mantel, walked back to Colin, mussed his Jew-fro, and said, "Listen, I'll be late. Long drive back from Memphis. I'll have my cell on. Y'all be safe."

By the time Lindsey got downstairs, wearing khaki shorts and a tight-fitting black GUTSHOT! T-shirt, Hassan was on the couch, watching reruns of *Saturday Night Live*.

"Who are our victims today?" asked Lindsey.

"The oldsters."

"That's cool, actually. I'm a veteran of that joint. Okay, off the couch, Hass."

"Sorry, Linds. I called in sick," he said. *I've never called her "Linds,"* Colin thought. Hassan laughed at some joke on the TV. Lindsey blew hair out of her face and then she grabbed Colin by his upper arm and led him out to the Hearse.

"I can't believe he's calling in sick," said Colin, but he started the car. "I'm fugging exhausted from staying up half the night reading a fugging book about the invention of the television,[61] and *he* gets to fugging call in sick?"

"Hey, why the fuck do you and Hassan say fug all the time?"

Colin exhaled slowly, his cheeks puffing out. "Have you ever read *The Naked and the Dead* by Norman Mailer?"

"I don't even know who that is."

"American novelist. Born in 1923. I was reading him when I first met

---

[61] Television was invented by a kid. In 1920, the memorably named Philo T. Farnsworth conceived the cathode ray vacuum tube used in most all twentieth-century TV sets. He was fourteen. Farnsworth built the first one when he was just twenty-one. (And shortly thereafter went on to a long and distinguished career of chronic alcoholism.)

Hassan. And then later Hassan ended up reading it because it's all about war, and Hassan likes actiony books. Anyway, it's 872 pages, and it uses the word *fug* or *fugging* or *fugger* or whatever about thirty-seven thousand times. Every other word is a fug, pretty much. So anyway, after I read a novel, I like to read some literary criticism of it."

"Color me surprised," she said.

"Right. Well, when Mailer wrote the book, he didn't use 'fug.' But then he sent it to the publisher and they were like, 'This is a really excellent book you've written, Mr. Mailer. But no one here in 1948 is going to buy it, because it contains even more F-bombs than it does Regular Bombs.' So Norman Mailer, as a kind of fug-you to the publisher, went through his 872-page book and changed every last F-word to 'fug.' So I told Hassan the story while he was reading the book and then he decided to start saying fug as an homage to Mailer—and because you can say it in class without getting in trouble."

"That's a good story. See? You can tell a story," she said, her smile like bright white firecrackers in a starless sky. "It doesn't have a moral, and it doesn't contain any romance or adventure, but—it's a story at least, and you didn't share any meditations on hydration." In his peripheral vision, Colin could see her smiling at him. "Turn left. We go down this fugging road forever and then—oh wait, wait, slow down that's Chase's car."

A two-toned Chevy Bronco approached from the other direction. Reluctantly, Colin brought the Hearse to a stop. TOC was behind the wheel. Colin rolled down the window as TOC rolled down his. Lindsey leaned across Colin to look up at her boyfriend. "Hey, Lass," TOC said.

"Not funny," Lindsey said emphatically, as Chase, riding shotgun, howled with laughter.

"Listen, Chase and me are gonna meet Fulton tonight at the Camp. See you there?"

"I think I'm gonna stay home tonight," she said, and then turned her head to Colin and said, "Go."

"Aww, Linds. I was just screwing with you."

"Go," she said again, and Colin hit the gas and shot off.

Colin was about to ask for an explanation of the scene when Lindsey turned to him and said very calmly, "It's nothing—just an inside joke. So anyway, I read your notebook. I don't really understand it all, but I at least *looked* at everything."

Colin quickly forgot about the weirdness with TOC and asked, "What'd you think?"

"Well, first, it kept making me think about what we talked about when you first got here. When I told you I thought it was a bad idea to matter. I think I gotta take that back, because looking at your notes, I kept wanting to find a way to improve on your Theorem. I had this total hard-on for fixing it and proving to you that relationships *could* be seen as a pattern. I mean, it ought to work. People are so damned predictable. And then the Theorem wouldn't be yours, it'd be ours, and I could—okay, this sounds retarded. But anyway, I guess I do want to matter a little—to be known outside Gutshot, or I wouldn't have thought so much about it. Maybe I just want to be big-time without leaving here."

Colin slowed as he approached a stop sign and then looked at her. "Sorry," he said.

"Why sorry?"

"Because you couldn't fix it."

"Oh, but I did," she said.

Colin brought the car to a full stop twenty feet in front of the stop sign and said, "Are you sure?" And she just kept smiling. "Well, *tell* me," he pleaded.

"Okay, well I didn't FIX it, but I have an idea. I suck at math—like really, really suck, so tell me if I have this wrong, but it seems like the only factor that goes into the formula is where each person fits on the Dumper/Dumpee scale, right?"

"Right. That's what the formula's about. It's about getting dumped."

"Yeah, but that's not the only factor in a relationship. There's, like, age. When you're nine, your relationships tend to be shorter and less serious and more random than when you're forty-one and desperate to get married before your flow-o'-eggs dries up, right?"

Colin turned away from Lindsey and looked at the intersecting roads before him, both utterly abandoned. He thought it through for a while. It seemed so obvious now—many discoveries do. "More variables," he announced enthusiastically.

"Right. Like I said—age, for starters. But a lot of things go into it. I'm sorry, but attractiveness matters. There's this guy who just joined the Marines, but last year he was a senior. He was like 210 pounds of chiseled muscle, and I love Colin and everything, but this guy was dead sexy and also really sweet and nice, and he drove a tricked-out Montero."

"I hate that guy," Colin said.

Lindsey laughed. "Right, you totally would. But anyway, total Dumper. Self-professed proponent of the 4 Fs: find 'em, feel 'em, fug 'em, and forget 'em. Only he made the mistake of dating the only person hotter than him in Middle Tennessee—Katrina. And he became the clingiest, neediest, whimperingest little puppy dog and finally Katrina had to ditch him."

"But it's not just physical attraction," Colin said, reaching into his pocket for his pencil and notepad. "It's how attractive you find the person and how attractive they find you. Like, say there's this girl who's very pretty, but as it happens, I have a weird fetish and only like girls with thirteen toes. Well, I might be the Dumper if she happens to be ten-toed and only gets turned on by skinny guys with glasses and Jew-fros."

"And really green eyes," Lindsey added nonchalantly.

"What?"

"I was complimenting you," she said.

"Oh. Mine. Green. Right." *Smooth, Singleton. Smooth.*

"Anyway, I think it needs to be way more complicated. It needs to be so complicated that a math tard like me won't understand it in the *least*."

A car pulled up behind them and honked, so Colin returned to driving, and by the time they were in the cavernous parking lot of the nursing home, they had settled on five variables:

Age (A)[62]
Popularity Differential (C)[63]
Attractiveness Differential (H)[64]
Dumper/Dumpee Differential (D)[65]
Introvert/Extrovert Differential (P)[66]

They sat in the car together with the windows down, the air warm and sticky but not stifling. Colin sketched possible new concepts and explained the math to Lindsey, who made suggestions and watched his sketching. Within thirty minutes, he was cranking out the basic she-broke-up-with-him frowny-face graph[67] for several Katherines. But he couldn't get the timing right. Katherine XVIII, who cost him months of his life, didn't look like she lasted any longer, or mattered any more, than the 3.5 days he spent in the arms of Katherine V. He was creating too simple a formula. And he was

---

[62] To get this variable, Colin took the two people's average age and subtracted five. By the way, all the footnotes on this page have math in them and are therefore *strictly optional*.
[63] Which Colin arrived at by calculating the popularity difference between Person A and Person B on a scale of 1 to 1,000 (you can approximate) and then dividing by 75—positive numbers if the girl is more popular; negative if the guy is.
[64] Which is calculated as a number between 0 and 5 based on the difference in attraction to each other. Positive numbers if the boy is more attracted to the girl; negative if vice versa.
[65] Between 0 and 1, the relative distance between the two people on the Dumper/Dumpee range. A negative number if the boy is more of a Dumper; positive number if the girl is.
[66] In the Theorem, this is the difference in outgoingness between two people calculated on a scale that goes from 0 to 5. Positive numbers if the girl is more outgoing; negative if the guy is.
[67]

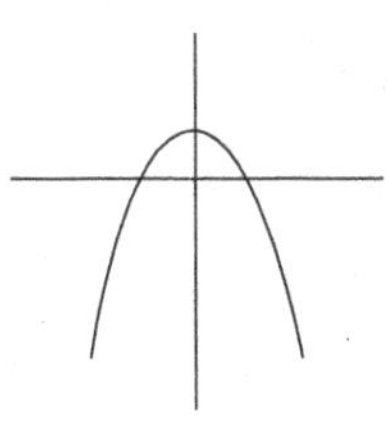

still trying to do it completely randomly. *What if I square the attractiveness variable? What if I put a sine wave here or a fraction there?* He needed to see the formula not as math, which he hated, but as language, which he loved.

So he started thinking of the formula as an attempt to communicate something. He started creating fractions within the variables so that they'd be easier to work with in a graph. He began to see before even inputting the variables how different formulas would render the Katherines, and as he did so the formula grew increasingly complicated, until it began to seem almost—how to put this not so dorkily—well, beautiful. After an hour parked in the car, the formula looked like this:

$$-D^7x^8+D^2x^3-\frac{x^4}{A^5}-Cx^2-Px+\frac{1}{A}+13P+\frac{\sin(2x)}{2}\left[1+(-1)^{H+1}\frac{\left(x+\frac{11\pi}{2}\right)^H}{\left|x+\frac{11\pi}{2}\right|^H}\right]$$[68]

"I think that's close," he said finally.

"And I sure as shit don't understand it at all, so you've succeeded in my eyes!" She laughed. "Okay, let's go hang with the oldsters."

Colin had only been in a nursing home once. He and his dad drove to Peoria, Illinois, one weekend when Colin was eleven to visit Colin's great-great-aunt Esther, who was in a coma at the time and therefore not very good company.

So he was pleasantly stunned by Sunset Acres. At a picnic table on the lawn outside, four old women, all wearing broad, straw hats, were playing a card game. "Is that Lindsey Lee Wells?" one of the women asked, and then Lindsey brightened and hastened over to the table. The women laid down

[68] That does not count as math, because one does not have to understand how it works or what it means in order to think that it looks sort of beautiful.

their cards to hug Lindsey and pat her puffy cheeks. Lindsey knew them all by name—Jolene, Gladys, Karen, and Mona—and introduced Colin to them, whereupon Jolene took off her hat, fanned her face, and said, "My, Lindsey, you *do* have a nice-looking boyfriend, don't you? No wonder you don't come 'round to visit us no more."

"Aw, Jolene, he ain't my boyfriend. I'm sorry I haven't been around as much. I been so busy with school, and Hollis works me like a dog down at the store."

And then they took to discussing Hollis. It took fifteen minutes before Colin could even get his tape recorder started to ask the four questions they'd come there to ask, but he didn't mind, first because Jolene thought he was "nice-looking," and second because they were such a relaxed bunch of old people. For example, Mona, a woman with liver spots and a gauze patch over her left eye, answered the question, "What's special about Gutshot?" by saying, "Well for starters that mill has got a right-good pension plan. I been retired for thirty years and Hollis Wells *still* buys my diapers. That's right, I use 'em! I pee myself when I laugh," she said gleefully, and then laughed disturbingly hard.

And Lindsey, it seemed to Colin, was some kind of rock star among the oldsters. As word filtered through the building that she'd arrived, more and more of them made their way to the picnic tables outside and hovered around Lindsey. Colin went from person to person, recording their answers to the questions. Eventually, he just sat down and let Lindsey throw people his way.

His favorite interview was with a man named Roy Walker. "Well I can't imagine," Roy said, "why on earth anyone would want to hear from me. But I'm happy to chat." Roy was starting to tell Colin about his former job as night-shift plant manager of Gutshot Textiles, but then he stopped suddenly and said, "Look how they're all loving on little Lindsey. We all raised that girl up. I used to see her once a week or more—we knew her when she was a baby and we knew her when you couldn't tell her from a boy and we knew her when she had blue hair. She used to sneak me in one Budweiser beer every Saturday, bless her heart. Son, if there's one thing I know," and Colin thought about how old people always like to tell you the one thing they know, "it's that there's some people in this world who you can just love and love and love no matter what."

Colin followed Roy over to Lindsey then. Lindsey was twisting a lock of her hair casually, but staring intently at Jolene.

"Jolene, what'd you just say?"

"I was telling Helen that your mama is selling two hundred acres of land up Bishops Hill to my boy Marcus."

"Hollis is selling land on Bishops Hill?"

"That's right. To Marcus. I think Marcus wants to build himself some houses up there, build a little—I don't remember what he calls it."

Lindsey half-closed her eyes and sighed. "A subdivision?" she asked.

"That's right. Subdivision. Up there on the hill, I guess. Nice views, anyway."

Lindsey became quiet after that, her big eyes staring off into the distance at the fields behind the nursing home. Colin sat there and listened to the old folks talking, and then finally Lindsey grabbed his arm just above the elbow and said, "We should get going."

As soon as the Hearse's doors were shut, Lindsey mumbled as if to herself, "Mom would never sell land. Never. Why is she doing that?" It occurred to Colin that he'd never before heard Lindsey refer to Hollis as Mom. "Why would she sell land to that guy?"

"Maybe she needs money," Colin offered.

"She needs money like I need a goddamned hole in my head. My great-grandfather *built* that factory. Dr. Fred N. Dinzanfar. We aren't hurting for money, I promise you."

"Was he Arab?"

"What?"

"Dinzanfar."

"No, he wasn't Arab. He was from Germany or something. Anyway, he spoke German—so does Hollis, that's how I know it. Why do you always ask such ridiculous questions?"

"Jeez. Sorry."

"Oh, whatever, I'm just confused. Who cares. On to other things. It's fun hanging out with the oldsters, isn't it? You wouldn't think it, but they're cool as hell. I used to visit those people at their houses—most of them weren't in the Home then—almost every day. I'd just go from house to house, getting fed and getting hugged on. Those were the pre-friend days."

"They certainly seemed to adore you," Colin said.

"Me? The ladies couldn't talk about anything but how hot you were. You're missing a whole demographic of Katherines by not chasing the over-eighty market."

"It's funny how they thought we were dating," Colin said, glancing over at her.

"How's that funny?" she asked, holding his gaze.

"Um," he said. Distracted from the road, Colin watched as she gave him the slightest version of her inimitable smile.

# (thirteen)

**That Sunday,** Hassan went "cruising" with Lindsey and Katrina and TOC and JATT and SOCT. The next night, he went cruising again, and came home after midnight to find Colin working on his Theorem, which now worked seventeen of nineteen times. He still couldn't get it to work for either Katherine III or, more importantly, Katherine XIX.

"'Sup?" asked Hassan.

"Sup is not a word," answered Colin without looking up.

"You're like sunshine on a cloudy day, Singleton. When it's cold outside, you're the month of May."

"I'm working," Colin said. He couldn't quite pinpoint when Hassan had started to become like everyone else on the planet, but it was clearly happening, and it was clearly annoying.

"I kissed Katrina," Hassan said. And then Colin put his pencil down and turned around in his chair and said, "You whated who?"

"Whated isn't a word," mimicked Hassan.

"On the lips?"

"No, dumbass, on her pupillary sphincter. Yes, on the lips."

"Why?"

"We were sitting in the back of Colin's truck and we were spinning this beer bottle, but it was bumpy as hell because we were riding up to this place in the woods. And so someone would spin the beer bottle, and it'd fly way the hell up and land on the other side of the truck bed, so no one was kissing anyone. So I figured it was safe to play, right? But then I spin the bottle and I swear to God it just spun in the tightest little circle even though we were still going over these bumps—I mean, only God could have kept that bottle from jumping up into the air—and then it stopped right in front of Katrina, and she said, 'Lucky me,' and she wasn't even being sarcastic, *kafir*! She was serious. And she leaned across the truck and we hit a bump and she just sort of landed in my arms, and then she made a beeline for my mouth and, I swear to God, her tongue was like *licking my teeth*." Colin just stared, incredulous. He wondered whether Hassan was making it up. "It was, uh, weird and wet and messy—but fun, I guess. The best part was having my hand on her face, and looking down at her and seeing her eyes closed. I guess she's a chubby chaser or something. Anyway, I'm taking her to the Taco Hell tomorrow night. She's picking me up. That's how I roll, baby." Hassan smirked. "The ladies come to Big Daddy, 'cause Big Daddy ain't got no car."

"You're serious," said Colin.

"I'm serious."

"Wait, you think the bottle staying still in the truck was a miracle?" Hassan nodded. Colin tapped his pencil eraser against the desk, and then stood up. "And God wouldn't lead you to kiss a girl unless you were supposed to marry her, so *God* wants you to marry the girl who believed I was a Frenchman suffering from hemorrhoidal Tourette's?"

"Don't be an asshole," said Hassan, almost threateningly.

"I'm just surprised that Mr. High and Mighty Religious is fugging around with girls in the back of a pickup truck, that's all. You were probably drinking shitty beer and wearing a football jersey."

"What the fug, dude? I kissed a girl. Finally. A *really hot, really sweet* girl. Dingleberries. Stop pushing it."

Colin didn't know why, but he felt compelled to keep pushing it. "Whatever. I just can't believe you made out with *Katrina*. Is she just not as dumb and ditzy as she seemed that day?"

And then Hassan reached out and grabbed a handful of Colin's Jewfro. He pulled Colin across the room by the hair, and then pushed him up against the wall. Hassan's jaw was clenched tight as he pressed into Colin's solar plexus, the precise location of the hole in Colin's gut. "I said dingleberries, *kafir*. You will respect the goddamned dingleberries. Now I'm going to bed before we get into a fight. And you want to know why I don't want to fight you? Because I'd lose." *Still joking*, Colin thought. *He's always joking, even when he's furious*. And as Hassan made his way through the bathroom toward his room, and Colin sat back down to work at the Theorem, Colin's face was bright and wet, the tears coming from frustration. Colin hated not being able to accomplish his "markers." He'd hated it since he was four and his dad set learning the Latin conjugations for twenty-five irregular verbs as a "daily marker," but by the end of the day, Colin only knew twenty-three. His dad didn't chastise him, but Colin knew he'd failed. And now the markers were more complicated, maybe, but they were still pretty simple: he wanted a best friend, a Katherine, and a Theorem. And after almost three weeks in Gutshot, it seemed he was becoming worse off than when he'd started.

Hassan and Colin managed not to speak the next morning—not once, and it was clear to Colin that Hassan still felt just as pissed off as Colin did. Colin watched in a lock-jawed silence as Hassan furiously stabbed at his breakfast, and later as Hassan slammed the mini-recorder down on the coffee table of some factory retiree who was old-but-not-old-enough-for-the-nursing home. Colin could hear the annoyance in Hassan's voice as he asked, in the monotone of the aggressively bored, what life had been like in Gutshot when the oldster was a kid. By now, it seemed, they'd run through the best storytellers and were left with people who took five minutes deciding whether they visited Asheville, North Carolina, in June or July of 1961. Colin still paid attention—it was, after all, what he did—but much of his brainpower was elsewhere. Mostly, he cataloged all the times Hassan had been an ass to him, all the times he'd been the butt of Hassan's jokes, all the snide little comments Hassan had made about his Katherining. And now that Hassan was Katrining, he'd become the kind of guy who cruises, leaving Colin behind.

Lindsey skipped that day to hang out with TOC at the store. So it was just Colin and Hassan and one single oldster who monopolized their entire day. Although the old man talked for seven hours almost without ceasing, Colin's world felt eerily quiet until he finally gave in as they left the old man's house to go pick up Lindsey.

"This sounds trite, but I just think you've changed," Colin said as they walked down the oldster's driveway. "And I'm tired of you hanging out with me only so you can make fun of me." Hassan said nothing in response, just climbed into the passenger seat and slammed the door shut. Colin got in and started the car, and *then* Hassan lost it.

"Has it ever crossed your mind, you ungrateful asshole, that when I was mopping up after all your breakups, when I was picking your sorry ass off the floor of your bedroom, when I was listening to your endless rantings and ravings about every fugging girl who ever gave you the time of day, that maybe I was actually doing it for you and not because I'm oh-so desperate to learn of the newest dumping in your life? What problems have you listened to of mine, dillhole? Have you ever sat with me for hours and listened to me whine about being a fat fugger whose best friend ditches him every time a Katherine comes along? Has it ever occurred to you even for the briefest goddamn moment that *my* life might be as bad as yours? Imagine if you weren't a fugging genius *and* you were lonely *and* nobody ever listened to you. So yeah. Kill me. I kissed a girl. And I came home with that story psyched to tell you because I've finally got a story of my own after four years of listening to yours. And you're such a self-involved asshole that you can't for one fugging second realize that my life doesn't spin around the star of Colin Singleton." Hassan paused for breath, and Colin mentioned the thing that had been bugging him most all day.

"You called him Colin," said Colin.

"Do you know what your problem is?" Hassan went on, not listening. "You can't live with the idea that someone might leave. So instead of being *happy* for me, like any normal person, you're pissed off because ooh, oh no, Hassan doesn't like me anymore. You're such a *sitzpinkler*. You're so goddamned scared of the idea that someone might dump you that your whole fugging life is built around not getting left behind. Well, it doesn't work, *kafir*. It just—it's not just dumb, it's ineffective. Because then you're not being a good friend or a good boyfriend or whatever, because you're only thinking they-might-not-like-me-they-might-not-like-me, and guess what? When you act like that, no one likes you. There's your goddamned Theorem."

"You called him Colin," repeated Colin, his voice catching now.

"Called who Colin?"

"TOC."

"No."

Colin nodded.

"Did I?"

Colin nodded.

"You're sure? Right, of course you're sure. Huh. Well, I'm sorry. That was an asshole move on my part."

Colin turned into the store's parking lot and stopped the car, but made no move to get out. "I know you're right. I mean, about me being a self-centered asshole."

"Well, it's only sometimes. But still. Just stop."

"I don't really know how," he said. "How do you just stop being terrified of getting left behind and ending up by yourself forever and not meaning anything to the world?"

"You're pretty fugging smart," Hassan answered. "I'm sure you can figure something out."

"It's great," Colin said after a while. "About Katrina, I mean. You fugging kissed a girl. A *girl*. I mean, I always sort of thought you were gay," Colin acknowledged.

"I might be gay if I had a better-looking best friend," said Hassan.

"And I might be gay if I could locate your penis under the fat rolls."

"Bitch, I could gain five hundred pounds and you could still see Thunderstick hanging to my knees."

Colin smiled. "She's a lucky girl."

"Too bad she'll never know just how lucky unless we get married."

And then Colin was back on the subject. "You *are* sort of a dick to me sometimes. It would be easier if you acted like you actually didn't hate me."

"Dude. Do you want me to sit here and say that you're my best friend and I love you and you're such a genius that I just want to cuddle up to you at night? Because I'm just not going to. That's *sitzpinklery*. But I do think you're a genius. No shit. I honestly do. I think you can do whatever the fug you want to do in your life, and that's a pretty sweet gig."

"Thanks," said Colin, and then they got out of the car, and they met in front of the hood, and Colin held his arms out a little, and Hassan shoved him playfully, and then they hustled into the store.

TOC was restocking some beef jerky sticks while Lindsey sat on the stool behind the counter reading a celebrity magazine, her bare feet up on the counter beside the cash register.

"Hey," TOC said. "Heard you got a date tonight, big guy."

"Yeah, and it's all thanks to your excellent driving. If you'd missed that pothole, she never would have ended up in my arms."

"Well, you're welcome. She's a hottie, ain't she?"

"Hey!" said Lindsey without looking up from her magazine. "I'm the hottie!"

"Oh, baby, hush," TOC said.

"So, Colin," said TOC. "Hass says you aren't much for cruising, but you gotta come out hunting with us next weekend."

"That's nice of you to offer," Colin said. And it *was* sorta nice. No quarterback or cornerback or anyone else in any way associated with football had ever invited him to do anything. But Colin thought immediately of the reason he chose Katherine XIX over Marie Caravolli. In this world, Colin figured, you're best off staying with your kind. "I don't know how to shoot, though."

"Oh, I bet you'll bag a hogzilla," said TOC. Colin glanced over at Hassan, who opened his eyes wide and nodded subtly. For a split second, Colin thought of passing on the hog hunt, but he figured he owed it to Hassan. Part of not being a self-centered asshole, Colin reasoned, is doing things with your friends even when you don't want to. Even if they could result in the death of a wild hog. "Okay," Colin said, looking not at TOC but at Hass.

And TOC said, "Sounds good. Listen, since y'all is here to look after the store till closing, I'm gonna head off. I gotta meet the boys down at the factory. We're going bowling."

Now Lindsey put down the magazine. "I like bowling," she said.

"Boys night out, baby."

Lindsey fake-pouted, then smiled, and stood up to kiss TOC good-bye. He leaned across the counter, pecked her on the mouth, and strode out.

They closed up the store early and went home, even though Hollis did not like to be interrupted before five-thirty. She was lying on the couch in the living room saying, "We need your help here. If you look at the price point—" and then she saw them walking in and said, "I need to call you back." She hung up the phone. "Now I've told y'all—I work until five-thirty and I can't be interrupted."

"Hollis, why are you selling land to that guy Marcus?"

"That's none of your business and I'll thank you not to try and change the subject. Y'all stay out of the house until five-thirty. I'm paying you to *work*, remember. And Lindsey Lee Wells, I know you weren't down at Mr. Jaffrey's house today. Don't think I don't find these things out."

"I've got a date tonight, so I'll be skipping dinner," Hassan interjected.

"And I'm taking Colin to dinner," Lindsey said. "This Colin," she clarified, her extended pointer finger poking his bicep. Hollis beamed; Colin looked over at Lindsey with equal parts surprise and confusion.

"Well, I guess I can do some work this evening with y'all out then," Hollis said.

Colin spent his remaining pre-"date" hours working on the Theorem. Within thirty minutes, he'd nailed K-19. The problem, as it turned out, was not so much bad math as false hope: Colin had been trying to tweak the Theorem to make K-19's graph look like:

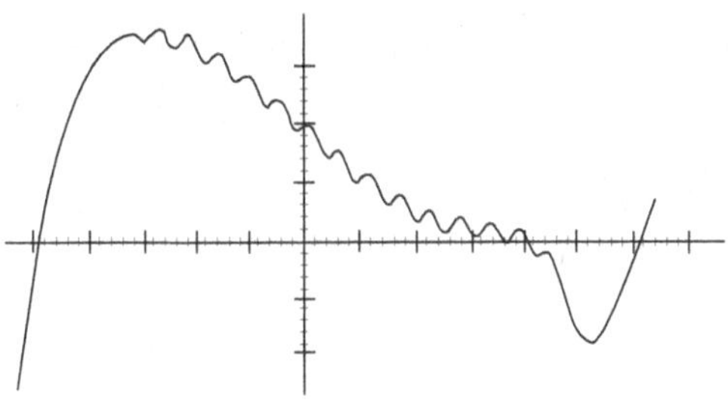

In short, he had been counting upon a reunion. He'd been assuming that the Theorem could see into the future, when K-19 would return to him. But the Theorem, he decided, couldn't take into account its own influence. So then with the same formula he'd worked out before, in the car with Lindsey,[69] Colin managed to get it to reflect his relationship with Katherine XIX up until now:

[69] The pretty one, with all the letters.

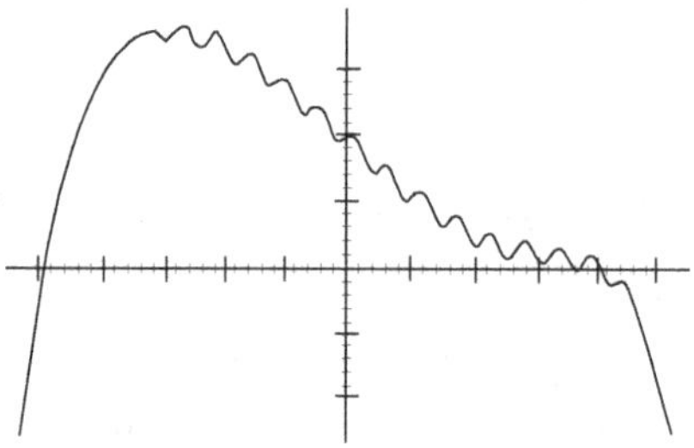

By five o'clock, he was perilously close. He had captured the Katherine roller coaster eighteen times. But what he *hadn't* done was quite important—he hadn't gotten Katherine III on paper, and one cannot take an equation that predicts eighteen out of nineteen Katherines to the Nobel Prize Committee.[70] For the next two hours, he thought of every facet of Katherine III (given name: Katherine Mutsensberger) with the precision and clarity that made his brain so unusual. And yet he could not fix what he came to call the III Anomaly. The equation that correctly predicted the other eighteen came out looking like this:

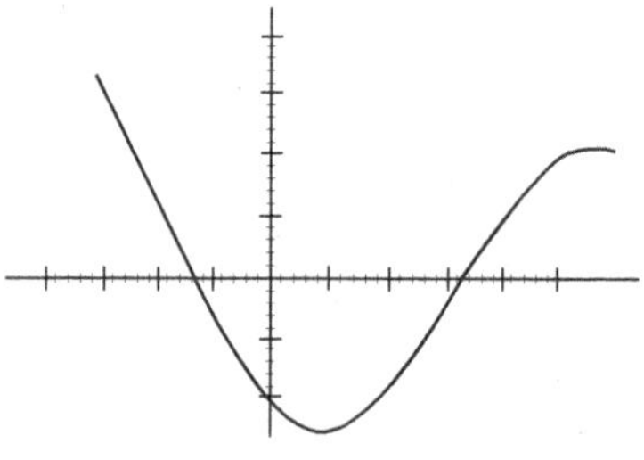

The graph's smiley-facedness indicated that Colin had not been dumped by III but had dumped her, which was ludicrous. He could remember *every-*

[70] Although there is not a Nobel Prize in Mathematics, he might have had an outside chance at the Peace Prize.

*thing* about Katherine III, and the rest of them, too, of course—he remembered everything about everything—and yet something about Katherine III clearly eluded him.

As he worked on the Theorem, Colin was so focused that the world outside his notebook seemed not to exist, so he jolted upright in surprise when he heard, from behind him, Lindsey say, "Time for dinner, dude." He turned around to see her head peeking through the open door. She wore a blue cotton tank top with tight blue jeans, Converse All Stars, and—as if she knew what he liked—no makeup. She looked, well, pretty—even not smiling. Colin glanced down at his jeans and yellow *KranialKidz* T-shirt. "Don't dress up on account of me," Lindsey said, smiling. "We gotta get going, anyway."

They came downstairs just in time to look through the screen door and see Hassan get into Katrina's SUV. Hassan handed her a sagging pink rose he'd plucked from the mansion's garden. She smiled, and then they kissed. *Lord.* Colin had seen it with his own eyes: Hassan kissing a girl who *had* to have been Homecoming Queen.

"Was Katrina Homecoming Queen?"

"No I was," Lindsey responded immediately.

"Really?"

Lindsey pursed her lips. "Well, no, but you don't have to sound so surprised about it! Katrina was on the Court, though." She stopped and shouted toward the kitchen, "Hey, Hollis! We're leaving. We might be back late. Hot sex and all!"

"Have fun!" replied Hollis. "Call if you'll be out past twelve!"

They drove downtown, to the gas station/Taco Hell, where they ordered at the drive-thru. They both peered through the accordion window, Lindsey leaning over Colin to catch a glimpse of Hassan and Katrina eating.

"She seems to really like him," Lindsey said. "I mean, I really like him, too. I don't want to sound mean. I'm just surprised. She usually goes for, um, the dumb, hot ones."

"So she's like you."

"Watch it. I'm paying for your dinner, after all."

They took their chicken soft tacos and drove off, and finally Colin decided to ask what was going on.

"Um, why are we going out for dinner together?"

"Well, three reasons. First, because I've been thinking about our Theorem and I have a question. How does it work if you're gay?"

"Huh?"

"Well it's all graph-going-up means boy dumps girl and graph-going-down means girl dumps boy, right? But what if they're both boys?"

"It doesn't matter. You just assign a position to each person. Instead of being 'b' and 'g,' it could just as easily be 'b1' and 'b2.' That's how algebra works."

"Which would explain my C-minus. Okay. Thank God. I was really worried that it would only help the straights, and that's not much of a Theorem. Reason two is I'm trying to get Hollis to like me, and she likes you, so if I like you, she'll like me." Colin was looking at her, confused. "C-minus in algebra; A-plus in coolology. See, popularity is complicated, yo. You have to spend a lot of time thinking about liking; you have to really like being liked, and also sorta like being disliked." Colin listened intently, nibbling the inside of his thumb. Listening to Lindsey talk about popularity made him feel a little bit of the *mysterium tremendum*. "Anyway," she went on, "I need to find out what's going on with her selling land. That guy Marcus built this cookie-cutter house subdivision south of Bradford. I mean, it's vomitous. Hollis would never stand for that shit."

"Oh, okay," Colin said, feeling a bit like a pawn.

"And reason three," Lindsey said, "is I gotta teach you how to shoot so you don't embarrass yourself."

"Shoot a gun?"

"A *shotgun*. I put one in your trunk this afternoon." Colin nervously glanced toward the back. "It won't *bite*," Lindsey said.

"Where did you get a gun?"

"Where did I *get* it? Smartypants, getting a gun in Gutshot, Tennessee, is easier than getting chlamydia from a hooker."

Twenty minutes later, they were sitting in a grassy field on the edge of a thick forested area that, Lindsey said, belonged to Hollis but would soon belong to Marcus. The field, overgrown with wildflowers and the occasional tree sapling, was nonetheless fenced in by an interweaving series of chopped logs.

"Why is there a fence?"

"Used to be we had a horse named Hobbit that grazed here, but then he died."

"He was your horse?"

"Yup. Well, Hollis's, too. Hollis got him from my father as a wedding present, and then when I was born—six months later—Hollis gave him to me. He was the gentlest horse, Hobbit. I could ride him from the time I was three."

"So are your parents divorced?"

"No, not officially. But you know what they say about Gutshot: the population never goes up and never goes down, because every time a woman gets pregnant, a man leaves town." Colin laughed. "He left when I was one. He calls a couple times a year, but Hollis never makes me talk to him. I don't know the guy, and I don't really care to. How 'bout you?"

"My parents are still married. I have to call them at the same time every night—in thirty minutes, actually. They're overprotective, I guess, but normal. We're really boring."

"You're not boring. You've got to stop saying that, or people will start believing you. Now, about the gun." Lindsey jumped up and ran back across the field and hurdled the fence. Colin followed her at a more sustainable pace. He did not, as a rule, believe in running. "Pop the trunk," Lindsey shouted.

Colin unlocked the trunk and found a long, double-barreled shotgun with a stained wooden handle. Lindsey picked up the gun, handed it to Colin, and said, "Point it at the sky." She grabbed a square paper box, and then they marched back, over the fence and across the field.

Looking like an expert, Lindsey cracked open the gun, pulled two cylindrical shells from the paper box, and inserted them. "When this shit is loaded, you don't point it at me, hear?" She snapped the gun shut, held it up to her shoulder, and then carefully handed it over to Colin.

She moved behind him and helped him hold the gun against his shoulder. He could feel her breasts against his shoulder blades, her feet by his feet, her stomach against his back. "Tuck it tight against your shoulder," she said, and he did. "The safety's here," she said, reaching up and guiding his hand to a steel switch on the side of the gun. He'd never held a gun before. It felt simultaneously exciting and deeply wrong.

"Now when you shoot it," she said, her breath against the nape of his neck, "you don't *pull* the trigger. You just reach in there and you *squeeze* it. Just squeeze it softly. I'm going to take a step back and then you just squeeze, okay?"

"What should I aim at?"

"You couldn't hit the broadside of a barn, so just aim straight ahead." Colin felt the absence of Lindsey on his back, and then he—ever so softly—squeezed the trigger.

The blast hit his ears at the same moment it hit his right shoulder, and the force of the gun caused his arm to pull up and his legs to fall out from under him and he found himself sitting on his ass in a field of wildflowers with the gun pointing to the sky. "Well," he said. "That was fun."

Lindsey was laughing. "See, that's why we're here, so you don't fall on your ass in front of Colin and Chase and everybody. You've got to learn to prepare for that kick."

And so over the course of the next hour, Colin shot the holy living hell out of the oak trees before him, pausing only to reload the gun and call his parents. He shot forty-four shells into the forest, and then, when his right arm was numb and he felt like he'd been punched repeatedly in the shoulder by a champion boxer, he said, "Why don't you try?" Lindsey shook her head and sat down on the grass. Colin followed her down.

"Oh, I don't shoot guns. I'm terrified of them," she said.

"Are you shitting me?"

"No. Plus that's a ten-gauge. I wouldn't shoot a ten-gauge for a thousand dollars. They kick like a goddamned mule."

"Then why did—"

"Like I said, I don't want you to look like a pussy."

Colin wanted to continue the conversation but didn't quite know how, so he lay back and rubbed his sore shoulder. On the whole, Gutshot had been physically unkind to him: a puffy scar above his eye, forty-four distinct shoulder bruises, and of course a still-painful gaping hole in his gut. And yet, somehow, he liked the place.

He noticed that she was lying next to him, her arms crossed beneath her head. She kicked at his shin playfully to get his attention. "What?" he asked.

"I was thinking about this girl you love so much," she said. "And this place I love so much. And how that happens. How you can just fall into it. This land Hollis is selling, the thing about it is—well, I'm partly mad because I don't want there to be some bullshit McMansion subdivision up there, but also partly because my secret hideout is up there."

"Your what?"

"My secret hideout. My super, incredibly top secret location that no one on earth knows about." Lindsey paused and turned her head away from the starstruck sky and toward Colin. "You wanna see it?"

### The End (of the Middle)

"I don't want to flatter myself," said Katherine I in between sips of coffee at *Café Sel Marie*, "but it does feel a little special, that it all began with me."

"Well," said Colin, who was drinking milk with a shot of coffee in it, "there's three ways to look at it. Either (1) it's a massive coincidence that all the girls I ever liked happen to share the same nine letters, or (2) I just happen to think it a particularly beautiful name, or (3) I never got over our two-and-a-half-minute relationship."

"You were very cute then, you know," she said. She blew on the coffee through pursed lips. "I remember thinking that. You were dork chic before dork chic was chic."

"I'm leaning toward explanation 3 at the moment." He smiled. Dishes clattered around them. The place was crowded. He could see into the kitchen, where their waiter was smoking a long, thin cigarette.

"I think maybe you try to be odd on purpose. I think you like that. It makes you *you* and not someone else."

"You sound like your father," he said, referencing Krazy Keith.

"I've found you insanely attractive since I saw you when I was freaking out about my French test," she answered. She didn't blink, didn't let go of his stare. Those eyes as blue as the sky ought to be. And then she smiled. "Do I sound like my father now?"

"Yeah, weirdly enough. He also sucks at French." She laughed. Colin saw the waiter put out his cigarette, and then he came over to their table and asked if they wanted anything more. Katherine I said no, and then she turned to Colin and said, "Do you know anything about Pythagoras?"

And Colin said, "I know his Theorem."

And she said, "No, I mean the guy. He was weird. He thought everything could be expressed numerically, that—like—math could unlock the world. I mean, *everything*."

"What, like, even love?" Colin asked, only vaguely annoyed that she knew something he didn't.

"Particularly love," Katherine I said. "And you've taught me enough French for me to say: 10-5 space 16-5-14-19-5 space 17-21-5 space 10-5 space 20-1-9-13-5." For a long moment Colin stared at her wordlessly. He cracked the code pretty quickly, but he stayed silent, trying to figure out when she'd come up with it, when she'd memorized it. Even he couldn't have translated French letters to Arabic numerals that quickly. *Je pense que je t'aime*, she'd said numerically—"I think that I like you." Or, "I think that I love you." The French verb *aimer* has two meanings. And that's why he liked her, and loved her. She spoke to him in a language that, no matter how hard you studied it, could not be completely understood.

He stayed quiet until he had a fully formulated response, one that would keep her interest alive without quite satiating it. Colin Singleton, let it be said, couldn't play the ninth inning of a relationship to save his life, but he could damn well score in the first.

"You're just saying that because I'm on a TV show that no one watches," he said.

"Maybe."

"Or maybe," he said, "you're saying it because you're flattered I've spent eight years of my life chasing after the nine letters in your name."

"Maybe," she allowed. And then Colin's phone rang. His mom. Their sneak-out was over. But by then it was too late. In his mind, Katherine I was already becoming Katherine XIX. She would soon retake the throne that, all along, had rightfully been hers.

# (fourteen)

**"The thing about your stories,"** Lindsey was saying in the darkness as they approached the forest in front of them, "is that they still don't have any morals, and you can't do a good girl voice, and you don't really talk enough about *everyone else*—the story's still about you. But anyway, I can imagine this Katherine now, a little bit. She's clever. And she's just a little mean to you. I think you get off on that. Most guys do. That's how I got Colin, really. Katrina was hotter and wanted him worse. They'd been dating for a while when he fell for me. But she was too easy. I know she's my friend and possibly Hassan's girlfriend and whatever, but Katrina's easier than a four-piece jigsaw puzzle."

Colin laughed, and Lindsey went on talking. "Getting people to like you is so easy, really. It's a wonder more people don't do it."

"It's not so easy for me."

"Whatever, *I* like you, and I never *really* like anybody. Hassan likes you, and I can tell that he never really likes anybody, either. You just need more people who don't like people."

"You don't ever really like anybody?"

They passed into the woods, following a narrow, periodically invisible trail. Lindsey motioned toward the trees and said, "You sure shot the holy hell out of this forest, Smartypants. Wouldn't that be something if you bagged a hog."

"I don't really *want* to kill a pig," Colin noted. He had read *Charlotte's Web*, see. Then he repeated himself. "You don't ever really like anybody?"

"Well, that's an exaggeration, I guess," she answered. "It's just that I learned a while ago that the best way to get people to like you is not to like them too much."

"Well, but you care about a lot of people. The oldsters?" Colin offered.

"Well, the oldsters are different," she said, and then stopped walking and turned around to Colin, who was already out of breath as he struggled up the hill behind her. "The thing about the oldsters, I think, is that they never screwed with me, so I don't worry about them. So yeah, oldsters and babies are the exceptions."

They walked in silence for a long time through dense, flat brush with thin trees rising straight and high all around them. The trail became increasingly steep, zigzagging up the hill, until they finally came to a rocky outcropping perhaps fifteen feet high, and Lindsey Lee Wells said, "Now comes the rock climbing."

Colin looked up at the craggy face of the stone. *There are probably people who can successfully negotiate their way up that rock*, he thought, *but I am not one of them.* "No way," he said. She turned back toward him, her cheeks flushed and glistening with sweat. "I'm kidding." She scampered up a wet, mossy boulder, and Colin followed. Immediately, he saw a narrow, chest-high crack covered over by a spiderweb. "See, I'm taking you here because you're the only guy I know who's skinny enough. Squeeze on through," she said.

Colin pushed the spiderweb aside—sorry, Charlotte. He turned sideways, crouched down, and inched away from the fading light outside. Soon he was completely blind, his knees and back and head all against the rock, and for a moment he panicked, thinking Lindsey had tricked him, and would leave him, wedged in here. But he kept shuffling his feet forward. Something glided against his back. He screamed.

"Relax. It's me," she said. Her hands found his shoulders, and she said, "Take one more step," and then he could no longer feel the rock pressing in on him. She turned him so that he was facing forward. "Keep walking," she said. "You can stand up straight now." And then her hands disappeared, and he heard her sweeping at the ground, and she said, "I keep a flashlight here, but I can't f—got it." She pressed the flashlight into his hands and he fumbled with it and then the world lit up.

"Wow," said Colin. Approximately square, the cave's only room was big enough to lie down comfortably in any direction, although the gray-brown ceiling sloped down toward the back, making it hard to stand in a lot of places. It contained a blanket, a sleeping bag, several old throw pillows, and one unmarked Mason jar filled with some sort of liquid. He nudged it with his foot. "Booze," Lindsey explained.

"Where'd you get it?"

"There's a guy out in Danville who makes corn whiskey moonshine. No shit. And he'll sell it to you if you've got ten dollars and are old enough to walk. Colin gave it to me. I told him I drank it, but really I brought it out here, 'cause it adds ambience." Colin moved the flashlight slowly around the cave's walls. "Sit down," Lindsey said. "And turn off the light."

And then it was the kind of dark your eyes never adjust to.

"How'd you find this place?"

"I was just hiking around. I used to love walking through Mom's land with all the oldsters when I was little. I started coming by myself during middle school, and I just stumbled across it one day in eighth grade. I must've walked past this rock a hundred times without ever noticing anything. It's weird talking to you; I can't see you at all."

"I can't see you either."

"We're invisible. I've never been here with someone else. It's different being invisible *with* someone."

"So what do you *do* here?"

"What do you mean?"

"Well, it's too dark to read. I guess you could get a head lamp or something, but other than that—"

"No, I just sit here. When I was a nerd, I came here to be somewhere where no one would find me. And now—I dunno, I guess the same reason."

". . ."

". . ."

"Do you want to drink it? The moonshine?"

"I never really drank before."

"Color me surprised."

"Also, moonshine can make you blind, and what I've seen of blindness so far hasn't really impressed me."

"Yeah that would suck for you if you couldn't read anymore. But how often are you going to find yourself in a cave with moonshine? Live a little."

"Says the girl who never wants to leave her hometown."

"Oh, burn. Okay I got the bottle. Talk to me and I'll come over to your voice."

"Um, hello my name is Colin Singleton and it's very dark and so you should come over here to my voice except the acoustics in this place are really w—oh that's me. That's my knee."

"Hi."

"Hi."

"Ladies first."

"All right. . . . Sweet holy shitstickers, it tastes like you're washing down a bite of corn with a pint of lighter fluid."

"Did it make you go blind?"

"I have absolutely no idea. Okay. Your turn."

". . . AkhhhhEchhhAhhhh. Kahhh. Ehhhhhh. Wow. Wow. Man. It's like French-kissing a dragon."

"That's the funniest thing you've ever said, Colin Singleton."

"I used to be funnier. I kinda lost all my confidence."

". . ."

". . ."

"Let me tell you a story."

"Ooh, a Lindsey Lee Wells story. Does it star an Archduke?"

"No it stars a Lindsey, but it's got all the elements of a top-notch story. Where are you? Oh, there. Hi. Hi, knee. Hi, calf. Okay. So we all went to Danville for elementary school and pretty much all the Gutshot kids stuck together because everyone else thought we were dirty and poor and spread lice. But then in about third grade—like I've said, I was ugly—Colin and all his friends started saying I was a dog."

"I hate that. I hate kids like that so fugging much."

"Rule Number One. No interrupting. But anyway, so they starting calling me Lass, short for Lassie."

"Hey, he called you that just the other day on the way to the oldsters!"

"Yeah, I recall. Also, to repeat myself: Rule. Number. One. So it's fourth grade, okay? And it's Valentine's Day. I really wanted to get some valentines. So I asked Hollis what I should do, and she said I should just make a valentine for everyone in the class and then people would respond. So Hollis bought a bunch of these Charlie Brown valentines, and I wrote one for every kid in the class even though my handwriting wasn't very good and it took me a shit-long time. And then, predictably, I didn't get any valentines.

"So then I went home and I was really upset but I didn't want to tell Hollis about it so I just sat in the chair by the window in my room and felt so—just horrible—I don't even want to think about it. And then I see Colin running up to my house with a little cardboard box. And he's the cutest boy in school and the only one from Gutshot who's popular. He puts the box on my doorstep and then rings the doorbell and runs off and I run down there and my heart's beating like crazy and I'm so hopeful that he's got this secret crush on me and I get down there and there's this really elaborately decorated cardboard box with red construction-paper hearts pasted all over it. . . . God, I hadn't thought about this in so long till he called me Lass."

"Wait, what was in the box?"

"Alpo. A can of Alpo. But I got him in the end, because now he dates that dog."

"Wow. Jesus Christ."

"What?"

"Nothing. Just, you know, I thought *my* romantic relationships were fugged up."

"Anyway, it became my life's goal to get him. To kiss him. To marry him. I can't explain it, but it did."

"And you did it."

"I did. And he's different now. I mean, we were eight. We were little kids. He's sweet now. Very protective and everything."

". . ."

". . ."

"Do you ever wonder whether people would like you more or less if they could see inside you? I mean, I've always felt like the Katherines dump me right when they start to see what I look like from the inside—well, except K-19. But I always wonder about that. If people could see me the way I see myself—if they could live in my memories—would anyone, *anyone*, love me?"

"Well, he doesn't love me now. We've been dating for two years and he's never once said it. But he would *really* not love me if he could see inside. Because he's so real about everything. I mean, you can say a lot of shit about Colin, but he is completely himself. He's going to work in that factory his whole life, and he's going to have the same friends, and he's really happy with that, and he thinks it matters. But if he knew . . ."

"What? Finish that sentence."

"I'm full of shit. I'm never myself. I've got a Southern accent around the oldsters; I'm a nerd for graphs and deep thoughts around you; I'm Miss Bubbly Pretty Princess with Colin. I'm nothing. The thing about chameleoning your way through life is that it gets to where nothing is real. *Your* problem is—how did you say it—that you're not significant?"

"Don't matter. I don't matter."

"Right, matter. Well, but at least you can get to the part where *you* don't matter. Things about you, and things about Colin, and things about Hassan and Katrina, are either true or they aren't true. Katrina *is* bubbly. Hassan *is* hilarious. But I'm not like that. I'm what I need to be at any moment to stay above the ground but below the radar. The only sentence that begins with 'I' that's true of me is *I'm full of shit.*"

". . ."

". . ."

". . ."

". . ."

"Well, I like you. And you aren't chameleoning in front of me. I just figured that out. Like, you bite your thumb in front of me, which is a private habit, but you do it in front of me, because I don't count as public. I'm at your secret hiding place. You're okay with me seeing inside you a little."

"A little, maybe."

"Because I pose no threat. I'm a dork."

"No, you're not. That's—"

"No, I am. And that's why."

"Maybe. I never thought about it."

"I don't mean to sound judgmental about it, it's just interesting. I'm not threatened by you either, because I never liked popular people before. But you're not really like them. It's more like you found a way to hijack their cool. That's awe—"

"Hi."

"Hi."

"We shouldn't."

"Well, you started it."

"Right, but I started it just so that I could say 'we shouldn't' really dramatically."

"Ha."

"We should leave it at our foreheads touching and our noses touching and your hand on my leg and we shouldn't, you know."

"Your breath smells like booze."

"Your breath smells like you just made out with a dragon."

"Hey, that's my joke."

"Sorry. Had to defuse tension."

". . ."

". . ."

"What are you doing?"

"Biting my goddamned thumb. My private habit."

They finally left the cave well after dark, but the moonlight was so bright, Colin found himself blinking it away. It was an awkward and largely quiet hike down the hill to the car. From there, they drove back to the Pink Mansion. They had just pulled into the driveway when Lindsey said, "I mean of course I like you and you're great, but let's just—it's just not to be," and he nodded, because he couldn't have a girlfriend without a finished Theorem. And anyway, she was a Lindsey.

They opened the door quietly, hoping not to disturb Hollis's work/QVC watching. The moment Colin closed the door, the phone rang.

"Hello," he heard Hollis say from inside the kitchen. Lindsey grabbed Colin then and pulled him over against the wall, where they could listen without being seen.

"Well, leave it out for the garbage men, then," Hollis said. "What a bunch of bullshit. . . . They can't charge you to pick up *trash*; that's why we pay taxes. . . . Well, I'm sorry, Roy, but that's bullshit. . . . No, we *can't* afford it, believe me. . . . No. Absolutely not. . . . Well, I don't know, Roy. . . . No, I *understand* the problem. . . . Hold on, I'm thinking. Christ, my daughter's gonna be home any second. . . . What about that field back there? We own that field, right? . . . Yeah, exactly. . . . All you need is a goddamned bulldozer and a forklift. . . . Well, I don't like it either, but unless you've got another idea. . . . Fine. I'll see you on Thursday." The phone clanked against the receiver.

"Hollis," Lindsey whispered, "owes a *shitload* of money to the swear jar." Then she led Colin through the hall and into the game room. "Out the window," she whispered. Colin raised the slim window facing the front yard as quietly as he could, and then motioned to the screen. He would have said something about the screen, but he knew he couldn't whisper.

"Christ, it's like you never snuck out of a house before," Lindsey whispered. She pressed at the corners of the screen and then lifted it up. She squirmed out headfirst, her skinny legs kicking slightly as she did a somersault onto the front lawn. Colin followed, feet first, trying a kind of limbo strategy that looked ridiculous.

Having successfully sneaked out of the house, Lindsey and Colin brushed themselves off, ambled to the front door, and opened it.

"Hollis," Lindsey called, "we're home!" Hollis was seated on the couch, a pile of papers in her lap. She turned to them and smiled.

"Hey," Hollis said, all trace of anger gone from her voice. "D'y'all have fun?"

Lindsey looked at Colin, and not at Hollis. "I've rarely had so much fun in my life," she said.

"I bet," said Hollis, who didn't seem to be listening.

"It was the warehouse." Colin spoke softly, conspiratorially, as they climbed the stairs. "She goes to the warehouse on Thursdays."

Lindsey smirked. "Yeah, I know. You've lived here three weeks; I've lived here seventeen years. I don't know what's going on, but between that and selling land and always being in a furious phone conversation whenever we show up at the house, I'm starting to think a road trip might be in order," said Lindsey.

"They can solve a surprising number of problems, road trips," Colin acknowledged.

"Road trip? Did somebody say road trip?" Hassan stood at the top of the staircase. "Because I'm in. So is Katrina. She's a college student, you know. I'm dating a *college girl*."

"She's getting her clinical nursing assistant license at Danville Community," Lindsey said dismissively.

"That's college; that's all I'm saying! And to think, Singleton, you thought I'd never get a college girl unless I *went* to college."

"How was the date?" Colin asked.

"Sorry, dude. Can't talk about it. My lips are too numb from all the kissing. That girl kisses like she wants to suck out your soul."

Colin sneaked into Hassan's room immediately after Lindsey went downstairs to bed, and they discussed Hassan's situation (second base over the shirt), and then Colin told him about Lindsey, minus the secret hideout, because it seemed private.

"I mean," Colin said, "it was dark and our whole faces were touching except our lips. She just brought her head against mine all of a sudden."

"Well, do you like her?"

"Um, I don't know. At that moment I kinda did."

"Dude, think about it. If you could make your Theorem work, you could predict how it would go." Colin smiled at the thought. "Now more than ever, you have to finish."

# (fifteen)

**The next few days** were slightly awkward with Lindsey. She and Colin remained friendly, but it was all so superficial, and Colin felt like they ought to be talking about the big issues of mattering and love and capital-t Truth and Alpo, but they only talked about the mundane business of taking oral histories. The sly jokes were gone; Hassan complained repeatedly that "all of a sudden, I've got to pull all the funny-weight in this family." But slowly, things returned to status quo: Lindsey had a boyfriend, and Colin had a broken heart and a Theorem to finish. Also, Hassan had a girlfriend and they were all preparing for a pig hunt—so, then again, things weren't *entirely* normal.

The day before his inaugural Feral Hog Hunt, Colin Singleton prepared the only way Colin Singleton would: by reading. He scanned through ten volumes of *Foxfire* books for information about the habits and habitat of the feral hog. Then he Googled "feral pig," from which he learned that wild pigs were so widely disliked that the state of Tennessee pretty much allowed you to shoot one whenever you came across it. The feral pig is considered a "pest animal," and as such is not subject to protections afforded, say, a deer, or a person.

But it was in Hollis's copy of a book called *Our Southern Highlands* that Colin found the most descriptive passage regarding the wild hog: "Anybody can see that when he[71] is not rooting or sleeping, he is studying devilment. He shows remarkable understanding of human speech, especially profane speech, and even an uncanny gift of reading men's thoughts, whenever those thoughts are directed against the peace and dignity of pigship." This, clearly, was not an enemy to take lightly.

Not that Colin intended to take any action against the peace and dignity of pigship. In the extremely unlikely event that he even came across a hog, he figured, he'd allow it to study devilment in peace. Which was how he justified not mentioning the hog hunt to his parents during their nightly phone conversation. He wasn't really going on a *hunt* anyway. He was going for a stroll through the woods. With a gun.

He awoke to his alarm the morning of the hunt at four-thirty. It was the first time since arriving in Gutshot that he'd beaten the rooster to waking. Immediately, he opened his bedroom window, pressed his face up against the screen, and shouted, "COCK-A-DOODLE DOO! HOW DO YOU LIKE IT FROM THE OTHER END, YOU LITTLE FUGGER?"

He brushed his teeth and then got in the shower. He kept the water coldish so as to wake up. Hassan came in to brush his teeth and shouted over the running water, "*Kafir*, I can say it with confidence: Today is a day that no pigs will die. I'm not even allowed to *eat* the motherfuggers;[72] I'm sure not going to *kill* one."

"Amen," Colin answered.

They were in the Hearse, with Lindsey and Princess in the backseat, by five.

"Why the dog?" asked Hassan.

"Chase and Fulton like to use her when they're hunting. She doesn't do a lick of good—poor Princess cares more about her curls than tracking pigs—but they enjoy it."

---

[71] That is, the hog.

[72] Eating pork is *Haram* in Islam. It is also forbidden in Judaism, but (a) Colin was only half-Jewish, and (b) he wasn't religious.

They drove a couple of miles past the store and then turned off onto a gravel road that wound up a small hill through thick foliage. "Hollis hasn't sold *this* land," she complained, "because *everybody* likes it."

The road dead-ended into a long, narrow, one-story wooden house. Two pickup trucks and JATT's Blazer were already parked by the lodge. TOC and JATT, whose jeans were again too tight, sat on the tailgate of one pickup, their legs dangling. Across from them, a middle-aged man was seated in what appeared to be a plastic chair stolen from a third-grade classroom, examining the muzzle of his shotgun. They all wore camouflage pants, long-sleeved camouflage shirts, and bright orange vests.

As the man turned to speak to them, Colin recognized him as Townsend Lyford, one of the people they'd interviewed at the factory. "How are y'all?" he asked as they got out. He shook hands with Colin and Hassan, then hugged Lindsey. "Pretty day for hunting hogs," said Mr. Lyford.

"It's a little early," Colin said, but by then light was just reaching the hillside. The sky was clear, and it did promise to be pretty—if hot.

Katrina peeked her head out from the lodge's front door and said, "Breakfast is on! Oh, hey cutie." Hassan winked at her.

"You're a smooth cat." Colin grinned.

Once Colin and Hassan were inside the lodge, SOCT handed them each camouflage outfits complete with ridiculous bright orange vests. "Y'all change in the bathroom," he said.

And by "bathroom," SOCT meant "outhouse." On the upside, the stench of the lodge's outhouse masked the smell of the camouflage clothes, which reminded Colin of all the worst parts of the Kalman School's gym. Still, he kicked off his shorts and slipped into the pants, the shirt, and the crossing-guard-orange vest. Before leaving the outhouse, Colin emptied out his pockets. Fortunately, the camo pants had huge cargo pockets—plenty of room for his wallet, his car keys, and the minirecorder, which he'd taken to carrying everywhere.

Once Hassan had changed, too, everyone settled down on one of the homemade benches and Mr. Lyford stood up. He spoke with a thick accent, and with authority. Mr. Lyford really seemed to *enjoy* placing *emphasis* on his *words*.

"The feral pig is an extremely *dangerous* creature. It is called the poor man's *grizzly bear*, and *not* for nothing. Now I hunt *without* dogs, choosing instead to *stalk* my prey as the *Indians* did. But Chase and Fulton—they're dog hunters, and that's a'ight, too. Either way, though, we must remember this is a dangerous sport." *Right*, Colin thought. *We have guns and the pigs have snouts. Dangerous, indeed.* "These pigs are *pests*—even the government says so—and they need to be *eradicated*. Now usually I would say you're gonna have trouble rootin' out a feral pig in the *daytime*, but it's been a while since we hunted around here, so I think we have an *excellent* chance. Now I'm going to go out with *Colin* and *Hassan*," which he pronounced HASS-in, "and we're going to go down into the flat land and see if we can't catch a trail. Y'all can split up as you wish. But *be safe* out there, and do not take the *dangers* of the *feral* pig lightly."

"Can we shoot 'em in the nuts?" asked JATT.

"No, you can *not*. A feral boar will charge if shot in the *testes*," answered Mr. Lyford.

"Jesus, Dad, he's kidding. We know how to hunt," said TOC. Before that, Colin didn't realize TOC and Mr. Lyford were related.

"Well, boy, I reckon I'm nervous sending you out *alone* with a bunch of *yahoos*."

Then he went over some boring stuff about guns, like which slugs to use in your shotgun and to always keep both barrels loaded. It turned out that Lindsey and TOC were going out together to a tree stand near a baited patch, whatever the hell that meant, and JATT and SOCT were going out in another direction with the adorably non-threatening labradoodle. Katrina would stay in camp, as she refused to hunt on moral grounds. She was, she told Colin as they sat at the cafeteria, a vegetarian. "I think it's right criminal," Katrina said of hog hunting. "Although those pigs *are* sort of horrible. But there wouldn't even *be* any wild hogs except we pen up so many pigs to eat."

"I've been thinking about going vegetarian," Hassan told her, his arm draped around her waist.

"Well just don't get *skinny*," Katrina answered, and then they kissed right in front of Colin, who still couldn't get his head around any of this.

"All right, boys," Mr. Lyford said, smacking Colin on the back rather too hard. "Ready for yer first *hunt*?"

Colin nodded with some reluctance, waved good-bye to Lindsey and the others, and headed out with Hassan, whose orange vest was not quite big enough to fit comfortably around his chest. They set off down the hill, not following a trail, just bushwacking. "We *begin* by looking for *rootings*," Mr. Lyford explained. "Places where a *hog* has been turning up the soil with his long *snout*." He talked to them like they were nine years old, and Colin was wondering if Mr. Lyford thought they were younger than they actually were when Mr. Lyford turned back to them with a can of chewing tobacco and offered them each a pinch. Colin and Hassan both politely declined.

Over the next hour, they hardly spoke, because "the *feral hog* may shy away from the *human* voice," Mr. Lyford said, as if the feral hog did not shy away from other voices, such as those of Martians. Instead they walked slowly through the woods, their eyes scanning the ground in search of rootings, their guns pointed down into the dirt, with one hand on the stock and the other sweating against the barrel. And then, finally, Hassan saw something.

"Uh, Mr. Lyford," Hassan whispered. He pointed to a patch of dirt that had been dug out haphazardly. Mr. Lyford knelt down and inspected it closely. He sniffed at the air. He dug his fingers into the dirt. "*This*," Mr.

Lyford whispered, "is a rooting. And you, HASS-in, have found a *fresh* one. Yes, a hog has been here recently. Now, we *track* it."

Mr. Lyford doubled the pace then, and Hassan struggled to keep up. Mr. Lyford found another rooting, and then another, and he felt sure he had the trail, so he took off in a kind of race-walk, his arms pumping so that the gun wiggled in the air like he was in color guard. After about five minutes of that, Hassan hussled up to Colin and said, "Please God, no more run-walking," and Colin said, "Seriously," and then they both together said, "Mr. Lyford?"

He turned around and walked several paces back to the boys. "What *is* it, boys? We're on the *trail* here. We've got a hog almost *in sight*, I can feel it."

"Can we slow down?" Hassan asked. "Or take a break? Or take a break and then slow down?"

Mr. Lyford sighed. "Boys, if you are not *serious* about hunting the *feral pig*, then I can just *leave* you here. We're on the trail of a hog," he whispered urgently. "This is no time for lollygaggin' or dillydallyin'."

"Well," suggested Colin, "maybe you should just leave us behind then. We can sort of protect your flank, in case the *feral pig* doubles back around."

Mr. Lyford looked extremely disappointed. He pursed his lips and shook his head sadly, as if he pitied the poor souls who were unwilling to push their bodies to the limit in search of the feral pig. "Very well, boys. I'll come back and get ya. And when I do, it'll be to get your help carryin' out a *gorgeous* hog." He started to walk off and then stopped and pulled out his can of chewing tobacco. "Here," he whispered, handing it to Colin. "I fear the *hog* will smell the *winter*green."

"Uh, thanks," said Colin, and Mr. Lyford ran off into the distance, weaving through the forest in search of more, fresher rootings.

"Well," Hassan said, squatting down to sit on a rotting fallen tree. "That was fun. Jesus, I didn't think hunting involved so much *walking*. We should have gotten the sweet gig Lindsey has, sitting in a tree and making out and waiting for a pig to walk by."

"Yeah," said Colin, absentmindedly.

"Hey, d'you bring the minirecorder?" asked Hassan.

"Yeah, why?"

"Gimme," he said. Colin pulled it out of his pocket and handed it over.

Hassan pressed record, and then started up with his best *Star Trek* voice. "Captain's log. Stardate 9326.5. Hog hunting is incredibly boring. I think I'll take a nap and trust in my brilliant Vulcan companion to let me know if any *extremely* dangerous *feral hogs* walk by." Hassan handed back the minirecorder and scooted over to lie down beside the fallen tree. Colin watched Hassan close his eyes. "Now *this*," Hassan said, "is *huntin'*."

Colin sat there for a while listening to the wind tease the trees as clouds moved in above them, and he let his mind wander. It went to a predictable place, and he missed her. She was at camp still, and they didn't let her use a cell phone, at least not last year, but just to be sure he pulled his phone out of his camouflage pants pocket. He got reception, amazingly, but had no missed calls. He thought of calling but decided against it.

He would call when he completed the Theorem, which led him back to it and the seemingly intractable III Anomaly. Eighteen out of nineteen Katherines worked, but this utterly insignificant blip on the Katherinadar came out looking like a jacked-up smiley face every time. He remembered her again, thought back to whether he'd failed to account for some facet of her personality in his calculations. Admittedly, he'd only known her for twelve days, but the whole idea of the Theorem was that you didn't have to know someone intimately in order for it to work. Katherine III. Katherine III. Who would have thought that she, among the least important to him, would prove the Theorem's downfall?

Colin spent the next ninety minutes thinking, without ceasing, about a girl he'd known for less than two weeks. But eventually, even he grew tired. To pass the time, he anagrammed her sprawling name: Katherine Mutsensberger. He'd never anagrammed her before, and he was fascinated to find the word "eighteen" within her. "Me returns eighteen barks; eighteen errs makes burnt." His favorite: "Remark eighteen, snub rest." But that didn't really make sense, because Colin had certainly remarked all nineteen.

Hassan sniffled and his eyes shot open and he looked around. "Fug, are we still hunting? Big Daddy needs some lunch." Hassan stood up, reached into the cargo pockets of his pants, and pulled out two badly smushed sandwiches in Ziploc bags. "Sorry, dude. I fell asleep on lunch." Colin opened the canteen hooked to his belt buckle, and they sat down for turkey sandwiches and water. "How long did I sleep?"

"Almost two hours," Colin said between bites.

"What the fug d'you do?"

"I should have brought a book. I just tried to finish the Theorem. The only problem left is Katherine III."

"Oo vat?" Hassan asked, his mouth full of a too-mayonnaisy sandwich.

"Summer after fourth grade. From Chicago, but she was homeschooled. Katherine Mutsensberger. One brother. Lived in Lincoln Square on Leavitt just south of Lawrence, but I never visited her there because she dumped me on the third-to-last day of smart kid camp in Michigan. She had dirty blond hair that was a little curly and she bit her nails and her favorite song when she was ten was 'Stuck with You' by Huey Lewis and the News and her mother was a curator at the Museum of Contemporary Art and when she grew up she wanted to be a veterinarian."

"How long d'you know her?" asked Hassan. His sandwich was finished, and he wiped the remnants of it on his pants.

"Twelve days."

"Huh. You know what's funny? I knew that girl."

"What?"

"Yeah. Mutsensberger. We went to all these lame-o homeschooling events together. Like, bring your homeschooled kid to the park so she learns how to be less nerdy. And, take your homeschooled kid for a homeschool picnic so the Muslim kid can get his ass kicked by all the evangelical Christians."

"Wait, you know her?"

"Well, I mean, we don't keep in touch or anything. But yeah. I could pick her out of a lineup."

"Well, was she quite introverted and a little dorky and she'd had one boyfriend when she was seven who dumped her?"

"Yup," said Hassan. "Well, I don't know about the boyfriend. She had a brother. He was a first-rate nutcase, actually. He was into spelling bees. Went to Nationals, I think."

"Weird. Well, the formula doesn't work for her."

"Maybe you're forgetting something. There can't be that many goddamned Mutsensbergers in Chicago. Why don't you call her and ask?" And the answer to that question—"because it literally has never occurred to me"—was so outrageously dumb that Colin just picked up the phone without another word and dialed 773.555.1212.

"What city?"

"Chicago," he said.

"What listing?"

"Mutsensberger. M U T S E N S B E R G E R."

"Hold."

The computer voice recited the number, and Colin pressed 1 to be connected immediately free of charge, and on the third ring, a girl picked up.

"Hello," she said.

"Hi. This is Colin Singleton. Is—is, uh, Katherine there?"

"Speaking. What did you say your name was?"

"Colin Singleton."

"That's so familiar," she said. "Do I know you?"

"When you were in fourth grade, I may have been your boyfriend for about two weeks at a summer program for gifted children."

"Colin Singleton! Oh yeah! Wow. Of all people . . ."

"Um, this is going to sound weird, but on a scale of one to five, how popular were you in fourth grade?"

"Uh, what?" she asked.

"And also do you have a brother who was into spelling bees?"

"Um, yeah, I do. Who is this?" she asked, suddenly sounding upset.

"This is Colin Singleton, I swear. I know it sounds weird."

"I was, I don't know. I mean, I had a few friends. We were kinda nerdy, I guess."

"Okay. Thanks, Katherine."

"Are you, like, writing a book?"

"No, I'm writing a mathematical formula that predicts which of two people will end a romantic relationship and when," he said.

"Um," she answered. "Where are you, anyway? Whatever happened to you?"

"What happened, indeed," he answered, and hung up.

"Well," said Hassan. "Boy. She must think that you're STARK RAVING BONKERS!"

But Colin was lost in thought. If Katherine III was who she claimed to be, and whom he remembered her to be, then what if. What if the formula—was right? He called her again.

"Katherine Mutsensberger," he said.

"Yes?"

"It's Colin Singleton again."

"Oh. Um, hi."

"This is the last question I'll ever ask you that sounds completely crazy, but did I by chance break up with you?"

"Um, uh-huh."

"I did?"

"Yeah. We were at a campfire sing-along and you came over to me in front of all my friends and said you'd never done this before, but you had to break up with me because you just didn't think it was going to work long-term. That's what you said. Long-term. God, I was devastated, too. I thought you hung the moon."

"I'm really sorry. I'm sorry I broke up with you," Colin said.

She laughed. "Well, we were ten. I've dealt with it."

"Yeah, but still. I'm sorry if I hurt your feelings."

"Well, thank you, Colin Singleton."

"No problem."

"Is there anything else?" she asked.

"I think that's it."

"Okay, well, you take care of yourself," she said, the way you might say it to a schizophrenic homeless person to whom you've just given a dollar.

"You too, Katherine Mutsensberger."

Hassan stared at Colin unblinkingly. "Well, dress me up in a tutu, put me on a unicycle, and call me Caroline the Dancing Bear. You're a fugging Dumper."

Colin leaned back against the rotten tree, his back arching over it until he was staring at the cloudy sky. Betrayed by his vaunted memory! He had, indeed, remarked eighteen and snubbed the rest. How could he remember everything about her and not remember that *he* dumped *her*? And for that matter, what kind of asshole was he to have dumped a perfectly nice girl like Katherine Mutsensberger? "I feel like I've only ever been two things," he said softly. "I'm a child prodigy, and I'm dumped by Katherines. But now I'm—"

"Neither," Hassan said. "And be grateful. You're a Dumper and I'm making out with a ridiculously hot girl. The whole world is turned upside down. I love it. It's like we're in a snow globe and God decided he wanted to see a blizzard so he shook us all the fug up."

Just as almost no true sentence beginning with *I* could be spoken by Lindsey, Colin was watching all the things he'd thought were true about himself, all his *I* sentences, fall away. Suddenly, there was not just one missing piece, but thousands of them.

Colin had to figure out what had gone wrong inside his brain, and fix it. He returned to the central question: how could he have completely forgotten dumping her? Or, almost completely, because Colin *had* experienced a dim flash of recognition when Katherine told him the story of his dumping her in front of her friends, a feeling vaguely like when a word is on the tip of your tongue and then someone says it.

Above him, the interweaving branches seemed to split the sky into a million little pieces. He felt like he had vertigo. The one facility he'd always trusted—memory—was a fraud. And he might have gone on thinking about it for hours, or at least until Mr. Lyford returned, except at that very moment he heard a weird grunting noise and simultaneously felt Hassan's hand tap his knee.

"Dude," said Hassan softly. "*Khanzeer.*"[73]

Colin shot up. Perhaps fifty yards in front of them, a brown-gray creature was pushing his long snout into the ground and snorting like he had a sinus infection. It looked like a cross between a vampire pig and a black bear—an absolutely massive animal with thick, matted fur and teeth that extended below its mouth.

"*Matha, al-khanazeer la yatakalamoon araby?*"[74] Colin asked.

"That's no pig," answered Hassan in English. "That's a goddamned monster." The pig stopped its rooting and looked up at them. "I mean,

---

[73]Arabic: "Pig"

[74]Arabic: "What, pigs don't speak Arabic?"

Wilbur is a fugging pig. Babe is a fugging pig. That thing was birthed from the loins of *Iblis*."[75] It was clear now the pig could see them. Colin could see the black in its eyes.

"Stop cursing. The feral hog shows a remarkable understanding of human speech, especially profane speech," he mumbled, quoting from the book.

"That's a bunch of bullshit," Hassan said, and then the pig took two lumbering steps toward them, and Hassan said, "Okay. Or not. Fine. No cursing. Listen, Satan Pig. We're cool. We don't want to shoot you. The guns are for show, dude."

"Stand up so he knows we're bigger than he is," Colin said.

"Did you read that in the book?" Hassan asked as he stood.

"No, I read it in a book about grizzly bears."

"We're gonna get gored to death by a feral fugging hog and your best strategy is to pretend it's a grizzly bear?"

Together, they stepped carefully backward, kicking their legs high to get over the fallen tree, which now offered their best protection against the hog. But Satan Pig didn't seem to think much of their strategy, because right then it took off running at them. For a squat-legged beast that couldn't have weighed less than four hundred pounds, the thing could run.

"Shoot it," Colin said, quite calmly.

"I don't know *how*," Hassan pointed out.

"Fug," said Colin. He leveled the gun, planted it tight against his exceedingly sore shoulder, turned off the safety, and took aim at the running pig. It was perhaps fifty feet away. He inhaled deeply and then slowly exhaled. And then he pointed the gun up and to the right, because he just couldn't bring himself to shoot at the pig. Calmly, he squeezed the trigger, just as Lindsey had taught him. The kick of the gun against his well-bruised

[75]Arabic: "Satan."

shoulder hurt so badly that tears welled up in his eyes, and in the shock of the pain he couldn't tell what had happened at first. But, amazingly, the pig stopped dead in its tracks, turned ninety degrees, and ran.

"You sure shot the living hell out of that gray thing," Hassan said.

"What gray thing?" asked Colin. Hassan pointed, and Colin followed the trajectory of his finger to an oak tree about fifteen feet away. Crooked between the trunk and a branch, a sort of gray paper cyclone contained a circular hole about an inch in diameter.

"What is that?" asked Hassan.

"Something's coming out of it," Colin said.

It doesn't take long for a thought to get from your brain to your vocal cords and out of your mouth, but it does take a moment. And in that moment, between when Colin thought *Hornets*! and when he would have said "Hornets," he felt a searing sting on the side of his neck. "Oh FUG!" shouted Colin, and then Hassan said, "AIEE! AH! AH! FU—FOOT—SHIT—HAND!" They took off running like a couple of spastic marathoners. Colin kicked his legs to the side with each step, like a heel-clicking leprechaun, trying to discourage the blood-thirsty hornets from attacking his legs. Simultaneously, he swatted around his face, which, as it happened, only indicated to the hornets that besides stinging his head and neck, they could also sting his hands. Waving his hands above his head crazily, Hassan ran considerably faster and with more agility than Colin had ever thought possible, weaving around trees and hurdling bushes in a vain attempt to discourage the hornets. They ran downhill, because that was easiest, but the hornets kept their pace, and Colin could hear their buzzing. For minutes, as they ran in random directions, the buzzing continued, Colin always following behind Hassan, because the only thing worse than getting stung to death in south-central Tennessee when your parents don't even know you're on a hog hunt is dying *alone*.

"*KAFIR* (breath) I'M (breath) FADING."

"THEY'RE STILL ON ME. GO GO GO GO GO GO GO GO," Colin answered. But just after that, the buzzing stopped. Having chased them for the better part of ten minutes, the hornets began the winding journey back to their decimated nest.

Hassan fell face-first into a brambly bush and then slowly rolled over onto the forest floor. Colin bent over, hands on knees, sucking air. Hassan was hyperventilating. "Real (breath) fat (breath) kid (breath) asthma (breath) attack," he finally said.

Colin pushed aside his fatigue and rushed up to his best friend. "No. No. Tell me you're not allergic to bees. Oh, shit." Colin pulled out his cell phone. He had reception, but what could he tell the 911 operator? "I'm somewhere in the woods. My friend's trachea is closing. I don't even have a knife to perform an emergency tracheotomy because stupid Mr. *Lyford* ran off with it into the woods to chase the same goddamned pig that started the whole fugging mess." He desperately wished Lindsey were there; she could deal with this. She'd have her first-aid kit. But before he could even register the consequences of such thoughts, Hassan said, "I'm not allergic to (breath) bees, *sitzpinkler*. I'm just (breath) out of (breath) breath."

"Ohhhhh. Thank God."

"You don't believe in God."

"Thank luck and DNA," Colin corrected himself quickly, and only then, with Hassan not-dying, did Colin begin to feel the stings. There were eight in all, each of them like a little fire burning just inside his skin. Four on his neck, three on his hands, and one on his left earlobe. "How many do you have?" he asked Hassan.

Hassan sat up and looked himself over. His hands were cut up from landing in the briar bush. He touched his stings, each in turn. "Three," said Hassan.

"Three?! I really took one for the team by staying behind you," he noted.

"Don't give me that martyr shit," said Hassan. "You shot the bees' nest."

"Hornets' nest," Colin corrected. "They were hornets, not bees. That's the kind of stuff you learn in college, you know."

"Dingleberries. Also, not interesting."[76] Hassan paused for a moment, then started talking. "God, these stings HURT. You know what I hate? The outdoors. I mean, generally. I don't like outside. I'm an inside person. I'm all about refrigeration and indoor plumbing and *Judge Judy*."

Colin laughed as he reached into his left pocket. He pulled out Mr. Lyford's can of chewing tobacco. He pinched a bit of tobacco, and pressed it against his own earlobe. It felt instantly, if only marginally, better. "It works," Colin said, surprised. "Remember, Mae Goodey told us about it when we interviewed her." Hassan said, "Really?" and Colin nodded, and then Hassan took the can of dip. Soon their stings were covered with blobs of wet tobacco dripping brown, wintergreen-flavored juice.

"Now see *that's* interesting," Hassan said. "You should focus less on who was prime minister of Canada in 1936[77] and focus more on shit that makes my life better."

Their idea was to walk downhill. They knew the camp was uphill, but Colin hadn't been paying attention to which way they ran, and while the cloudy sky made it bearable to walk around in long sleeves and an orange vest, he couldn't navigate by the sun. So they walked downhill, because (a) it was easier, and (b) they knew the gravel road was down there somewhere, and

---

[76] But there is an important difference, and that important difference was manifested in Colin's throbbing pain. Bees sting people only once, and then die. Hornets, on the other hand, can sting repeatedly. Also, hornets, at least the way Colin figured it, are meaner. Bees just want to make honey. Hornets want to kill you.

[77] William Lyon Mackenzie King, who had enough names for two people (or four Madonnas) but was only one man.

since it was longer than the camp, they figured they had a better chance of finding it.

And maybe they did have a better chance of finding the road than the lodge, but they never found it, either. Instead, they walked through a forest that seemed endless, and their progress was slow, as they had to step through kudzu and over trees and hop the occasional dribbling creek. "If we just keep walking in one direction," Colin said, "we'll find civilization." Meanwhile, Hassan was singing a song entitled: "We're on a Trail / a Trail of Tears / There's Dip on My Chin / and We're Gonna Die Here."

Just after 6 P.M., tired and hornet-bitten and sweaty and generally in a poor mood, Colin spotted a house a short walk to their left. "I know that house," Colin said.

"What, we interviewed someone there?"

"No, it's one of the houses you can see when you walk to the grave of the Archduke," Colin stated with great confidence. Colin gathered his last bit of energy and jogged up to the house. The place itself was windowless, weather-beaten, and abandoned. But from the front of the house, Colin could—yes—see the graveyard in the distance. In fact, there seemed to be some movement down there.

Hassan came up behind him and whistled. "*Wallahi,*[78] *kafir,* you're lucky we're unlost, because I was about ten minutes away from killing and eating you."

They hustled down an easy slope and then fast-walked toward the store, ready to bypass the cemetery. But then Colin caught sight of movement in the graveyard again, turned his head, and stopped dead. Hassan seemed to notice it at precisely the same moment.

"Colin," said Hassan.

"Yeah," Colin answered calmly.

---

[78] Arabic: "I swear to God."

"Tell me if I'm mistaken, but isn't that my girlfriend in the graveyard?"

"You are not mistaken."

"And she's straddling some guy."

"That's correct," said Colin.

Hassan pursed his lips and nodded. "And—I just want to make sure we have our facts straight here—she's naked."

"She certainly is."

# (sixteen)

**She was facing away** from them, her back arched, her butt bobbing in and out of visibility. Colin had never seen actual people having actual sex before. From his angle, it looked a little ridiculous, but he suspected it might appear different if he were in the guy's position.

Hassan laughed silently, and he seemed so amused by the situation that Colin felt okay laughing, too. "This is some fugging snow globe of a day," Hassan said. And then he raced forward about ten paces, cupped his hands over his mouth, and screamed, "I AM BREAKING UP WITH YOU!" Still, though, a goofy grin was on his face. *Hassan takes so little seriously*, Colin thought. As Katrina turned back toward them, her face shocked and scared, her arms crossed over her chest, Hassan turned away.

Hassan looked back at Colin, who finally tore his gaze away from the inarguably quite fetching naked girl before him. "Give her some privacy," Hassan said. And then he laughed again. This time, Colin didn't join in. "You gotta see the humor in it, baby. I'm bug-bit, hornet-stung, bramble-cut, covered in chaw, and wearing camouflage. A feral hog, some hornets, and a prodigy led me through the woods so that I might stumble upon the first girl I ever kissed riding TOC like he's a thoroughbred next to the grave of an Austro-Hungarian Archduke. That," Hassan said to Colin emphatically, "is funny."

"Wait, TOC?" Colin's head swiveled back to the Archduke's obelisk, where he saw—holy shit—TOC, his very self, slithering into some camo pants. "The. Rat. Bastard." For reasons that he didn't understand, Colin felt a pulsing rage, and he took off toward the graveyard. He didn't stop running until he got to the knee-high stone wall, and was staring TOC dead in the eye. And then he didn't quite know what to do.

"Is my dad with you?" TOC asked coolly. Colin shook his head, and TOC sighed. "Thank God," he said. "He'd have my ass in a sling. Have a seat." Colin stepped over the wall and sat down. Katrina was leaning against the obelisk, dressed now, her hands shaking slightly as she smoked a cigarette. TOC started talking. "You're not gonna say a word. Because this ain't none of your business. Now your little Arab friend can have his words with Kat, and that's fine, and they'll keep it 'tween themselves. But I don't reckon you want Lindsey to know anything."

Colin stared at the Archduke's obelisk. He was tired and thirsty and sort of needed to pee. "I think I have to tell her," he said, a trace of the philosophical in his tone. "She's my friend. And if I were in her position, I'd expect her to tell me. It's just basic Golden Rule stuff, really."

TOC stood up and walked over to Colin. He was a sizable presence. "Let me tell you both," and only then did Colin realize Hassan was standing behind him, "why you aren't going to say a word. If you do, I will beat your asses so bad, you'll be the only guys in hell walking with a limp."

Hassan mumbled, "*Sajill*."[79] Colin quietly reached into his cargo pocket and fiddled with the device for a moment, then kept his hand in his pocket so it wouldn't look suspicious. "I just want to know," Hassan said to Katrina, "how long this has been going on."

Katrina put her cigarette out against the Archduke's obelisk, stood up, and walked over to stand next to TOC. "A long time," she said. "I mean, we dated when we were sophomores and we've been hooking up occasionally ever since. But we came out here and I was going to end it. Honestly. And

---

[79] Arabic: "Record."

I'm sorry because I really do like you and I haven't really liked anyone since him," she said, glancing up at TOC, "and I wouldn't have even done it this time except, I don't know. It was, like a good-bye or something. But I'm really sorry."

Hassan nodded. "We can still be friends," he said, and it was the first time Colin had ever heard those words spoken sincerely. "No big whup, really." Hassan looked at TOC then. "I mean," Hassan said, "it's not like *we* had agreed not to see other people."

TOC shot back, "Look, she just said it's over, okay? So that's it. It's over. I'm not cheating."

"Well," Colin pointed out, "you were cheating five minutes ago. That's a pretty narrow definition of cheating."

"Shut up before I knock your goddamned teeth in," TOC said angrily. Colin glanced down at his muddy shoes. "Now listen," TOC continued, "they're all coming back here from Bradford in a little while. So we're all just gonna sit here like a big happy family, and then when they show up, you're going to make your retarded jokes and hunch over and look like the shitsucking pussy you are. And the same goes for you, Hass."

This is what Colin thought in the long silence that followed: *would* he want to know? *If* he were dating Katherine XIX, and *if* she'd cheated on him, and *if* Lindsey knew, and *if* Lindsey would get physically injured as a result of sharing the information. Then no, he would not want to know. So perhaps the Golden Rule indicated that he *should* stay mum, and the Golden Rule was really Colin's only Rule. It was because of the Golden Rule, actually, that he hated himself for Katherine III: he'd believed that Katherines did unto him as he would never have done unto them.

But there was more to consider than the Golden Rule: there was the small matter of liking Lindsey. That shouldn't factor in to an ethical decision, of course. But it did.

He hadn't quite made up his mind when Lindsey, trailed by SOCT and

JATT, came running up with a six-pack of Natural Light beer in each hand. "When'd you get here?" she asked TOC.

"Oh, just a minute ago. Kat picked me up as I was walkin', and then we ran into them," TOC said, his head gesturing toward Colin and Hassan, who were seated together on the stone wall.

"There was some concern that you might be dead," Lindsey said to Hassan matter-of-factly.

"Believe me," Hassan answered, "you weren't the only one concerned." Lindsey leaned in toward Colin then, and he thought for a second she might kiss him on the cheek, and then she said, "Is that *dip*?"

He touched his ear. "It is," he acknowledged.

Lindsey laughed. "It ain't supposed to go in your ear, Colin."

"Hornet sting," Colin said morosely. He felt so horrible for her, cheery and smiling and holding beer she'd brought for her boyfriend. He just wanted to take her to her cave and tell her there, so she wouldn't have to go through it all in the light.

"Hey, by the way, did anyone kill a feral hog?" Hassan asked.

"Nope. Well, not unless you did," SOCT said. And then he laughed. "Me and Chase shot us a squirrel, though. Blew the damned thing to bits. Princess treed it for us."

"*We* didn't shoot it," JATT corrected. "I shot it."

"Well, whatever. I saw it first."

"They're like an old married couple," explained Lindsey. "Except instead of being in love with each other, they're both in love with Colin." TOC laughed heartily, while the two other boys repeatedly asserted their heterosexuality.

For a while, they drank. Even Colin stomached down the better part of a beer. Only Hassan abstained. "I'm back on the wagon," he said. By then the sun was sinking fast toward the horizon and the mosquitoes had come out. Colin, already sweaty and bloody, seemed to be their favorite target. Lindsey was cuddled up against TOC, her head nestled between his pec and shoulder, his arm around her waist. Hassan sat next to Katrina, chatting with her in whispers, but they did not touch. Colin was still thinking.

"You're not so talkative today," Lindsey said to Colin eventually. "Stings getting to you?"

"They burn like the fire of ten thousand suns," Colin said, deadpan.

"Pussy," TOC said, showing the grace and eloquence for which he was widely famous.

And maybe it was for the right reasons and maybe it wasn't. But right then, Colin pulled the minirecorder out of his pocket and rewound it. To Lindsey, he said, "I'm really, really sorry." And then he hit play.

"*. . . dated when we were sophomores and we've been hooking up occasionally ever since. But we came out here and I was going to end it.*"

Lindsey bolted upright, staring at Katrina with a gathering malice. TOC, strangely, was frozen. He'd never expected Colin Singleton, noted *sitzpinkler*, to say a word. Colin hit fast-forward, then play again.

"*. . . she just said it's over, okay? So that's it. It's over. I'm not cheating.*"

Lindsey raised her beer, chugging it, and then crumpled the can and dropped it. She stood up and stepped toward TOC, who was still leaning, in a state of apparent calm, against the obelisk. "Baby," he said, "you don't understand. I said I wasn't cheating and I'm *not*."

"Screw you," she said, and then she turned around and walked away. TOC caught her in his arms from behind, and she wrestled to get free of him. "Get off me right now," she shouted, but he held on tight, and then she sounded panicked, screaming, "GET OFF! GET HIM OFF ME."

"Let her go," Colin said softly. And then behind him, he heard JATT. "Yeah, Colin, get off her." Colin turned around, and saw JATT march up to TOC and grab him by the collar. "Calm the hell down," JATT said, and then TOC threw Lindsey to the ground. TOC hit JATT in the face with a right cross, and JATT fell to the ground like a dead man. As JATT lay there, unmoving, Colin wondered at the fact that *JATT* had gone after TOC; Colin had underestimated him. TOC quickly turned around and grabbed Lindsey by the ankle.

"Let her go," Colin said, standing now. "You *paardenlul*."[80]

She was kicking against his grip, but he was persistent, holding her tighter, saying, "Baby, stop. You don't understand."

Hassan looked at Colin. Together, they ran toward TOC, Hassan aiming for a body slam in the midsection and Colin going for a crazed punch to the head. At the last moment, TOC reached one hand out and hit Colin in the jaw so hard that the hornet stings didn't sting anymore. And then with his leg, TOC swept Hassan's feet out from under him. They weren't much for damsel-in-distress saving, Colin and Hassan.

But then again, Lindsey wasn't much for being a damsel in distress. After Colin hit the ground, he opened his eyes and saw Lindsey reach up, grab TOC's nuts, squeeze, and turn. TOC fell to his knees, hunched over, and released Lindsey.

His head scrambled, Colin crawled to the Archduke's obelisk, the only geographical location in the world that wasn't currently spinning. He grabbed hold of the obelisk with both hands and clung to it. Opening his eyes, he saw JATT still facedown. Lindsey and Katrina were kneeling over him.

And then Colin felt angels lifting him by the armpits, pulling him toward their home in the sky, and he felt light and free. He turned to his left, and saw Hassan. He turned to his right, and saw SOCT.

"Hey," said SOCT, "you all right?"

"Yeah," Colin said. "That was nice of your friend to, uh, get hit like that."

"He's a good guy. This is f'ed up, man. We been dealin' with this Colin

[80] Dutch. Literally, "horse's penis."

and Kat crap for two years. I love Colin, but this is ridiculous. Lindsey's good people."

TOC interrupted. He seemed to have recovered. "Stop talking to that little bitch."

"Aw, c'mon, Col. You screwed this one up, bro, not him."

"You're all such goddamned pussies!" TOC shouted, and then Hassan said, "It's three on one," and charged TOC.

And sure, it was three on one. But what a one. Hassan's run was met by a body punch that entered cartoonishly far into his gut. Hassan started to fall but couldn't, because TOC had his hand wrapped around Hass's neck. Colin rushed in then with an overhand right. The punch connected, but (1) Colin forgot to close his fist, so he was slapping not hitting, and (2) instead of slapping TOC, he ended up slapping Hassan flush across the cheek, whereupon Hassan finally succeeded in falling down.

SOCT jumped on TOC's back then, and for a brief moment, it seemed the fight might be a draw. Then TOC grabbed SOCT by one arm and threw him halfway across the graveyard, leaving Colin and TOC standing more or less toe to toe.

Colin began by employing a strategy he'd just invented called the "windmill," which involved windmilling his arms around to keep his attacker at bay. The strategy worked brilliantly, for about eight seconds, until TOC caught hold of his arms. And then TOC's square, reddened face was inches from Colin's. "I didn't want to do it, dude," explained TOC with a remarkable calm. "But, you know, you made me."

"Technically," Colin mumbled. "I kept my promise. *I* didn't *say* anyth—" but his thoughtful explanation was cut off by a fast-coming kick. In the moment before the strike, Colin felt it in his loins—phantom pain—and then TOC's knee came up into Colin's groin so hard that Colin briefly left the ground. *Flying*, he thought. *On the wings of a knee.* And then, before he'd even fallen, Colin vomited.

Which turned out to be a fairly good idea, since TOC ceased to pursue him. Colin fell to the ground, moaning, waves of pain radiating from his middle. It felt as if the Franz Ferdinandian hole in his gut had now torn, and the pain grew and grew from a bullet hole to a canyon until finally Colin himself was the hole. He'd become a wracking, all-over vacuum of pain.

"Oh God," Colin said finally. "Oh God, my balls."

Colin misspoke. In a better state, he would have recognized that it wasn't his *balls* that hurt, but rather his brain. Nerve impulses flew from his testes to his brain, where the brain's pain receptors were triggered, and the brain told Colin to feel pain in his balls, which Colin did, because the body always listens to the brain. Nuts, arms, stomachs—they never hurt. All hurt is brain hurt.

The pain made him dizzy and faint, and he lay on his side, crouched in the fetal position, his eyes closed. His head swam with the nauseating ache, and for a moment he fell asleep. But he had to get up, because he could hear Hassan grunting as he received blow after blow, so Colin crawled to the obelisk, and slowly dragged himself up, his hands walking up the Archduke's grave.

"I'm still here," Colin said feebly, his eyes shut as he held onto the obelisk for balance. "Come and get me." But when he opened his eyes, TOC was gone. Colin could hear the cicadas out in force, humming to a rhythm that matched his still-throbbing balls. Through the gray twilight, Colin saw Lindsey Lee Wells and her red-crossed first-aid kit tending to a seated Hassan, whose camouflage shirt and orange vest were covered with blood. SOCT and JATT were sitting together sharing a cigarette—there was a lump above JATT's eye that literally looked like his forehead was about to birth a chicken egg. Colin got dizzy, and then turned back around, hugging the obelisk. When he opened his eyes again, he realized his glasses were gone, and between the dizziness and his astigmatism, the letters before him started dancing. The Archduke *Franz Ferdinand*. He anagrammed to dull the pain. "Huh," he mumbled after a moment. "That's a hell of a coincidence."

"The *kafir* has awoken," Hassan noted. Lindsey rushed over to Colin, wiped the last flecks of chaw from his earlobe, and whispered into his ear. "*Mein held*,[81] thanks for defending my honor. So where'd he get ya?"

"In the brain," Colin said, getting it right this time.

[81]German: My hero.

# (seventeen)

**The next morning,** a Monday, was their twenty-second morning in Gutshot, and indubitably the worst. Aside from the residual tenderness in and around his nuts, Colin's entire body was sore from a day spent walking and running and shooting and getting hit. And his head hurt—each time he opened his eyes, beams of feverish, demonic pain shot through his brain. The night before, Paramedic (in Training) Lindsey Lee Wells had diagnosed him with moderate contusions and "sprained balls" after an exhaustive search of medical Websites. She diagnosed TOC as suffering from "I'm-an-asshole-and-Lindsey's-never-going-to-speak-to-me-again-itis."

Keeping his eyes closed as much as possible, Colin stumbled toward the bathroom that morning, where he found Hassan staring at himself in the mirror. Hassan's lower lip was hideously busted—he looked like he was chewing a fat wad of tobacco—and his right eye was very nearly swollen shut.

"How ya doing?" asked Colin. Hassan turned to him and gave Colin the full view of his well-punched face, as if to answer the question.

"Yeah, sure," Colin said, reaching in to turn on the shower. "But you should see the other guy."

Hass managed a wan smile. "If I could do it all over again," he said, his speech slow and vaguely mangled by his massive lower lip, "I'd just let myself be trampled to death by the Satan Pig."

• • •

As Colin came down the stairs to breakfast, he saw Lindsey sitting at the oak table sipping a glass of orange juice. "I really don't want to talk about it," Lindsey said, preemptively. "But I do hope your balls are okay."

"Me too," said Colin. He'd checked on them during his shower. They felt the same, only tenderer.

Their assignment that day—left in note form by Hollis—was to interview a woman named Mabel Bartrand. "Oh, man," Lindsey said when Colin read the name to her. "She's at the other home, the one for when you're *really* old. I can't take that today. I can't—God. Let's just skip. Let's just all go back to sleep."

"I'm for that," Hassan mumbled through his meaty lips.

"She could probably use the company," Colin said, trying to use his familiarity with loneliness for the powers of good.

"Lord, you do know how to lay on the guilt," Lindsey said. "Let's go."

Mabel Bartrand lived in an assisted living facility about fifteen miles outside of Gutshot, one exit south of the Hardee's. Lindsey knew the way, so she drove the Hearse. On the drive, no one talked. There was too much to discuss. And anyway, Colin's whole body felt like pure, undiluted crap. But his life had finally calmed down enough to return to the troubling question of Katherine III, and the failure of his memory. His head, however, hurt too much to make any sense of it.

A male nurse met them at reception and guided them to Mabel's room. This place was significantly more depressing than Sunset Acres. Here the only sound was the whirring of machines, and the halls were mostly empty of people. A TV blaring the Weather Channel in the common room went unwatched; the doors were mostly closed; the few people seated in the common room looked confused or blank or—worst of all—scared.

"*Ms. Mabel*," the nurse said singsongily, condescendingly. "You have some visitors." Colin turned on the minirecorder. He was using the same tape from the day before, taping over TOC's confession.

"Hello," Mabel said. She was seated in a leather recliner in what looked like a dorm room, with one twin bed, one chair, a long-ignored wooden desk, and a minifridge. Her thinning, curly white hair was styled into a kind of old lady Jew-fro. She hunched forward, and she smelled old, vaguely like formaldehyde. Lindsey leaned forward, her arms around Ms. Mabel, and kissed her cheek. Colin and Hassan introduced themselves, and Ms. Mabel smiled but didn't speak.

Belatedly, Mabel asked, "Is that Lindsey Wells?"

"Yes'm," said Lindsey, sitting down next to her.

"Oh, Lindsey darling, I ain't seen you in so long. It's been *years*, hasn't it? Oh, but Lord it's good to see you."

"You too, Mabel."

"I've thought about you so much and wished on you visitin', but you never did. Don't you look so good and grown-up. No more blue hair for you, uh-uh. How've you been, baby?"

"I've been good, Mabel. How about yourself?"

"I'm ninety-four! How you think I'm doing?" Mabel laughed, and so did Colin. "What's your name?" she asked Colin, and he told her.

"Hollis," she said to Lindsey. "Is that Dr. Dinzanfar's son-in-law?" Ms. Mabel leaned forward and pointed a finger that would not straighten in Hassan's direction.

"No, Ms. Mabel. I'm Hollis's daughter, Lindsey. Dr. Dinzanfar's daughter, Grace, was my grandma, and Corville Wells was my grandpa. This is Hassan, a friend of mine who wants to talk to you about the old days in Gutshot."

"Oh, well that's fine," Ms. Mabel said. "I get confused sometimes," she explained.

"That's okay," said Lindsey. "It's awful good to see you."

"And you, Lindsey. I can't get over how pretty you look. You right grew into that face, didn't you?" Lindsey smiled, and now Colin noticed that Lindsey had tears in her eyes.

"Tell us a story about the old days in Gutshot," Lindsey said, and it became clear to Colin that this was not an occasion to be asking Hollis's four questions.

"I've been thinking on Dr. Dinzanfar. Before he started that tactilery, he owned the General Store. I was just a little thing, knee-high to a bird dog. And he's only got one eye, you know. Fought in the first War. Well one day, we was at the store and Daddy gave me one red penny and I ran up to the counter there and I said, 'Doctor Dinzanfar, do you have any penny candy?' And he looked down at me, and he said, 'I'm sorry, Mabel. We don't have any penny candy in Gutshot. All we got is *free* candy.'" Mabel closed her eyes as they all let the story sink in a bit. She seemed almost asleep, her breathing slow and rhythmic, but then her eyes snapped open and she said, "Lindsey, I sure missed seeing you. I missed holding this hand."

And then Lindsey began crying in earnest. "Ms. Mabel, we gotta go, but I'm-a gonna come back later this week and see you again, I promise. I'm s—I'm sorry I haven't visited in so long."

"Well that's fine, sweetie. Don't you go gettin' upset about it. Next time you come, show up 'tween twelve-thirty and one and I'll give you my Jell-O. Sugar free, but it ain't bad." Mabel finally let go of Lindsey's hand, and Lindsey blew a kiss and left.

Colin and Hassan lingered behind to say good-bye, and when they got into the common room, they found Lindsey sobbing—death-cry-of-a-hyena sobbing. She disappeared into a bathroom, and Colin followed Hassan out the door. Hassan sat down on the curb. "I can't handle that place," he said. "We're never going back in there."

"What's wrong with it?"

"It's sad, and not in a funny way," Hassan said. "It's not the least bit fugging funny. And it's really getting to me."

"Why does everything have to be funny to you?" asked Colin. "So you don't have to ever really care about anything?"

"Dingleberries, Dr. Freud. I'm actually just going to issue a blanket dingleberries on all attempts to psychoanalyze me."

"Aye, aye, Cap'n Funnypants."

Lindsey showed up outside then, seeming to be fully recovered. "I'm fine and don't need to talk about it," she said, unprompted.

That night he finished the Theorem. It proved relatively easy, actually, because for the first time in several days, he had no distractions. Lindsey was locked in her room. Hollis was downstairs, so entranced in her work/TV that she never so much as said a word about Hassan's blue-black eye or the fist-shaped bruise on Colin's jaw. Hassan was off somewhere, too. A lot of people could lose themselves in the Pink Mansion, and that night, a lot of people did.

It proved almost unfairly easy to finish it—now that he knew about his time as a Dumper, the formula as he had it was very close to accurate. He needed only to tweak a radical to finalize the formula.

$$-D^7x^8+D^2x^3-\frac{x^2}{A^3}-Cx^2-Px+\frac{1}{A}+13P+\frac{\sin(2x)}{2}\left[1+(-1)^{H+1}\frac{\left(x+\frac{11\pi}{2}\right)^H}{\left|x+\frac{11\pi}{2}\right|^H}\right]$$

Everyone came out looking correct, which is to say that Katherine Mutsensberger looked like so:

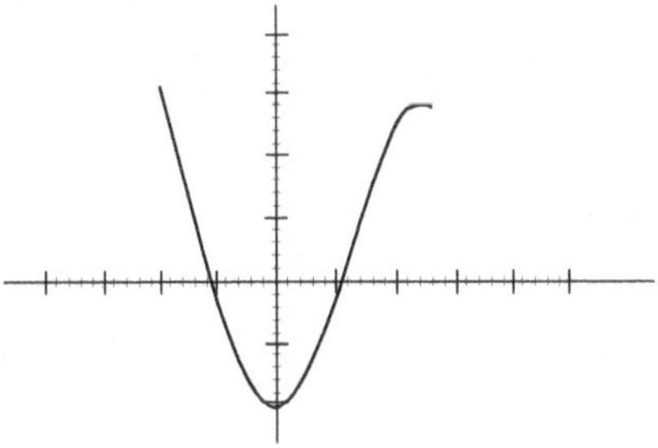

A perfect graph for a fourth-grade love story.

Upon putting down his pencil, he held up his hands, fists clenched tight. Like a marathoner winning a race. Like the hare, coming from behind and screwing up the story by beating the tortoise.

He went looking for Lindsey and Hassan, and eventually found them in the Game Room. "I finished our Theorem," he told Lindsey, who was seated on the pink felt of the pool table, her brown eyes still puffy. Hassan was ensconced in the green leather couch.

"Really?" asked Lindsey.

"Yeah. It took like eight seconds. I actually almost finished it like two weeks ago; I just didn't realize it worked."

"*Kafir*," said Hassan, "that is such good news that I almost want to get off the couch and shake your hand. But God, it's comfortable. So now can you use it for, like, anything? Like for any two people?"

"Yeah, I think so."

"Are you going to use it to predict the future?"

"Sure," offered Colin. "Who are you looking to date?"

"Uh-uh, dude. I tried it your way with the dating and the girls and the kissing and the drama, and man, I didn't like it. Plus, my best friend is a walking cautionary tale of what happens to you when romantic relationships don't involve marriage. Like you always say, *kafir*, everything ends in breakup, divorce, or death. I want to narrow my misery options to divorce or death—that's all. That said, you could do it for me and Lindsay Lohan. I wouldn't mind converting her to Islam, if you catch my drift."

Colin laughed but otherwise ignored the diatribe.

"Do me and Colin," Lindsey said softly, her eyes staring down at her bare, tan knees. "The other Colin, I mean," she added.

And so Colin did. He sat down and balanced a book on his knees, then pulled out his notebook and pencil. As he filled in the variables, he said, "Now just so you know, getting cheated on counts as getting dumped. I don't want you to get pissed off about it; that's just the way the Theorem works."

"Fair," Lindsey said curtly. Colin had played with the Theorem so much that he knew from the numbers what it would look like, but he still went through the motions of plotting each point.

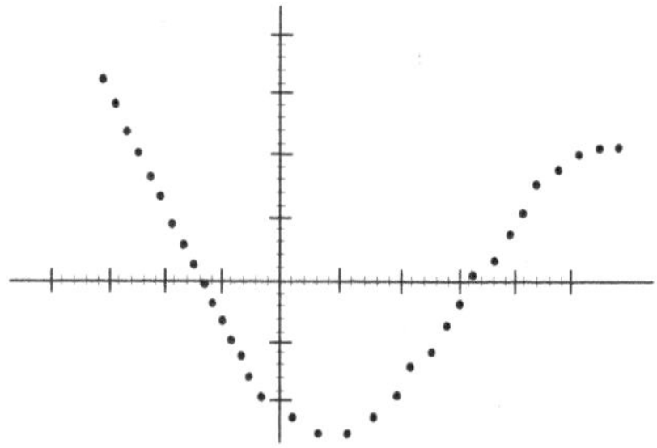

When he showed it to her, she said, "Wait, what's that?"

"That's TOC dumping you," answered Colin.

"So it works," she said, her voice empty of emotion. "It's weird—I feel sad, but not about him. All I feel about breaking up is—I'm just relieved."

"Relief is a Dumper emotion," Colin noted with some concern.

Lindsey hopped off the pool table and plopped down on the couch beside Colin. "I think I just realized that I don't actually want to date an asshole I'm not even attracted to. Those are two separate revelations: I don't want to date assholes, and I'm not actually turned on by big muscles. Although I did cry like a two-year-old in the nursing home, so the relief is possibly temporary."

Hassan grabbed the notebook from Colin. "It really fugging seems to work."

"Yeah, I know."

"Well, although, not to poop on your party, but you proved what I already knew—that guys who play football know how to play the mother-fugging field, and that Katherines dump Colins like Hassans eat Monster Thickburgers: voraciously, passionately, and often."

"Well, the real test is whether it can *predict* the arc of a relationship," Colin acknowledged.

"Oh, hey," Lindsey said, seeming to remember something. "Ask Hassan what he was doing in the Game Room about twenty minutes before you showed up."

"What were you doing in the Game Room about twenty min—"

"God, don't take her so literally," said Hassan. "I was on the Internet."

"Why were you on the Internet?"

Hassan stood up, smiling through his busted lip. He rubbed the Jew-fro as he walked by, and then paused at the doorway and said, "Me and Thunderstick decided to take our show to college," Hassan said, and Colin opened his mouth to talk, but Hassan said, "I only registered for two classes in the fall, so don't start creaming yourself. I've got to ease my way into it. Don't tell me how fugging happy you are. I know."[82]

---

[82] And sure enough, that September ninth, Hassan would sit down in a class called English Composition at ten in the morning, even though it directly conflicted with his beloved companion, friend, and possible fantasy lover, Judge Judy.

# (eighteen)

**Colin slept through the rooster** that Thursday morning but not through Lindsey jumping onto his bed and saying, "Get up. We're going to Memphis."

She gracefully jumped down, her butt landing on the bed, and sang, "Memphis. Memphis. We're skipping work and going to Memphis. To spy on Hollis and find out why she was filling the swear jar."

"Mm-hmm," Colin mumbled as if he were sleepy, but he wasn't. Her presence made him shoot immediately awake.

When Colin got downstairs, Hassan was up and dressed and fed. With a few days of healing, his face had returned mostly to normal. He was searching through a mess of papers. "*Kafir,*" he said loudly, "help me find the warehouse's address. I'm lost in a sea of spreadsheets."

It took Colin about thirty seconds to find the address of the warehouse in Memphis. He found it at the top of a business letter addressed to Gutshot Textiles, Inc.

Hassan shouted, "MapQuest 2246 Trial Boulevard, Memphis, Tennessee 37501," and Lindsey Lee Wells shouted back, "Awesome! Good work, Hassan!"

"Well, technically, it was my work," Colin noted.

"Let me take the credit. I've had a tough week." Hassan said as he collapsed, dramatically, on the couch. "Hey, how do you like that, Singleton? You're the only nonrecent Dumpee in this house."

This was true. But Hassan seemed to get over Katrina immediately, and Lindsey had just burst into Colin's room in song, so he still felt he could lay claim to the Household's Most Devastated Dumpee, even if he had to admit that he didn't exactly want K-19 back anymore. He wanted her to call; he wanted her to miss him; but as it turned out, he was okay. He'd never found single life so interesting before.

Hassan called driving and Lindsey called shotgun, so even though it was his car, Colin was relegated to the backseat, where he curled up against the window and read J. D. Salinger's *Seymour: An Introduction*. He finished it just as the Memphis skyline came into view. It was no Chicago, but Colin had missed skyscrapers.

They drove through downtown and then got off the interstate in a part of the city that seemed to be comprised entirely of low-lying buildings with few windows and even fewer signs informing visitors of their function. A few blocks from the exit, Lindsey motioned to one, and Hassan pulled into a four-car parking lot, which was empty.

"You're sure this is it?"

"It's the address you found," Lindsey answered.

They walked into a small office with a receptionist's desk, which contained no receptionist, so then they left and made their way around the side of the warehouse.

It was a hot day but windy enough to feel mild. Colin heard a rumbling, looked up, and saw a bulldozer out in a dirt field behind the warehouse. The only two guys in sight were the guy driving the bulldozer and the fellow behind him, who was driving a forklift. The forklift contained three massive cardboard boxes. Colin frowned.

"D'you see Hollis anywhere?" Lindsey whispered.

"No."

"Go ask those guys if they've ever heard of Gutshot Textiles," Lindsey said. Colin didn't particularly enjoy talking to strangers driving forklifts, but he silently started to walk out into the field.

The bulldozer hauled up a final mound of dirt and then puttered away to make room for the forklift. And as it approached the hole, Colin did too. He was spitting distance[83] from the hole when the forklift came to a stop and the guy came around, reached up, and toppled the first box into the ground. It landed with a thud. Colin kept walking.

"How you?" asked the man, a short black guy with white hair at his temples.

"Okay," said Colin. "Do you work for Gutshot Textiles?"

"Yup."

"Whatcha throwing in the hole?"

"Don't know that it's any of your business, on account of how you don't own the hole."

Colin didn't really have a response to that—it *wasn't* his hole. The wind picked up then, and the dry dirt whipped up from the ground and passed over them in a cloud. Colin turned 180 degrees to put his back to the dust, and then he saw Hassan and Lindsey walking briskly toward him. Colin heard the crash of another box, but he didn't want to turn around. He didn't want that dust in his eyes.

But then he did turn, because it wasn't only dust flying. The second box had cracked open, and thousands of finely braided tampon strings were whipping past him, and past Hassan and Lindsey—blowing around and over them. And he looked up and watched the strings rush by as he became immersed in a cloud of them. They looked like garfish or brilliant white light. Colin thought of Einstein. A certifiable genius (who was definitely

---

[83] The world record for watermelon seed spitting is held by Jim Dietz, who in 1978 spit a watermelon seed 68 feet, 11 inches. Colin was closer to the hole than that for sure.

never a prodigy), Einstein had figured out that light can act, in a seeming paradox, both as a discrete particle and as a wave. Colin had never understood this before, but now thousands of strings were fluttering over and around and past him, and they were both tiny broken beams of light and endless, undulating waves.

He reached up to grab one and came down with several, and they kept coming, washing over him, floating all around him. Never have tampon strings seemed so beautiful as they rolled up and down with the wind, landing on the ground and then twirling and floating up again, falling and rising and falling and rising.

"Shit," said the man. "Ain't that pretty, though?"

"It sure is," said Lindsey, suddenly beside Colin, the back of her hand touching the back of his. A few straggling strings were still blowing up from the box, but most of the army of unleashed tampon strings were fading into the distance.

"You look just like your momma," the man said to her.

"I wish you wouldn't say that," said Lindsey. "Who are you, by the way?"

"I'm Roy," he said. "I'm the director of operations for Gutshot Textiles. Your mom'll be here soon. Best let her talk to you. Y'all come in with me and get a drink." They'd wanted to *spy* on Hollis, not beat her to the warehouse, but Colin figured the element of secrecy was now more or less totally lost.

Roy pushed the last box into the hole, and that one held together. Then he reached his thumb and finger into his mouth, issued a piercing whistle, and motioned to the bulldozer, which lumbered to life.

They walked back to the unair-conditioned warehouse. Roy told them to sit tight, and then returned to the field.

"She's gone nuts," Lindsey said. "Her 'Director of Operations' is some guy I've never seen and she's telling him to bury our damned product out behind the warehouse? She's bonkers. What does she want, to run the town into the ground?"

"I don't think so," said Colin. "I mean, I do think she's bonkers. But I don't think she wants to run the—"

"Baby," Colin heard from behind him, and he wheeled around and saw Hollis Wells in her trademark Thursday pink pantsuit. "What are you *doing* here?" Hollis asked, not sounding very angry.

"What the hell's wrong with you, Hollis? Have you gone nuts? Who the hell is Roy? And why are you *burying* everything?"

"Lindsey, baby, the company ain't doing so well."

"Jesus, Hollis, do you stay up all night every night trying to figure out how to ruin my life? Sell the land, put the factory out of business, and then the town will die and then I'll for sure have to leave?"

Hollis scrunched her face up. "What? Lindsey Lee Wells, no. No! There's no one to *buy* them, Lindsey. We have one client—StaSure, and they buy a quarter of what we can produce. We've lost everything else to companies overseas. Everything."

"Wait, what?" Lindsey asked quietly, although Colin figured she'd heard.

"They stacked up in the warehouse. Up and up and up. And it's just gotten worse and worse, until it came to this."

And then Lindsey understood. "You don't want to fire anyone."

"That's right, baby. If we cut production down to what we were selling, we'd lose most our people. It'd kill Gutshot."

"Wait, then why the heck did you hire *them* to do some little made-up job?" Lindsey asked, nodding toward Colin and Hassan. "If we're so broke, I mean."

"It's not made up. A generation from now there might not be a factory and I want your kids and their kids to know what it was like, what *we* were like. And I liked them. I thought they'd be good for you. The world ain't gonna stay like you imagine it, sweetheart."

Lindsey took a step toward her mother. "Now I know why you work at home," she said. "So no one will know what's going on. No one knows?"

"Just Roy," said Hollis. "And you can't tell anyone. We can go on like this for at least five more years, so that's what we're gonna do," Hollis said. "And between now and then I'm gonna work like hell to find new ways of making money."

Lindsey put her arms around her mom's waist and pressed her face against her chest. "Five years is a long time, Mom," she said.

"It is and it isn't," Hollis answered, stroking Lindsey's hair. "It is and it isn't. But it's not your fight; it's mine. I'm sorry, sweetie. I know I've been busier than a mom ought to be."

And this, unlike TOC's cheating, was a secret best kept, Colin thought. People don't like to know that three quarters of their tampon strings are being buried, or that their paychecks have less to do with their company's profitability than its owner's compassion.

Hollis and Lindsey ended up riding home together, leaving Colin and Hassan alone in the Hearse. They weren't five miles outside of Memphis when Hassan said, "I had a, um, blinding light spiritual awakening."

Colin glanced at him. "Huh?"

"Watch the road, *kafir*. It started a few nights ago, actually, so I guess it wasn't that dramatic—at the old folks' home, when you said I was Mr. Funnypants because I wanted to avoid getting hurt."

"No doubt about it," Colin said.

"Yeah, well, that's bullshit, and I knew it was bullshit, but then I started wondering exactly why I am Mr. Funnypants, and I didn't have a very good answer. But then, back there, I started thinking about what Hollis is doing. I mean, she's giving up all her time and her money so people can keep jobs. She's *doing* something."

"Okay . . ." said Colin, not getting it.

"And I'm a not-doer. Like, I'm lazy, but I'm also good at not-doing things I'm not supposed to do. I never drank or did drugs or hooked up with girls or beat people up or stole or anything. I was always good at that, although not so much this particular summer. But then doing all that stuff here felt weird and wrong, so now I'm back to happily not-doing. But I've never been a *doer.* I never *did* anything that helped anybody. Even the religious things that involve doing, I don't do. I don't do *zakat.*[84] I don't do Ramadan. I'm a total non-doer. I'm just sucking food and water and money out of the world, and all I'm giving back is, 'Hey, I'm really good at not-doing. Look at all the bad things I'm not doing! Now I'm going to tell you some jokes!'"

Colin glanced over and saw Hassan sipping Mountain Dew. Feeling that he should say something, Colin said, "That's a good spiritual revelation."

"I'm not done yet, fugger. I was just drinking. So but anyway, being funny is a way of not-doing. Sit around and make jokes and be Mr. Funnypants and just make fun of everyone else's attempts to do something. Make fun of you when you get back up and try to love yourself another Katherine. Or make fun of Hollis for falling asleep covered in her work every night. Or get on your case for shooting at the hornets' nest, when I didn't shoot at all. So that's it. I'm going to start doing." Hassan finished his can of Mountain Dew, crumpled it, and dropped it beneath his feet. "See, I just did something. Usually," he said, "I would have thrown that shit in the backseat, where I wouldn't have to look at it and you'd have to clean it up the next time you had a date with a Katherine. But I'm leaving it here, so I remember to pick it up when we get to the Pink Mansion. God, someone should give me a Congressional Medal of Honor for Doing."

Colin laughed. "You're still funny," Colin said. "And you have been doing stuff. You registered for college."

"Yeah, I'm getting there. Although—if I'm going to be an all-out, full-on doer," Hassan noted, faux morose, "I should probably register for *three* classes. It's a hard life, *kafir.*"

---

[84] Giving to the poor, one of the pillars of Islamic faith.

# (nineteen)

**Lindsey and Hollis** beat them home, on account of how Colin and Hassan had to stop at the Hardee's for a Monster Thickburger. As they stood in the Pink Mansion's living room, Hollis said, "Lindsey went to spend the night at her friend Janet's. She was pretty broken up on the car ride home. It's about the boy, I guess."

Hassan nodded, and sat down on the sectional couch with her. Colin's brain started working. He had to find an unsuspicious way out of the Pink Mansion as soon as possible, he realized.

"Can I do anything to help you?" asked Hassan, and Hollis brightened and said, "Sure. Sure. You can sit here with me and brainstorm—all night, if you've got the time." And Hassan said, "Cool."

Colin sort of half-coughed, and started speaking rapidly. "I may go out for a while. I think I'm going to go camping. I'll probably *sitzpinkler* out and sleep in the car, but still—I'm gonna give it a try."

"What?" asked Hassan, incredulous.

"Camping," Colin said.

"With the pigs and the hornets and the TOCs and the whatnot?"

"Yes, camping," said Colin, and then he tried to give Hassan an extremely meaningful look.

After staring back quizzically for a moment, Hassan's eyes shot open, and he said, "Well, I'm not going with you. As we've learned, I'm an inside cat."

"Keep your phone on," Hollis said. "Do you have a tent?"

"No, but it's pretty out and I'll just take a sleeping bag if that's all right."

And then before Hollis could further object, he climbed the stairs two at a time, grabbed his supplies, and headed out.

It was early evening—the fields receding into a pink invisibility as they rose back into the horizon. Colin felt his heart slamming in his chest. He wondered if she even wanted to see him. He'd taken "sleeping over at Janet's" as a hint, but maybe it wasn't. Maybe she really *was* sleeping at Janet's, whoever that was—which would mean a lot of hiking for naught.

After five minutes of driving, he reached the fenced-in field that had once been home to Hobbit the horse. He climbed over the tri-logged fence and jogged across the field. Colin, of course, did not believe in running when walking would suffice—but here and now, walking would not. He slowed down, however, as he made his way up the hill, the flashlight a thin and shaky beam of yellow light against the darkening landscape. He kept it directly before him as he picked through bushes and vines and trees, the thick rotting floor of the forest crunching beneath his feet, reminding him of where we all go. To seed, to ground. And even then he couldn't help but anagram. To ground—Run, Godot; Donor Gut. And the magic through which "to ground" can become "donor gut," combined with his newfound feeling that he had at some recent point *received* a donor gut, kept his pace quick. Even as the darkness became so complete that trees and rocks became not objects but mere shadows, he climbed, until finally he reached the stone outcropping. He walked along the rock, his flashlight scanning up and down, until the light passed over the crack. He leaned his head in and said, "Lindsey?"

"Christ, I thought you were a bear."

"Quite the opposite. I was just in the neighborhood and I thought I'd drop by," he said. He heard her laugh echo through the cave. "But I don't want to impose."

"Come on in," she said, and he squeezed through the jagged crack and shuffled sideways until he reached the room. She turned on her flashlight; they were blinding each other. "I thought you might come," she said.

"Well you told your mom you were sleeping at Janet's."

"Yeah," she said. "It was kind of a code."

Lindsey pointed the light next to her, and then drew a line back to Colin, like she was bringing an airplane into the gate. He walked over, and she arranged a couple of pillows into a chair, and he sat beside her.

"Out, damn light," she said, and it was dark again.

"The most upsetting part of it is that I'm not even upset. About Colin, I mean. Because I—in the end I just didn't care. About him, about his liking me, about his screwing Katrina. I just—don't care. Hey, are you there?"

"Yes."

"Where?"

"Here. Hi."

"Oh, hi."

"So go on."

"Right. So, I don't know. It was just so easy to dismiss. I keep thinking I'm going to get upset, but it's been three days, and I just don't even think about him. Remember when I told you that unlike me, he was *real*? I don't think he is, actually. I think he's just boring. I'm so pissed off about it, because—I mean, I wasted so much of my life with him and then he *cheats* on me and I'm not even particularly, like, *depressed* about it?"

"I would love to be like that."

"Yeah, except you wouldn't, I don't think. People are *supposed* to care. It's good that people mean something to you, that you miss people when they're gone. I don't miss Colin at all. I mean, literally. I only ever liked the *idea* of being his girlfriend—and that is just such a goddamned waste! That's what I realized—*that's* what I cried about the whole way home. Here's Hollis, really doing something for people. I mean, she works all the goddamned time and now I know it's not for herself; it's for all these fugging people in Sunset Acres who get a pension that pays for their diapers. And it's for everybody at the factory."

"..."

"I used to be an okay person, you know. But now I. Never. Do. Anything. For anybody. Except retards I don't even give a shit about."

"But people still like you. All the oldsters, everybody at the factory . . ."

"Right. Yeah. But they like me as they remember me, not as I am now. I mean, honestly, Colin, I'm the world's most self-centered person."

"..."

"Are you there?"

"It just occurred to me that in point of fact what you just said can't be true because *I* am the world's most self-centered person."

"Huh?"

"Or maybe we're tied. Because I'm the same, right? What did I ever do for anyone?"

"Didn't you stay behind Hassan and let, like, a thousand hornets sting you?"

"Oh. Yeah. There was that. Okay, you're the world's most self-centered person after all. But I'm close!"

"Come here."

"I am here."

"More here."

"Okay. There?"

"Yes. Better."

"So what do you do about it? How do you fix it?"

"That's what I was thinking about before you came. I was thinking about your mattering business. I feel like, like, how you matter is defined by the things that matter to you. You matter as much as the things that matter to you do. And I got so backwards, trying to make myself matter to him. All this time, there were real things to care about: real, good people who care about me, and this place. It's so easy to get stuck. You just get caught in being something, being special or cool or whatever, to the point where you don't even know why you need it; you just think you do."

"You don't even know why you need to be world-famous; you just think you do."

"Yeah. Exactly. We're in the same boat, Colin Singleton. But it didn't really fix the problem, getting popular."

"I don't think you can ever fill the empty space with the thing you lost. Like getting TOC to date you doesn't fix the Alpo event. I don't think your missing pieces ever fit inside you again once they go missing. Like Katherine. That's what I realized: if I did get her back somehow, she wouldn't fill the hole that losing her created."

"Maybe no girl can fill it."

"Right. Being a world-famous Theorem-creator wouldn't, either. That's what I've been thinking, that maybe life is not about accomplishing some bullshit markers. Wait, what's funny?"

"Nothing it's just, like—I was thinking that your realization is like if a heroin addict suddenly said, 'You know, maybe instead of always doing *more* heroin, I should, like, *not* do heroin.'"

". . ."

". . ."

". . ."

". . ."

"I think I know who's buried in the Archduke Franz Ferdinand's tomb, and I don't think it's the Archduke."

"I knew you'd figure it out! Yeah, I already know. My great-grandfather."

"You knew?! Fred N. Dinzanfar, that anagramming bastard."

"All the old-timers here know. He insisted on it in his will, supposedly. But then a couple years ago, Hollis had us put up the sign and start giving tours—now I realize it was probably for the money."

"It's funny, what people will do to be remembered."

"Well, or to be forgotten, because someday no one will know who's really buried there. Already a lot of kids at school and stuff think the Archduke is really buried here, and I like that. I like knowing one story and having everyone else know another. That's why those tapes we made are going to be so great one day, because they'll tell stories that time has swallowed up or distorted or whatever."

"Where'd your hand go?"

"It's sweaty."

"I don't mi—oh hi."

"Hi."

". . ."

". . ."

"Did I tell you I dumped one of the Katherines?"

"You what? No."

"I did, apparently. Katherine the Third. I just completely misremembered it. I mean, I always assumed that all the things I *did* remember were *true*."

"Huh."

"What?"

"Well, but it's not as good a story if you dumped her. That's how I remember things, anyway. I remember stories. I connect the dots and then out of that comes a story. And the dots that don't fit into the story just slide away, maybe. Like when you spot a constellation. You look up and you don't see all the stars. All the stars just look like the big fugging random mess that they are. But you want to see shapes; you want to see stories, so you pick them out of the sky. Hassan told me once you think like that, too—that you see connections everywhere—so you're a natural born storyteller, it turns out."

"I never thought about it like that. I—huh. It makes sense."

"So tell me the story."

"What? The whole thing?"

"Yeah. Romance, adventure, morals, everything."

#### The Beginning, and the Middle, and the End

"Katherine I was the daughter of my tutor Krazy Keith, and she asked me to be her boyfriend one night at my house, and I said yes, and then about two minutes and thirty seconds later she dumped me, which seemed funny at the time, but now, in retrospect, it's possible that those two minutes and thirty seconds were among the most significant time periods of my life.

"K-2 was a slightly pudgy eight-year-old from school, and she showed up at my house one day and said there was a dead rat in the alley and, being eight, I ran outside to see the dead rat, but instead I found only her best friend Amy, and Amy said, 'Katherine likes you and will you be her boyfriend?' and I said yes, and then eight days later Amy showed up at my door again to say that Katherine didn't like me anymore and wouldn't be going with me from there on out.

"Katherine III was a perfectly charming little brunette whom I met my first summer at smart-kid camp, which would in time come to be *the* place for child prodigies to pick up chicks, and since it makes a better story, I choose to remember that she dumped me one morning on the archery course after this math prodigy named Jerome ran in front of her bow and fell to the ground, claiming he'd been shot by Cupid's arrow.

"Katherine IV, aka Katherine the Red, was a mousy redhead with red plastic-rimmed glasses whom I met in Suzuki violin lessons and she played beautifully and I played hardly at all because I could never be bothered to practice and so after four days she dumped me for a piano prodigy named Robert Vaughan who ended up playing a solo concert at Carnegie Hall when he was eleven, so I guess she made the right call there.

"In fifth grade, I went out with K-5, widely reputed to be the nastiest girl in school because she always seemed to be the one who started lice outbreaks, and she kissed me on the lips out of nowhere during recess one day while I was trying to read *Huck Finn* in the sandbox, and that was my first kiss, and later that day she dumped me because boys were gross.

"Then after a six-month dry spell, I met Katherine VI during my third year at smart-kid summer camp, and we went together for a record seventeen days and she was excellent at both pottery and pull-ups, two fields of endeavor at which I have never excelled, and although between us we could have made an unstoppable force of intelligence and upper-body strength and coffee mug-making, she dumped me anyway.

"And then came middle school and the severe unpopularity commenced in earnest, but the nice thing about being on the near end of the cool curve is that periodically people will take pity on you, such as sixth grade's Katherine the Kind, a sweetheart who wore a frequently snapped training bra and whom everyone called pizza face due to an acne problem that wasn't even that bad, and who eventually broke up with me not because she realized I was damaging what minuscule social standing she had but because she felt that our month-long relationship had hurt my academic pursuits, which she believed to be very important.

"The Eighth wasn't quite so sweet, and maybe I should have known it since her name, Katherine Barker, anagrams into Heart Breaker, Ink, like she's a veritable CEO of Dumping, but anyway she asked me out on a date and then I said yes and then she called me a freak and said I didn't have any pubes and that she would never seriously go out with me—all of which, to be fair, was true.

"K-9 was in sixth grade when I was in seventh, and she was by far the best-looking Katherine to date with her cute chin and the dimples in her cheeks, and her skin perennially tan, not unlike you, and she thought that dating an older man might be good for her social status, but she was wrong.

"Katherine X—and yes by then I had realized certainly that this was an awfully odd statistical anomaly, but I wasn't actively pursuing Katherines so much as I was actively pursuing girlfriends—was a smart-kid-summer-camp conquer, and I won her heart by, you guessed it, running in front of her bow on the archery course and claiming I'd been shot by Cupid's arrow, and she was the first girl I ever French-kissed, and I didn't know what to do so I sort of kept darting my tongue out from behind closed lips like I was a snake, and it didn't take very much of that for her to want to be just friends.

"K-11 wasn't so much a dating thing as a going-to-the-movies-once-and-holding-hands-and-then-me-calling-and-her-mother-saying-she-wasn't-home-and-then-her-never-calling-me-back thing, but I'd argue it counts, due to hand-holding and also due to the fact that she called me a genius.

"At the start of the second semester of ninth grade, a new girl showed up from New York and she was as rich as they come, but she hated being rich and loved *The Catcher in the Rye*, and she said I reminded her of Holden Caulfield, presumably because we were both self-absorbed losers, and she liked me because I knew a lot of languages and had read a lot of books, and then she broke up with me after twenty-five days because she wanted a boyfriend who didn't spend so much time reading and learning languages.

"By then I had met Hassan, and for about ten years, I'd had an obsessive crush on this brunette with blue eyes from school whom I'd always called Katherine the Best and Hassan played like Cyrano and told me exactly how to woo her because as we know from Katrina, Hassan is actually quite good at that stuff, and it worked and I loved her and she loved me and it lasted for three months, until November of tenth grade, when she finally broke up with me because she said, and I am quoting directly here, that I was both 'too smart and too dumb' for her, which marked the beginning of Katherines having ridiculous, idiotic, and frequently oxymoronic reasons for breaking up with me.

"A pattern that continued with the always-clad-in-black Katherine XIV, who I met that spring when she came up to me at a coffee shop and asked if I was reading Camus, which I was, and I said I was, and then she asked if I had ever read Kierkegaard, and I said I had because I had, and then by the time we left the coffee shop we were holding hands and her phone number was in my brand-new cell phone, and she liked to take me for walks on the lakeshore, where we'd watch the waves crashing against the rocks on the shoreline, and she said there was only one metaphor, and that the metaphor was water beating against rocks—because, she said, both the water and the rocks ended up worse off in the bargain, and then when she dumped me in the same coffee shop where we'd met three months before, she said she was the water and I was the rocks and we were just going to keep going at each other till there was nothing left of either of us—and when I pointed out that, really, water doesn't suffer any negative effects whatsoever from slowly eroding the rocks on the lakeshore, she allowed as to how that was true but dumped me anyway.

"And then that summer at camp I met K-15, who had that kind of puppy-dog face with the big brown eyes and drooping eyelids that just sort of made you want to take care of her, only she didn't want me to take care of her, because she was a very empowered feminist who liked me because she thought I was the great mind of my generation, but then she decided I would never be—and again I'm quoting—'an artist,' which was apparently cause for dismissal even though I had never claimed to be an artist—and in fact if you have listened closely you have already heard me freely admit that I suck at pottery.

"And then after a horrendous dry spell, I met Katherine XVI on the roof deck of a hotel in Newark, New Jersey, during an Academic Decathlon tournament in October of my junior year, and we had about as wild and torrid an affair as you can possibly have over the course of fourteen hours at an Academic Decathlon tournament, which is to say that at one point we had to kick her three roommates out of her hotel room so we could make out properly, but then even after I emerged from the tournament with nine gold medals—I sucked at Speech—she dumped me on account of how she had a boyfriend back home in Kansas and she didn't want to dump *him*, so I was the next logical person to dump.

"Katherine XVII I met—I'm not going to lie about it—on the Internet the next January, and she had a pierced nose with a ring in it and had this immensely impressive vocabulary with which she was able to talk about indie rock—one of the words she used that I didn't initially know the definition of was, in fact, 'indie'—and it was fun to listen to her talk about music and one time I helped her dye her hair, but then she broke up with me after three weeks because I was sort of 'emo nerd' and she was more looking for 'emo core.'

"While I generally don't like to use the word 'heart' unless I'm referring to the blood-pumping, beat-beat-beating organ, there's no question that Katherine XVIII broke my heart, because I loved her immensely from the very moment I saw her at a concert Hassan made me attend during Spring Break, and she was this short fiery woman who hated being called a girl, and she liked me and at first it seemed she shared my massive sense of insecurity, and so I just built up my hopes ridiculously and found myself writing her these extravagantly long and painfully philosophical e-mails, and then she dumped me over e-mail after only two actual dates and four actual kisses, whereupon I found myself writing her these extravagantly long and painfully pathetic e-mails.

"And just two weeks after that, Katherine I showed up on my doorstep and soon enough she became K-19, and she was a nice girl with a good heart who liked helping people, and none of them ever lit my heart—God, I can't stop it with that word now—on fire like she did, but I just needed her so much and it never felt like enough and she wasn't consistent and her inconsistency and my insecurity were this horrible match for each other, but I still loved her, because all of me was wrapped up in her, because I'd put all my eggs in someone else's basket, and in the end, after 343 days, I was left with an empty basket and this gnawing endless hole in my gut, but then now I find myself deciding to remember her as a good person with whom I had some good times until we, both of us, got ourselves into an ineradicably bad situation.

"And the moral of the story is that you don't remember what happened.

What you remember becomes what happened. And the second moral of the story, if a story can have multiple morals, is that Dumpers are not inherently worse than Dumpees—breaking up isn't something that gets done *to* you; it's something that happens *with* you."

"And the other moral of the story is that you, Smartypants, just told an *amazing* story, proving that given enough time, and enough coaching, and enough hearing stories from current and former associates of Gutshot Textiles, anyone—*anyone*—can learn to tell a damned good story."

"Something about telling that story made my gut grow back together."

"What?"

"Oh, nothing. Thinking out loud."

"That's who you really like. The people you can think out loud in front of."

"The people who've been in your secret hiding places."

"The people you bite your thumb in front of."

"Hi."

"Hi."

". . ."

". . ."

"Wow. My first Lindsey."

"My second Colin."

"That was fun. Let's try it again."

"Sold."

". . ."

". . ."

". . ."

". . ."

". . ."

". . ."

". . ."

". . ."

• • •

They left the cave together very late that night, and drove home separately, Colin in the Hearse and Lindsey in the pink pickup. They kissed once more in the driveway—that kiss as good as her smile hinted it would be—and then snuck into the house for a few hours of sleep.

# (epilogue, or the lindsey lee wells chapter)

**Colin woke up,** exhausted, to the rooster, and rolled around in bed for a solid hour before making his way downstairs. Hassan was already sitting at the oak table with a collection of papers in front of him. Colin noticed that Hollis was not asleep on the couch; maybe she actually had a bedroom somewhere.

"Profit/Loss Margins," Hassan explained. "It's actually really interesting stuff. Hollis explained it to me last night. So, d'you hook up with her or what?"

Colin smiled.

Hassan got up, grinning goofily, and smacked Colin on the back gleefully. "You're such a vulture, Singleton. You just circle, baby. You circle, and you just slowly fly lower and lower, always circling, waiting for the moment when you can just land on the carcass of a relationship and fugging feast. It's a beautiful thing to watch—particularly this time, because I like the girl."

"Let's go out to breakfast," said Colin. "Hardee's?"

"Hardee's," agreed Hassan excitedly. "Linds, get up we're going to Hardee's!"

"Gotta go visit Mabel this morning," Lindsey called back. "Eat seven Monster Thickburgers for me, though."

"Will do!" Hassan promised.

"So listen. When I got home last night, I plugged Lindsey and me into the formula," Colin said. "She dumps me. The curve was longer than

K-1 but shorter than K-4. That means she's going to dump me within four days."

"Could happen. It's a crazy fugging snow globe of a world."

Three days later, the day the Theorem indicated Lindsey and Colin would not survive together, Colin woke up to the rooster and rolled over groggily only to find a piece of notebook paper against his cheek. It was folded in the shape of an envelope.

And, for once, Colin saw it coming. As he carefully unfolded the paper, he knew that the Theorem's prophecy had been fulfilled. And yet, knowing it was going to happen made it no less horrible. *Why? It's been so amazing. The best first four days ever. Am I crazy? I must be crazy.* As he opened the note, he was already debating whether to leave Gutshot immediately.

Colin,
I hate to fulfill the Theorem, but I don't think we should be involved romantically. The problem is that I am secretly in love with Hassan. I can't help myself. I hold your bony shoulder blades in my hands and think of his fleshy back. I kiss your stomach and I think of his awe-inspiring gut. I like you, Colin. I really do. But—I'm sorry. It's just not going to work.
I hope we can still be friends.
Sincerely,
Lindsey Lee Wells
P.S. Just kidding.

Colin wanted to be all-the-way happy, he really did—because ever since he saw the steepness of the curve with Lindsey, he'd been hoping that it'd be wrong. But as he sat there on the bed, the note in his still-shaky hands, he couldn't help but feel that he would never be a genius. For as much as he believed Lindsey that what matters to you defines your mattering, he still wanted the Theorem to work, still wanted to be as special as everyone had always told him he was.

The next day, Colin was feverishly trying to fix the Theorem while Hassan and Lindsey played Hold 'Em poker for pennies in the Pink Mansion's screened-in porch. A ceiling fan blew the warm air around without really cooling it. Colin was half paying attention to the game while scribbling graphs, trying to make the Theorem account for the fact that Lindsey Lee Wells was, quite clearly, still his girlfriend. And then poker finally clarified the Theorem's unfixable flaw.

Hassan shouted, "She's all in for thirteen cents, Singleton! It's a huge bet. Should I call?"

"She does tend to bluff," Colin answered without looking up.

"You better be right, Singleton. I call. Okay, turn 'em over, kid! Gutshot Dolly has trip Queens! It's a hell of a hand, but will it beat—A FULL HOUSE?!" Lindsey groaned with disappointment as Hassan flipped over his hand.

Colin knew nothing about poker except that it was a game of human behavior and probability, and therefore the kind of quasi-closed system in which a Theorem similar to the Theorem of Underlying Katherine Predictability ought to work. And when Hassan turned over his full house, Colin all of a sudden realized: you can make a Theorem that explains why you won or lost past poker hands, but you can never make one to predict *future* poker hands. The past, like Lindsey had told him, is a logical story. It's the sense of what happened. But since it is not yet remembered, the future need not make any fugging sense at all.

In that moment, the future—uncontainable by any Theorem mathematical or otherwise—stretched out before Colin: infinite and unknowable and beautiful. "*Eureka,*" Colin said, and only in saying it did he realize he had just successfully whispered.

"I figured something out," he said aloud. "The future is unpredictable."

Hassan said, "Sometimes the *kafir* likes to say massively obvious things in a really profound voice."

Colin laughed as Hassan returned to counting the pennies of victory, but Colin's brain was spinning with the implications: *if the future is forever,* he thought, *then eventually it will swallow us all up.* Even Colin could only name a handful of people who lived, say, 2,400 years ago. In another 2,400 years, even Socrates, the most well-known genius of that century, might be forgotten. The future will erase everything—there's no level of fame or genius that allows you to transcend oblivion. The infinite future makes that kind of mattering impossible.

But there's another way. There are stories. Colin was looking at Lindsey, whose eyes were crinkling into a smile as Hassan loaned her nine cents so they could keep playing. Colin thought of Lindsey's storytelling lessons. The stories they'd told each other were so much a part of the how and why of his liking her. Okay. Loving. Four days in, and already, indisputably: loving. And he found himself thinking that maybe stories don't just make us matter to each other—maybe they're also the only way to the infinite mattering he'd been after for so long.

And Colin thought: *Because like say I tell someone about my feral hog hunt. Even if it's a dumb story, telling it changes other people just the slightest little bit, just as living the story changes me. An infinitesimal change. And that infinitesimal change ripples outward—ever smaller but everlasting. I will get forgotten, but the stories will last. And so we all matter—maybe less than a lot, but always more than none.*

And it wasn't only the remembered stories that mattered. That was the true meaning of the K-3 anomaly: Having the correct graph from the start proved not that the Theorem was accurate, but that there's a place in the brain for knowing what cannot be remembered.

Almost without knowing it, he'd started writing. The graphs in his notebook had been replaced by words. Colin looked up then and wiped a single bead of sweat from his tanned, scarred forehead. Hassan turned around to Colin and said, "I realize the future is unpredictable, but I'm wondering if the future might possibly feature a Monster Thickburger."

"I predict it will," Lindsey said.

As they hustled out the door, Lindsey shouted, "Shotgun," and Colin said, "Driver," and Hassan said, "Crap," and then Linds ran past Colin, beating him to the door. She held it open for him, leaning up to peck his lips.

That brief walk—from the screened-in porch outside to the Hearse—was one of those moments he knew he'd remember and look back on, one of those moments that he'd try to capture in the stories he told. Nothing was happening, really, but the moment was thick with mattering. Lindsey laced her fingers in Colin's hand, and Hassan sang a song called, "I love the / Monster Thickburger at Ha-ar-dee's / For my stomach / It's a wonderful pa-ar-ty," and they piled into the Hearse.

They'd just driven past the General Store when Hassan said, "We don't have to go to Hardee's, really. We could go anywhere."

"Oh good because I really don't want to go to Hardee's," Lindsey said. "It's sort of horrible. There's a Wendy's two exits down the interstate, in Milan. Wendy's is way better. They have, like, salads."

So Colin drove past the Hardee's and out onto the interstate headed north. As the staggered lines rushed past him, he thought about the space between what we remember and what happened, the space between what we predict and what will happen. And in that space, Colin thought, there was room enough to reinvent himself—room enough to make himself into something other than a prodigy, to remake his story better and different—room enough to be reborn again and again. A snake killer, an Archduke, a slayer of TOCs—a genius, even. There was room enough to be anyone—anyone except whom he'd already been, for if Colin had learned one thing from Gutshot, it's that you can't stop the future from coming. And for the first time in his life, he smiled thinking about the always-coming infinite future stretching out before him.

And they drove on. Lindsey turned to Colin and said, "You know, we could just keep going. We don't have to stop." Hassan in the back leaned forward between the seats and said, "Yeah. Yeah. Let's just keep driving for a while." Colin pressed down hard on the accelerator, and he was thinking of all the places they might go, and all the days left in their summer. Beside him, Lindsey Lee Wells's fingers were on his forearm, and she was saying, "Yeah. God. We could, couldn't we? We could just keep going."

Colin's skin was alive with the feeling of connection to everyone in that car and everyone not in it. And he was feeling not-unique in the very best possible way.

# (author's note)

The footnotes of the novel you just read (unless you haven't finished reading it and are skipping ahead, in which case you should go back and read everything in order and not try to find out what happens, you sneaky little sneakster) promise a math-laden appendix. And so here it is.

As it happens, I got a C-minus in pre calc despite the heroic efforts of my eleventh-grade math teacher, Mr. Lantrip, and then I went on to take something called "finite mathematics," because it was supposed to be easier than calculus. I picked the college I attended partly because it had no math requirement. But then shortly after college, I became—and I know this is weird—kind of *into* math. Unfortunately, I still suck at it. I'm into math the way my nine-year-old self was into skateboarding. I talk about it a lot, and I think about it a lot, but I can't actually, like, *do* it.

Fortunately, I am friends with this guy Daniel Biss, who happens to be one of the best young mathematicians in America. Daniel is world famous in the math world, partly because of a paper he published a few years ago that apparently proves that circles are basically fat, bloated triangles. He is also one of my dearest friends. Daniel is pretty much entirely responsible for the fact that the formula is real math that really works within the context of the book. I asked him to write an appendix about the math behind Colin's Theorem. This appendix, like all appendices, is strictly optional reading, of course. But boy, is it fascinating. Enjoy.

—John Green

# (the appendix)

Colin's Eureka moment was made up of three ingredients.

First of all, he noticed that a relationship is something you can draw a graph of; one such graph might look something like this:

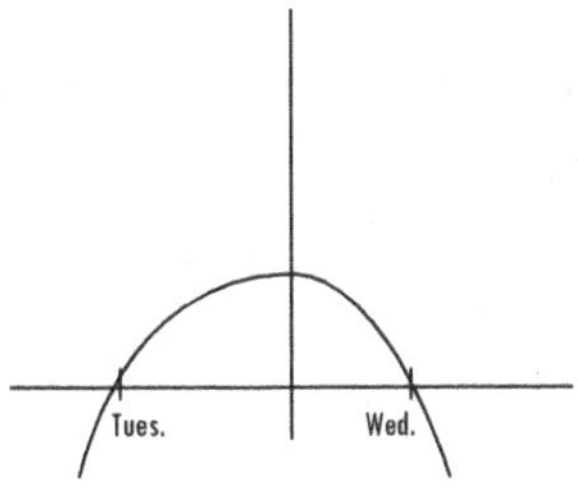


According to Colin's thesis, the horizontal line (which we call the *x*-axis) represents time. The first time the curve crosses the *x*-axis corresponds to the beginning of the relationship, and the second crossing indicates the conclusion of the relationship. If the curve spends the intermediate time above the *x*-axis (as is the case in our example), then the girl dumps the boy; if, instead, the curve passes below the *x*-axis, that means that the boy dumps the girl. ("Boy" and "girl," for our purposes, contain no gender-specific meaning; for same-sex relationships, you could as easily call them "boy1" and "boy2" or "girl1" and "girl2.") So in our diagram, the couple's first kiss is on a Tuesday, and then the girl dumps the boy on Wednesday. (All in all, a fairly typical Colin-Katherine affair.)

Since the curve crosses the *x*-axis only at the beginning and end of the relationship, we should expect that at any point in time, the farther the curve strays from the *x*-axis, the farther the relationship is from breakup, or, put another way, the better the relationship seems to be going. Here's a more complicated example, the graph of my relationship with one of *my* ex-girlfriends:

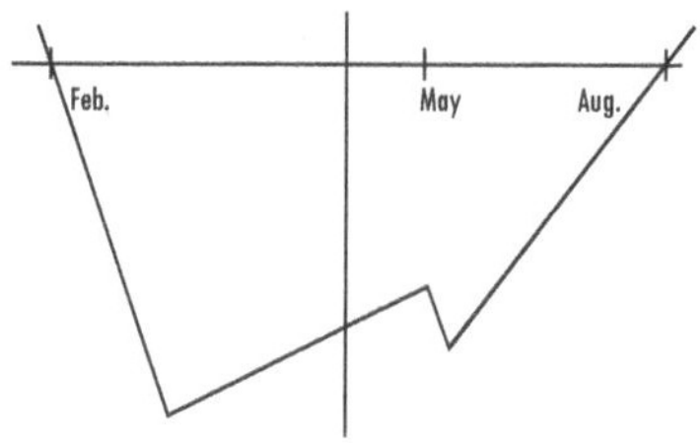


The initial burst came in February when, all in a matter of hours, we met, a blizzard started, and she totaled her car on an icy highway, breaking her wrist in the process. We suddenly found ourselves snowed in at my apartment, she an invalid doped up on painkillers, and me distracted and intoxicated by my new jobs as nurse and boyfriend. That phase ended abruptly when, two weeks later, the snow melted, her hand healed, and we had to leave my apartment and interact with the world, whereupon we immediately discovered that we led radically different lives and didn't have all that much in common. The next, smaller spike occurred when we went to Budapest for vacation. That ended, moments later, when we noticed that we were spending about twenty-three hours of each romantically Budapestian day bickering about absolutely everything. The curve finally crosses the *x*-axis somewhere in August, which is when I dumped her and she threw me out of her apartment and onto the streets of Berkeley, homeless and penniless, at midnight.

• • •

The second ingredient in Colin's Eureka moment is the fact that graphs (including graphs of romantic relationships) can be represented by functions. This one will take a bit of explaining; bear with me.

The first thing to say is that when we draw a diagram like this,

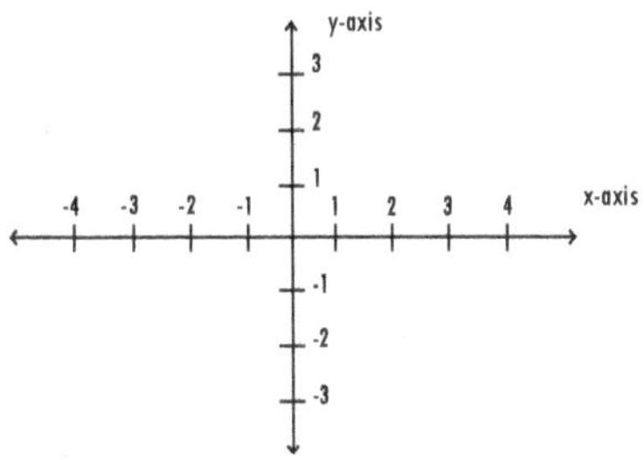


each point can be represented by numbers. That is, the horizontal line (the $x$-axis) has little numbers marked on it, as does the vertical line (the $y$-axis). Now, to specify a single point somewhere in the plane, it's enough to just list two numbers: one that tells us how far along the $x$-axis the point lies, and the other that tells us where it's situated along the $y$-axis. For example, the point (2,1) should correspond to the spot marked "2" on the $x$-axis and the spot marked "1" on the $y$-axis. Equivalently, it's located two units to the right and one unit above the location where the $x$- and $y$-axes cross, which location is called (0,0). Similarly, the point (0,–2) is located on the $y$-axis two units below the crossing, and the point (–3,2) is situated three units to the left and two units above the crossing.

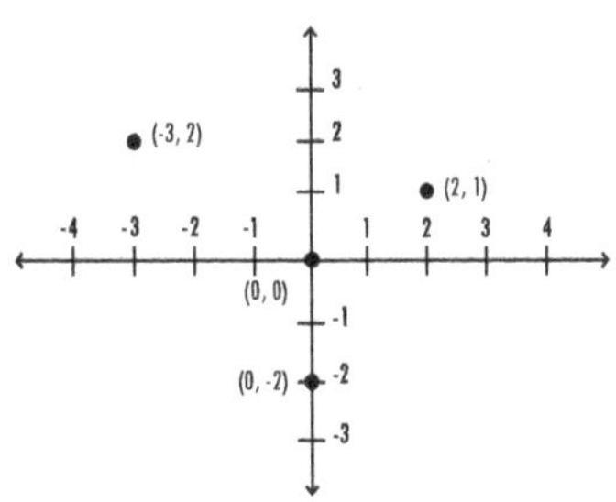

Okay, so functions: a function is a kind of machine for turning one number into another. It's a rulebook for a very simple game: I give you any number I want and you always give me back some other number. For instance, a function might say, "Take the number and multiply it by itself (i.e., square it)." Then our conversation would go something like this:

ME: 1
YOU: 1
ME: 2
YOU: 4
ME: 3
YOU: 9
ME: 9,252,459,984
YOU: 85,608,015,755,521,280,256

Now, many functions can be written using algebraic equations. For example, the function above would be written

$$f(x) = x^2$$

which means that when I give you the number $x$, the function instructs you to take $x$ and multiply it by itself (i.e., to compute $x^2$) and return that new number to me. Using the function, we can plot *all* points of the form $(x,f(x))$. Those points together will form some kind of curve in the plane, and we call that curve the "graph of the function." Consider the function $f(x) = x^2$. We can plot the points (1,1), (2,4), and (3,9).

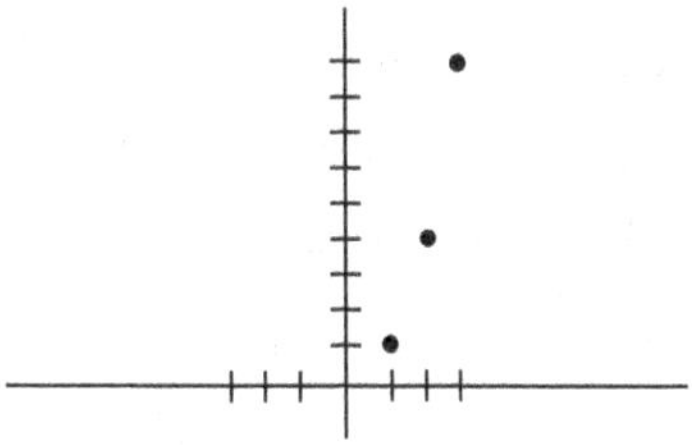

In this case, it might help to plot the additional points (0,0), (–1,1), (–2,4), and (–3,9). (Remember that if you take a negative number and multiply it by itself, you get a positive number.)

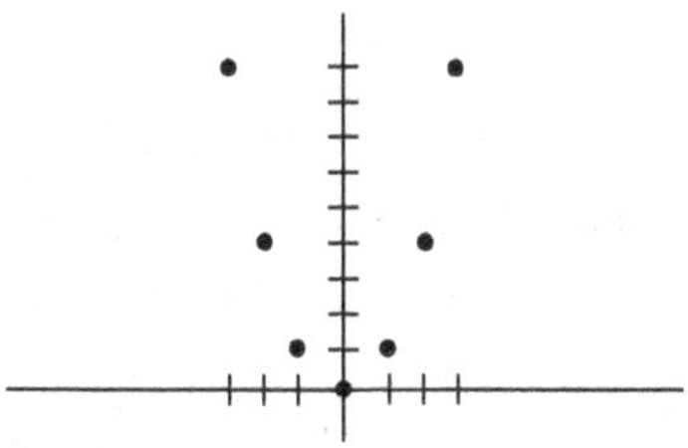

Now, you can probably guess that the graph will be a curve that looks something like this:

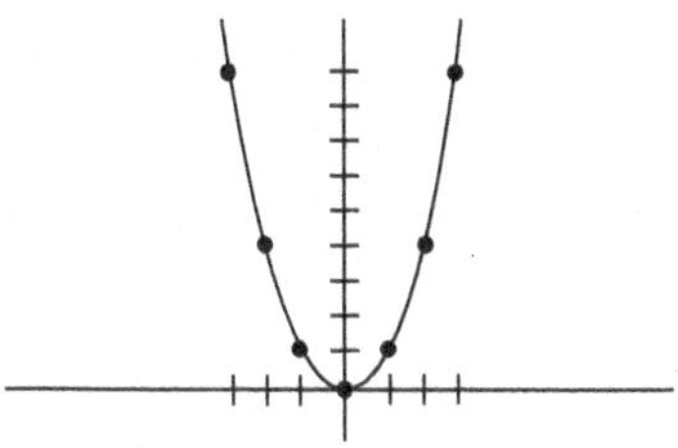

Unfortunately, you'll notice that this graph doesn't do a particularly good job of representing relationships. The graphs that Colin wants to use for his Theorem all need to cross the $x$-axis twice (once for when a couple starts dating, and once for the dumping), whereas the graph we drew only touched it once. But this can easily be fixed by using slightly more complicated functions. Consider, for example, the function $f(x) = 1 - x^2$.

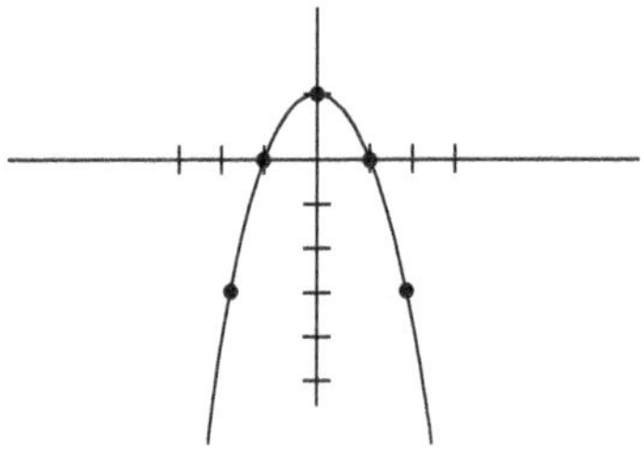

This graph is quite familiar to Colin—it's a graph of a short relationship in which he's dumped by the girl (we know that the girl dumps Colin because the graph is above the $x$-axis between the first kiss and the dumping). It's the graph that tells an outline of the story of Colin's life. Now all we need to do is figure out how to modify it so as to flesh out some details.

One of the great themes of twentieth-century mathematics has been the drive to study everything in "families." (When mathematicians use the word "family," they mean "any collection of like or related objects." E.g., a chair and a desk are both members of the "furniture family.")

Here's the idea: a line is nothing more than a collection (a "family") of points; a plane is simply a family of lines, and so forth. This is supposed to convince you that if one object (like a point) is interesting, then it will be even more interesting to study a whole family of similar objects (like a line). This point of view has come to completely dominate mathematical research over the last sixty years.

This brings us to the third piece of Colin's Eureka puzzle. Every Katherine is different, so each dumping that Colin receives at the hands of a new

Katherine is different from all the previous ones. This means that no matter how carefully Colin crafts a *single* function, a *single* graph, he'll only ever be learning about a *single* Katherine. What Colin really needs is to study all possible Katherines and their functions, all at once. What he needs, in other words, is to study the *family* of all Katherine functions.

And this, at last, was Colin's complete insight: that relationships can be graphed, that graphs come from functions, and that it might be possible to study all such functions at once, with a single (very complicated) formula, in such a way that would enable him to predict when (and, more importantly, whether), any prospective Katherine would dump him.[85]

Let's give an example of what this might mean; in fact, we'll talk about the first example that Colin tried. The formula looks like this:

$$f(x) = D^3x^2 - D$$

In explaining this expression, I certainly have a lot of questions to answer: first off, what on earth is $D$? It's the Dumper/Dumpee differential: you can give anybody a score between 0 and 5 depending on where they fall on the spectrum of heartbreak. Now, if you're trying to predict how a relationship between a boy and a girl will work out, you begin by taking the boy's D/D differential score and subtracting from it the girl's D/D differential score and calling the answer A. (So if the boy is a 2 and the girl is a 4, you get D = −2.)

Now, let's see what effect this has on the graph. In the example I just gave where the boy gets a 2 and the girl gets a 4, so that $D = -2$, we have

$$f(x) = -8x^2 + 2$$

[85]Yeah, I know, that's a lot to keep in your head all at once. Look, John *told* you that Colin was a prodigy.

whose graph looks like this:

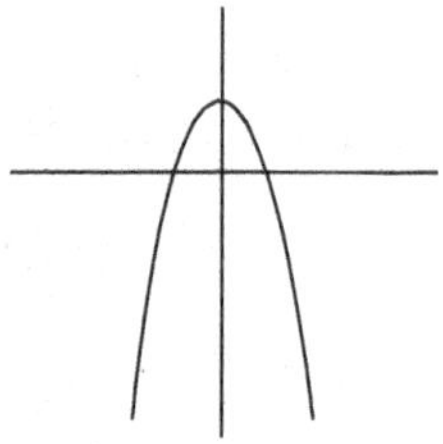

As you can see, the relationship doesn't last too long, and the girl ends up dumping the boy (a situation Colin is quite familiar with).

If, instead, the boy was a 5 and the girl was a 1, we'd have D = 4, so that

$$f(x) = 64x^2 - 4$$

which has the following graph:

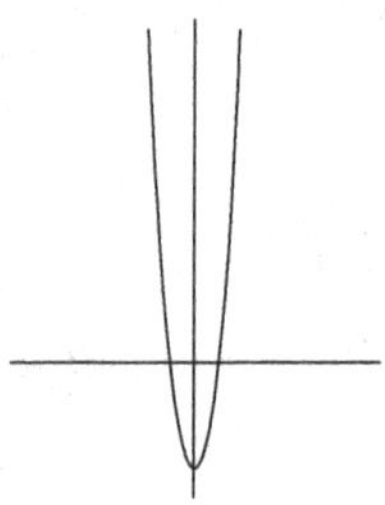

This relationship is even shorter, but it seems even more intense (the peak is remarkably steep), and this time the boy dumps the girl.

Unfortunately, this formula has problems. For one thing, if D = 0, that is, if they're equal Dumpers or Dumpees, then we get

$$f(x) = 0$$

whose graph is just a horizontal line, so you can't tell where the relationship begins or ends. The more basic problem is that it's patently absurd to suggest that relationships are so simple, that their graphs are so uniform, which is what Lindsey Lee Wells eventually helps Colin to figure out. And so Colin's final formula ends up being far more subtle.

But the main point is already visible in this case: because $D$ can vary, this *single* formula is capable of specifying a whole *family* of functions, each of which can be used to describe a different Colin-Katherine affair. So all Colin needs to do now is add more and more variables (more ingredients along the lines of $D$) to this formula so that the family of functions it encompasses is bigger and more complicated, and therefore has a hope of encapsulating the complex and challenging world of Katherine-dumpings, which is what Colin eventually realizes thanks to Lindsey's insight.

So that's the story of Colin Singleton and his Eureka moment and the Theorem of Underlying Katherine Predictability. I should briefly point out that although no reasonable adult mathematician (at least not one with a soul) would seriously suggest that you can predict romance with a single formula, there actually has been some recent work that points in this direction. To be specific, psychologist John Gottman (and longtime head of the University of Washington's "Love Lab") and a group of coauthors, including the mathematician James Murray, have published a book entitled *The Mathematics of Marriage* that purports to use math to predict whether marriages will break up. The basic philosophy is, in its outline, not unlike Colin's Theorem, but the math that goes into it is far more sophisticated, and the claimed outcome is far more modest (these people aren't pretending that they can predict *every* divorce, just that they can make some educated guesses[86]).[87]

[86] Right, big deal—I can also make educated guesses about whether my friends' relationships will last. I guess the point here is that they were able to mathematically justify the educated-guessing process.

[87] This work is too technical for me to summarize here (for example, I don't understand a word of it), but if you want to read about it, you can either try the colossal and impenetrable book *The Mathematics of Marriage* by Gottman, Murray, Swanson, Tyson, and (yet another) Swanson, or else the much more manageable and fun online review and summary by Jordan Ellenberg, available at *http://slate.msn.com/id/2081484/*.

There's one last thing I'd like to mention: notwithstanding John's notorious tendency to cannibalize his friends' lives for literary material, and notwithstanding the fact that I was somewhat accelerated in school as a kid, Colin's character was in no way inspired by me. For one thing, I've only ever kissed two girls named Katherine. Interestingly, though, throughout my whole career as a pathological Dumper, the Katherines were the only two women who ever dumped me. Strange. It almost makes me wonder if there's a formula out there somewhere . . .

—Daniel Biss
*Assistant Professor, University of Chicago,*
*and Research Fellow at the Clay Mathematics Institute*

# (acknowledgments)


1. My incomparable editor and friend, Julie Strauss-Gabel, who worked on this book when she was, literally, *in labor.* I rely so much on Julie's editing that—this is a true story—I once made her edit an e-mail I wrote the woman with whom I was then "just friends" and with whom I am now "living in holy matrimony." Which reminds me . . .
2. Sarah. (See dedication.)
3. My mentor and collaborator and alter ego and BFF Ilene Cooper, who is responsible for most of the good things that have ever happened to me. And also, come to think of it, helped me woo Acknowledgee #2.
4. My dear friend Daniel Biss, who fortunately for me is one of the best mathematicians in America—and also one of the best teachers on the subject. I could never have imagined this book without Daniel, let alone written it.
5. My family—Mike, Sydney, and Hank Green.
6. Sarah Shumway, my very talented *in loco editoris* at Dutton. Also everyone else at Dutton, particularly Margaret "Double Letters" Woollatt.
7. My man in the United Arab Emirates, Hassan al-Rawas, who has been providing me with Arabic translations and his wonderful friendship for many years now.
8. Adrian Loudermilk.
9. Bill Ott, 10. Lindsay Robertson, 11. Shannon James and Sam Hallgren, 12. David Levithan and Holly Black, 13. Jessica Tuchinsky, 14. Bryan Doerries, 15. Levin O'Connor and Randy Riggs, 16. Rosemary Sandberg, 17. *Booklist*, 18. All librarians everywhere, and of course . . .
19. The Katherines. I wish I could name them all, but (a) I lack the space, and (b) I fear the libel suits.

A READERS GUIDE TO

# AN ABUNDANCE OF KATHERINES

JOHN GREEN

**Were you a child prodigy?**

No! I was not a very good student when I was in high school. I wanted to write about a child prodigy because Colin's experience seemed to me like an exaggerated version of what we all go through in adolescence—we all wonder whether we matter, and how we can establish our mattering in a very big world. Also, many of us find in high school that we must grapple with the reality that we are perhaps less special than we previously believed ourselves to be. (In that respect, Colin and I are quite similar!)

**How do your high school experiences shape your writing?**

I attended a small and wonderful boarding school in Alabama called Indian Springs School, and I'm certainly not above borrowing from my own high school experiences. I also think that my particular high school experience pushed me toward writing about (1) the South, (2) smart kids, and (3) teenagers removed from direct parental control, and I also probably—(4)—owe this whole numbered-list-inside-a-sentence construction to high school, since I stole it from my friend Todd Cartee.

**In high school, how did you spend your free time?**

Mostly, I sat around with my friends and talked. I mean, we would play video games or watch TV or sneak out into the woods or play ultimate Frisbee, but all of these activities were just vehicles for talking.[1] Whenever I'm asked what advice I have for young writers, I always say that the first thing is to read, and to read a lot. The second thing is to write. And the third thing, which I think is absolutely vital, is to tell stories and listen closely to the stories you're being told.

Other than talking, I spent a lot of time getting dumped. As any dumpee can tell you, getting dumped is extraordinarily time-consuming.

**_Katherines_ was first published in 2006. Looking back on it now, how do you remember the writing and publication of it?**

It was immensely fun to write. Colin can be a very annoying person, but I had such fondness for him, and I particularly loved Hassan—every minute that I spent with Hassan was such a pleasure, and I've often wished that I could write a whole book about him (and who knows, maybe I will someday). When I wrote this book, I was working for mental_floss magazine, researching gobs of trivia every day, and so it was a wonderful release to have a place to write about: for instance, how shower curtains are affected by vortexes.

**Anagrams play a huge role in _An Abundance of Katherines_—why?**

Well, anagrams say something about the malleability of language. We always think of language as an immovable object, as this set of codified and unbreakable rules. But when you consider that one can rearrange the letters in PRESBYTERIANS and spell

[1] Example: I was on the ultimate Frisbee team at my high school, and I was of course the worst member of the team by a very wide margin, which is really saying something, because we were all pretty bad. And all I remember of playing ultimate Frisbee is running up and down a field, listening to my friends' stories, and telling my own. I suppose that now and again I must have caught or thrown a Frisbee, but I only remember us telling each other these stories between heaving breaths as we ran back and forth across the field.

BRITNEY SPEARS,[2] it reminds us that language (and the stories we tell with language) can be twisted and molded. Words are not static. Language shapes our memories, and it is also shaped by our memories.

**How's your anagramming?**

Terrible. Whenever I play Scrabble now, my friends who have read *Katherines* expect me to be some kind of Scrabble genius, and I invariably fail to spell anything more impressive than "zap." I also don't speak any of the foreign languages that Colin speaks. Nor have I ever been good at math. The wonderful thing about writing stories is that you get to pretend to be people you could never actually be.

**What inspired the town of Gutshot, Tennessee?**

Gutshot is a mixture of places I often visited when I was growing up. Both my mother's parents are from small towns in Tennessee.

My grandmother grew up in the tiny town of Skullbone, Tennessee, and here is a completely true story: When I was in college, I visited Skullbone with my girlfriend at the time, and we were hanging out on the bridge that leads into town, just looking at the river below and chatting. Suddenly, a minivan pulled up and parked beside our car. A big guy with a thick beard got out of the minivan. He appeared to be wearing nothing but very dirty overalls and brand-new white sneakers. Without saying a word to us, the guy reached into the minivan, emerged with a pair of very old shoes, and then threw them into the river.

---

[2] The whole Britney/Presbyterians thing fascinates me because "Britney" is such an odd spelling. (It is less common than either Brittany or Brittney.) This begs a question: Did Britney Spears's parents choose to spell her name eccentrically because of its anagrammatic potential?

The man watched his shoes bob in the river until they went under the bridge, and only then did he seem to notice us. "I moved to Nashville twenty years ago," he said. "Every year I come back and toss last year's shoes into the river, so they walk the country even though I can't anymore."

Then he got back in the minivan and drove away.

**Why the Archduke Franz Ferdinand?**

He's a good example of someone who mattered very much to human history, but didn't really do anything to matter. History came for Franz Ferdinand, not the other way around. That interested me because Colin is obsessed with how you matter (and whether the extent to which you matter historically is the measure of one's life).

**Toward the end of the book, Colin thinks about how he wants "to be as special as everyone had always told him he was . . ." What's meaningful about that to you?**

I think most people have had that experience, whether it's about academic performance or baseball or writing or cheerleading or whatever.

I think in some ways that's what adolescence is—the emerging knowledge that you are not alone, both in exciting and in disappointing ways.

At some point in adolescence, you realize that you are not the center of the universe, which is a bummer of a thing to discover. But it's only through this discovery that you can build the kind of deep and lasting and sustaining relationships with peers that are so central to adulthood.

**_Katherines_ is written in third person, unlike the rest of your books. Why? Did you ever try writing in first person?**

I felt like *Katherines* needed to be written in third person, because it's about a guy whose brain does not lend itself to narratives, and who struggles to tell stories in ways that other people find interesting.

For a while I tried to write it in first person with all these tangents and footnotes to the footnotes and the story never really moving forward.

But it was infuriating to read, and I felt like it was already challenging enough to empathize with Colin. My hope was that creating a little narrative distance would make it easier to understand Colin.

**Why did you choose to use footnotes?**

In college, I often felt like most of the really interesting stuff in academic nonfiction was in the footnotes, because that's where the author's voice came through.

Also, I'd read *Infinite Jest* by David Foster Wallace, which contains a lot of endnotes, and I loved them, because:

1. They can function as a kind of competing narrative that comments upon and—for lack of a better word—problematizes the central narrative.

2. Also, sometimes exceptionally intelligent people (like David Foster Wallace or Colin or E. Lockhart's Ruby Oliver) feel this need to qualify and refine and analyze everything they say, because they feel this urge to be both understood and intellectually precise. They want to be both very clear and very accurate.

Footnotes can serve as a way of attempting to achieve that precision and clarity. But I think that at least on some levels, precision and clarity are in competition with each other.[3] As discussed in the novel, human memory is not in the accuracy business; it's in the narrative business. Colin eventually starts to feel that when it comes to being understood, telling stories empathetically works best.

**This book's cover was designed by one of your readers. How do you feel about that?**

I love the cover so much, and I am so grateful and astonished to have such passionate and creative readers. My publisher was kind enough to hand the cover-making reins over to readers of *Katherines*, who came up with hundreds of really excellent designs, but the winner was a young woman named Sarah Turbin. Her design captures so much about the book—its nerdiness, its heart, and its love of footnotes.

**What's new with Daniel Biss?**

Daniel Biss, the mathematician who wrote the formulae in *An Abundance of Katherines* and taught me to understand enough abstract mathematics to be able to write the book, was working happily as a professor of mathematics when this book came out. But then he discovered, of all things, politics, and in 2010, he became the only professional mathematician in the Illinois State House of Representatives. He went on to become a state senator in Illinois before leaving elected office to work on increasing

---

[3] Like, eventually footnotes and endnotes and footnotes-within-footnotes and so on in the ceaseless attempt to be clear in precisely what you are trying to say leads to the reader being confused and annoyed and altogether less engaged.

civic engagement and support of progressive candidates in the Midwest. Daniel and I have remained friends, and I have great admiration for him.

**Does the formula work?**

Yes, in the sense that you can input variables and see a graph. But no, it cannot tell you how the story will end. Nobody can.

## QUESTIONS FOR DISCUSSION

1. Colin's theory is that relationships are inherently predictable. Do you agree? If there was a formula to predict romantic success, would you use it?

2. What is the difference between Colin's memory of the past and what actually happened? Why does he forget he dumped Katherine III?

3. Do you agree that Colin was always the dumpee?

4. What purpose does anagramming words serve for Colin? In what ways does this activity connect or isolate him from others?

5. Lindsey Lee Wells feels like she's constantly chameleoning, and never really acting like herself in front of other people. Why? What does it mean to be your authentic self?

6. Hassan says, "I'm a not-doer." How does passivity affect himself and others?

7. What is the importance of storytelling in the novel? How does understanding story change Colin's understanding of his past and current relationships?

8. Throughout the book, Colin worries about mattering, but in the last chapter he feels "not unique in the best possible way." What's the significance of this evolution?

9. What does it mean to you to matter? Do you think it's important?

10. Lindsey tells Colin, "How you matter is defined by the things that matter to you." Do you agree?

Turn the page to read an excerpt from John Green's #1 *New York Times* bestselling novel

# TURTLES ALL THE WAY DOWN

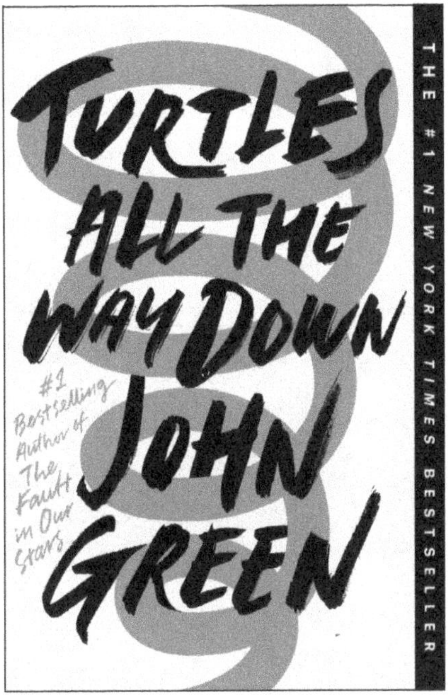


**A *NEW YORK TIMES* NOTABLE BOOK • A *NEW YORK TIMES* CRITICS' TOP BOOK OF THE YEAR • AN NPR BEST BOOK OF THE YEAR • A *TIME* BEST BOOK OF THE YEAR • A *WALL STREET JOURNAL* BEST BOOK OF THE YEAR • AN *ENTERTAINMENT WEEKLY* BEST BOOK OF THE YEAR**

"Wrenching and revelatory." —*NEW YORK TIMES*

"A sometimes heartbreaking, always illuminating, glimpse into how it feels to live with mental illness." —NPR, BEST BOOKS OF THE YEAR

"Green finds the language to describe the indescribable—the particular pain that accompanies mental illness—through his remarkable narrator, Aza Holmes. A must-read for those struggling with mental illness, or for their friends and family." —*SAN FRANCISCO CHRONICLE*

★ "Superb." —*BOOKLIST*

# ONE

**AT THE TIME I FIRST REALIZED** I might be fictional, my weekdays were spent at a publicly funded institution on the north side of Indianapolis called White River High School, where I was required to eat lunch at a particular time—between 12:37 P.M. and 1:14 P.M.—by forces so much larger than myself that I couldn't even begin to identify them. If those forces had given me a different lunch period, or if the tablemates who helped author my fate had chosen a different topic of conversation that September day, I would've met a different end—or at least a different middle. But I was beginning to learn that your life is a story told about you, not one that you tell.

Of course, you pretend to be the author. You have to. You

think, *I now choose to go to lunch*, when that monotone beep rings from on high at 12:37. But really, the bell decides. You think you're the painter, but you're the canvas.

Hundreds of voices were shouting over one another in the cafeteria, so that the conversation became mere sound, the rushing of a river over rocks. And as I sat beneath fluorescent cylinders spewing aggressively artificial light, I thought about how we all believed ourselves to be the hero of some personal epic, when in fact we were basically identical organisms colonizing a vast and windowless room that smelled of Lysol and lard.

I was eating a peanut butter and honey sandwich and drinking a Dr Pepper. To be honest, I find the whole process of masticating plants and animals and then shoving them down my esophagus kind of disgusting, so I was trying not to think about the fact that I was eating, which is a form of thinking about it.

Across the table from me, Mychal Turner was scribbling in a yellow-paper notebook. Our lunch table was like a long-running play on Broadway: The cast changed over the years, but the roles never did. Mychal was The Artsy One. He was talking with Daisy Ramirez, who'd played the role of my Best and Most Fearless Friend since elementary school, but I couldn't follow their conversation over the noise of all the others.

What was my part in this play? The Sidekick. I was

Daisy's Friend, or Ms. Holmes's Daughter. I was somebody's something.

I felt my stomach begin to work on the sandwich, and even over everybody's talking, I could *hear* it digesting, all the bacteria chewing the slime of peanut butter—the students inside of me eating at my internal cafeteria. A shiver convulsed through me.

"Didn't you go to camp with him?" Daisy asked me.

"With who?"

"Davis Pickett," she said.

"Yeah," I said. "Why?"

"Aren't you listening?" Daisy asked. *I am listening*, I thought, *to the cacophony of my digestive tract*. Of course I'd long known that I was playing host to a massive collection of parasitic organisms, but I didn't much like being reminded of it. By cell count, humans are approximately 50 percent microbial, meaning that about half of the cells that make you up are not yours at all. There are something like a thousand times more microbes living in my particular biome than there are human beings on earth, and it often seems like I can *feel* them living and breeding and dying in and on me. I wiped my sweaty palms on my jeans and tried to control my breathing. Admittedly, I have some anxiety problems, but I would argue it isn't irrational to be concerned about the fact that you are a skin-encased bacterial colony.

Mychal said, "His dad was about to be arrested for bribery

or something, but the night before the raid he disappeared. There's a hundred-thousand-dollar reward out for him."

"And you know his kid," Daisy said.

"*Knew* him," I answered.

I watched Daisy attack her school-provided rectangular pizza and green beans with a fork. She kept glancing up at me, her eyes widening as if to say, *Well?* I could tell she wanted me to ask her about something, but I couldn't tell what, because my stomach wouldn't shut up, which was forcing me deep inside a worry that I'd somehow contracted a parasitic infection.

I could half hear Mychal telling Daisy about his new art project, in which he was using Photoshop to average the faces of a hundred people named Mychal, and the average of their faces would be this new, one-hundred-and-first Mychal, which was an interesting idea, and I wanted to listen, but the cafeteria was so loud, and I couldn't stop wondering whether there was something wrong with the microbial balance of power inside me.

Excessive abdominal noise is an uncommon, but not unprecedented, presenting symptom of infection with the bacteria *Clostridium difficile*, which can be fatal. I pulled out my phone and searched "human microbiome" to reread Wikipedia's introduction to the trillions of microorganisms currently inside me. I clicked over to the article about *C. diff*, scrolling to the part about how most *C. diff* infections occur in hospitals. I scrolled down farther to a list of symptoms, none of which I had, except for the excessive abdominal noises, although I knew from previous searches that the Cleveland Clinic had reported the case of one person who'd died of *C. diff* after presenting at the hospital with only abdominal pain and fever. I reminded myself that I didn't have a fever, and my self replied: *You don't have a fever YET*.

At the cafeteria, where a shrinking slice of my consciousness still resided, Daisy was telling Mychal that his averaging project shouldn't be about people named Mychal but about imprisoned men who'd later been exonerated. "It'll be easier, anyway," she said, "because they all have mug shots taken from the same angle, and then it's not just about names but about race and class and mass incarceration," and Mychal was like, "You're a genius, Daisy," and she said, "You sound surprised," and meanwhile I was thinking that if half the cells inside of you are not you, doesn't that challenge the whole notion of *me* as a singular pronoun, let alone as the author of my fate? And I fell pretty far down that recursive wormhole until it transported me completely out of the White River High School cafeteria into some non-sensorial place only properly crazy people get to visit.

Ever since I was little, I've pressed my right thumbnail into the finger pad of my middle finger, and so now there's this weird callus over my fingerprint. After so many years of doing this, I can open up a crack in the skin really easily, so I cover it up with a Band-Aid to try to prevent infection. But sometimes I get worried that there already is an infection, and so I need to drain it, and the only way to do that is to reopen the wound and press out any blood that will come. Once I start thinking about splitting the skin apart, I literally cannot not do it. I apologize for the double negative, but it's a real double negative of a situation, a bind from which negating the negation is truly the only escape. So anyway, I started to want to feel my thumbnail biting into the skin of my finger pad, and I knew that resistance was more or less futile, so beneath the cafeteria table, I slipped the Band-Aid off my finger and dug my thumbnail into the callused skin until I felt the crack open.

"Holmesy," Daisy said. I looked up at her. "We're almost through lunch and you haven't even mentioned my hair." She shook out her hair, with so-red-they-were-pink highlights. Right. She'd dyed her hair.

I swum up out of the depths and said, "It's bold."

"I know, right? It says, 'Ladies and gentlemen and also people who do not identify as ladies or gentlemen, Daisy Ramirez won't break her promises, but she will break your heart.'" Daisy's self-proclaimed life motto was "Break Hearts, Not Promises." She kept threatening to get it tattooed on her ankle when she turned eighteen. Daisy turned back to Mychal, and I to my thoughts. The stomach grumbling had grown, if anything, louder. I felt like I might vomit. For someone who actively dislikes bodily fluids, I throw up quite a lot.

"Holmesy, you okay?" Daisy asked. I nodded. Sometimes I wondered why she liked me, or at least tolerated me. Why any of them did. Even I found myself annoying.

I could feel sweat sprouting from my forehead, and once I begin to sweat, it's impossible to stop. I'll keep sweating for hours, and not just my face or my armpits. My neck sweats. My boobs sweat. My calves sweat. Maybe I did have a fever.

Beneath the table, I slid the old Band-Aid into my pocket and, without looking, pulled out a new one, unwrapped it, and then glanced down to apply it to my finger. All the while, I was breathing in through my nose and out through my mouth, in the manner advised by Dr. Karen Singh, exhaling at a pace "that would make a candle flicker but not go out. Imagine that candle, Aza, flickering from your breath but still there, always there." So I tried that, but the thought spiral kept tightening anyway. I could hear Dr. Singh saying I shouldn't get out my phone, that I mustn't look up the same questions over and over, but I got it out anyway, and reread the "Human Microbiota" Wikipedia article.

The thing about a spiral is, if you follow it inward, it never actually ends. It just keeps tightening, infinitely.

I sealed the Ziploc bag around the last quarter of my sandwich, got up, and tossed it into an overfilled trash can. I heard a voice from behind me. "How concerned should I be that you haven't said more than two words in a row all day?"

"Thought spiral," I mumbled in reply. Daisy had known me since we were six, long enough to get it.

"I figured. Sorry, man. Let's hang out today."

This girl Molly walked up to us, smiling, and said, "Uh, Daisy, just FYI, your Kool-Aid dye job is staining your shirt."

Daisy looked down at her shoulders, and indeed, her striped top had turned pink in spots. She flinched for a second, then straightened her spine. "Yeah, it's part of the look, Molly. Stained shirts are huge in Paris right now." She turned away from Molly and said, "Right, so we'll go to your house and watch *Star Wars: Rebels*." Daisy was really into Star Wars—and not just the movies, but also the books and the animated shows and the kids' show where they're all made out of Lego. Like, she wrote fan fiction about Chewbacca's love life. "And we will improve your mood until you are able to say three or even four words in a row; sound good?"

"Sounds good."

"And then you can take me to work. Sorry, but I need a ride."

"Okay." I wanted to say more, but the thoughts kept coming, unbidden and unwanted. If I'd been the author, I would've stopped thinking about my microbiome. I would've told Daisy how much I liked her idea for Mychal's art project, and I would've told her that I did remember Davis Pickett, that I remembered being eleven and carrying a vague but constant fear. I would've told her that I remembered once at camp lying next to Davis on the edge of a dock, our legs dangling over, our backs against the rough-hewn planks of wood, staring together up at a cloudless summer sky. I would've told her that Davis and I never talked much, or even looked at each other, but it didn't matter, because we were looking at the same sky together, which is maybe more intimate than eye contact anyway. Anybody can look at you. It's quite rare to find someone who sees the same world you see.

MARINA WATERS

**JOHN GREEN** is the author of *Looking for Alaska*; *An Abundance of Katherines*; *Paper Towns*; *Will Grayson, Will Grayson* (with David Levithan); and *The Fault in Our Stars*. His books have received many accolades, including a Printz Medal, a Printz Honor, and an Edgar Award. John has twice been a finalist for the LA Times Book Prize and was selected by *TIME* magazine as one of the 100 Most Influential People in the World. With his brother, Hank, John has co-created many online video projects, including Vlogbrothers and the educational channel Crash Course. He lives with his family in Indianapolis, Indiana.

You can visit John online at *johngreenbooks.com*

# Paper Towns

**WINNER OF THE EDGAR AWARD FOR BEST YOUNG ADULT MYSTERY**
**#1 *NEW YORK TIMES* BESTSELLER • A *USA TODAY* BESTSELLER**

When Margo Roth Spiegelman beckons Quentin Jacobsen in the middle of the night—dressed like a ninja and plotting an ingenious campaign of revenge—he follows her. Margo's always planned extravagantly, and, until now, she's always planned solo. After a lifetime of loving Margo from afar, things are finally looking up for Q. . . until day breaks and she has vanished. Always an enigma, Margo has now become a mystery. But there are clues. And they're for Q.

★ **"Green's prose is astounding—from hilarious, hyperintellectual trash talk and shtick, to complex philosophizing, to devastating observation and truths. . . . Profoundly moving."**
—*SLJ*

★ **"Stellar, with deliciously intelligent dialogue and plenty of mind-twisting insights . . . a powerfully great read."**
—*VOYA*

PB: 978-0-14-241493-4 • HC: 978-0-525-47818-8

# The Fault in Our Stars

***TIME* MAGAZINE'S #1 FICTION BOOK OF THE YEAR**
**A *TODAY SHOW* BOOK CLUB PICK • #1 *NEW YORK TIMES* BESTSELLER**
**#1 *WALL STREET JOURNAL* BESTSELLER • #1 *USA TODAY* BESTSELLER**
**#1 INTERNATIONAL BESTSELLER**

Despite the tumor-shrinking medical miracle that has bought her a few years, Hazel has never been anything but terminal, her final chapter inscribed upon diagnosis. But when a gorgeous plot twist named Augustus Waters suddenly appears at Cancer Kid Support Group, Hazel's story is about to be completely rewritten.

Insightful, bold, irreverent, and raw, *The Fault in Our Stars* brilliantly explores the funny, thrilling, and tragic business of being alive and in love.

**"Damn near genius . . . *The Fault in Our Stars* is a love story, one of the most genuine and moving ones in recent American fiction, but it's also an existential tragedy of tremendous intelligence and courage and sadness."**
**—LEV GROSSMAN, *TIME* MAGAZINE**

**"The greatest romance story of this decade."**
***—ENTERTAINMENT WEEKLY***

**"This is a book that breaks your heart—not by wearing it down, but by making it bigger until it bursts."**
***—ATLANTIC***

**★ "In its every aspect, this novel is a triumph."**
***—BOOKLIST***

PB: 978-0-14-242417-9 • HC: 978-0-525-47881-2